Praise for Shannon Curtis

"This is a fun spy caper book with a great and very competent heroine."
—*Dear Author* on *Viper's Kiss*

"The characters are well written and the story line is enjoyable."
—*Harlequin Junkie* on *Warrior Untamed*

"The chemistry between them is intense and exciting, making an excellent complement to the suspenseful aspects of the story, which are superb in their own right."
—*RT Book Reviews* on *For Her Eyes Only*

"A bodyguard, a stalker and a prim and proper heroine...it just sounded like a recipe for success, and I enjoyed it very much!"
—*The Book Pushers* on *Guarding Jess*

"*Heart Breaker* is engrossing to the end and readers who like a bit of sensual romance with their crime will enjoy it greatly."
—*Sisters in Crime*

Shannon Curtis grew up picnicking in graveyards (long story) and reading by torchlight, and has worked in various roles, such as office admin manager, logistics supervisor and betting agent, to mention a few. Her first love—after reading, and her husband—is writing, and she writes romantic suspense, paranormal and contemporary romance. From faeries to cowboys, military men to business tycoons, she loves crafting stories of thrills, chills, kills and kisses. She divides her time between being an office administrator for the Romance Writers of Australia and creating spellbinding tales of mischief, mayhem and the occasional murder. She lives in Sydney, Australia, with her best-friend husband, three children, a woolly dog and a very disdainful cat. Shannon can be found lurking on Twitter, @2bshannoncurtis, and Facebook, or you can email her at contactme@shannoncurtis.com—she loves hearing from readers. Like...LOVES it. Disturbingly so.

Books by Shannon Curtis

Harlequin Nocturne

Lycan Unleashed
Warrior Untamed
Vampire Undone
Wolf Undaunted

WITCH HUNTER

—

SHANNON CURTIS

HARLEQUIN® NOCTURNE™

Recycling programs
for this product may
not exist in your area.

ISBN-13: 978-1-335-62965-4

Witch Hunter

Copyright © 2018 by Shannon Curtis

This edition published by arrangement with Harlequin Books S.A.

For questions and comments about the quality of this book,
please contact us at CustomerService@Harlequin.com.

Printed in U.S.A.

www.Harlequin.com

Dear Reader,

I wanted to take this opportunity to thank all of you for coming along on this ride with me. You have embraced the Shadow Breeds world and characters, which is a very humbling experience for this writer.

Witch Hunter is a bittersweet book for me, as it signifies the final chapter (at this time—and in the Shadow Breeds world, the end may not always be the end!) of the Shadow Breeds series. I have loved these characters, dreamed of these characters, railed at these characters and wept over these characters. It seemed only fitting to conclude this part of the series with Dave's story.

Dave Carter was a requested creation from a friend, reader and writer. He has made an appearance in each novel, and admittedly he's got a few traits that have intrigued me, so it was a great pleasure to flesh him out further for his own story.

Dave needed a partner who could match him in strength, but also in heart, and be just as intriguing, and I've loved getting to know Sully—and I hope you do, too!

Writing this final installment of the Shadow Breeds series brought me a lot of smiles and a lot of feels, and I'm so glad I got a chance to share that with you.

Happy reading!

Warm regards,

Shannon Curtis

This book is dedicated to all the readers who have supported me by reading this series.
You have no idea how meaningful and humbling your consideration and time have meant to me.

And thank you to Coleen, for the inspiration that has become Dave Carter, tattoo artist and witch hunter.

Chapter 1

"Why do you have so many tattoos?"

Dave lifted the tip of his needle from his client's inner wrist and gently dabbed at the skin. The woman was looking up at the ceiling, and she was exhaling slowly through her lips, as though trying not to flinch. Scream. Pee. Puke. Whatever.

"I'm a tattoo artist. Perks of the job." He eyed the intricate linework he'd inked onto her wrist. He just needed to close the top of the loop of one twist of the knot, and he was finished.

He dabbed at the skin again. He was only doing a simple line tattoo for this woman. It was her first tattoo, and she didn't think she could stand a lot of shading. He had to agree. The whole time she'd breathed as though she was in a Lamaze class. He was surprised she hadn't hyperventilated.

"I can't quite make it out…?" Her tone was raised in query.

He leaned forward, gently pressing his foot on the pedal, and the woman snapped her gaze from the mark on his arm to the ceiling again. The skin on his left breast itched.

Damn.

"I can, and that's what matters," he said, smiling at the woman as he carefully pressed the needle against her skin. He focused intently, despite the itch that was getting more annoying—and bound to become more so.

He worked as quickly as he could, his lips tightening as the itch became warm. He didn't have long.

"Are you sure you can see with those glasses on?" The woman bit her lip as he wiped petroleum jelly across her wrist to hydrate the skin, and then pressed the needle against her, concentrating on drawing out the ink.

"I'm nearly finished and you're asking me that now?" Dave raised an eyebrow, but didn't stop his work. The itch began to heat. Sweat broke out on his forehead and upper lip, and he worked faster, gritting his teeth at the burn.

He finished the line perfectly, closing the loop and preventing any breach to the protection spell he'd drawn into her tattoo.

"Right, that's done," he rasped, reaching for the anti-septic liquid soap on his table. He washed her skin and gently held her arm so that she could see the intricate linework. It looked like a delicate lace band around her wrist.

"And this will stop him…?" she asked tentatively.

He nodded. "He won't be able to raise his hand against you." He worked quickly, placing low adherent bandages over her new tattoo and taping them carefully into place. "Leave those on for about twenty-four hours—or until tomorrow morning at the earliest. It will probably look shiny and gross—don't worry, that's normal." Damn, what had started as an itch now felt like someone was directing a heat lamp on his chest. "Shower and soap it up—antiseptic soap only, nothing scented, and for God's sake, no scrubs, and don't scratch it."

Ow. Crap. The burn! He'd run out of time.

He reached over with his left hand to pick up a flyer he'd had printed. "Here are the instructions for aftercare, call me if you need anything and leave your money on the counter on the way out."

He rose from his wheeled stool, and she gaped at him, her gaze dropping to his torso. "Hey, are you all rig—?"

"Fine," he said brusquely, leaving his room and jogging down the hall. He flung open a door marked Private and ran down the metal stairs to the apartment below his tattoo parlor, below street level. He raised his hand, pushing the door at the bottom of the stairs open with his magic, and then flicking it closed behind him. He jogged down the rock-hewn corridor to the door to his private quarters, and thrust it open, kicking it closed behind him, swearing in a soft hiss as he pulled the fabric of his gray T-shirt away from the blooming stain over his left pectoral muscle. He lifted the garment over his head, moving his left arm gingerly as he removed the T-shirt.

He always left the lamp next to his armchair on in his subterranean quarters, and it gave out a low, warm light. At the moment, it was just enough light to show him the damage.

The skin on his breast was blistered, bleeding. He

sucked in and held his breath, trying not to yell or scream as it happened again.

The marking glowed as it seared into his skin, and he gritted his teeth, closing his eyes and tilting his head back as his skin was branded. The name was scorched into the very fiber of his being, and he let out a soft, pained growl as the searing seemed to continue forever. He started breathing like his recent client, short hitched gasps that stopped him from crying like a baby. The heat, the pain—it was excruciating, and left him temporarily powerless until the etching was complete.

He opened his eyes and stared at the bare-chested figure in the mirror on the wall by the door. The glow was beginning to darken, and he tried to slow his breathing down as the mark was completed, the wound glistening with his blood. He swallowed, his shoulders sagging.

Christ. That was a long name.

He stumbled closer to the mirror, and tilted his head to the side as he translated the script. *S. U.* double letters…more double letters. He turned back to the natural-edged hardwood table that was his dining table, kitchen prep, spellcasting, office desk and anything else he thought to use it for. He grabbed the pencil and notepad, then turned back to the mirror.

S.U.L.L… He jotted down the letters, gaze flicking between the notepad and the mirror, until he was sure he'd gotten it right—because he sure as hell couldn't get this wrong. Of course, it would be much easier if the Ancestors would try scripting their messages in English, and not in a language that hadn't been spoken in seven hundred years.

He held the paper in front of him and closely compared the lettering. Yep, he was right.

It was damn long name.

Sullivan Timmerman.

Dave's lips tightened. So what was Timmerman's crime?

He removed the sunglasses he always wore and took a deep breath.

"Sullivan Timmerman."

Bright light lanced his vision, and then all of a sudden he could see not his rock-walled apartment beneath his tattoo parlor, but a dark alley instead, as he gazed through Timmerman's eyes. He gazed down at the body he knelt over, and removed the blade from the man's heart. Dave watched as gloved hands picked up the limp right wrist and used the intricately carved blade to incise a rough X into the skin, and held a— Dave squinted—a horn?

Timmerman drained some blood into the horn and— Dave's stomach heaved as the killer drank the blood. He couldn't hear the words that were uttered, but the X on the wrist turned an inky black—and then Dave's vision went dark, and he blinked, his vision clearing to reveal his dim apartment.

What the—how had Timmerman kicked him out? He was usually able to piggyback on the vision of the killer until he could identify his location. This time, though, Timmerman had consumed the blood, said a few words and then blocked him.

Dave pressed his lips together. It was easy to see the witch was using dark magic, and he'd taken a life. No wonder the Ancestors had assigned him a new target.

Well, tracking the damned was part of his job, and he was good at it. He'd start looking—right after he'd patched himself up. He winced as he looked down at the brand that was already beginning to heal. Damn. It was over his heart, too. He shook his head as he stalked over to his bathroom door. The Ancestors didn't seem to care where he got the message, as long as he got it. Well, he'd received it, loud and clear.

He had a witch to kill.

Sully Timmerman glanced cautiously about the schoolroom.

"Relax, Sully. The kids are having their lunch outside," Jenny Forsyth said with a smile as she set out test papers on the students' desks.

"The day I relax is the day I get caught," Sully said, then smiled as she leaned her hip against the teacher's desk. "How are the munchkins?"

Jenny smiled. "They're good, right now. They don't know they have a math test this afternoon."

Sully grinned. "You are such a cruel woman."

"And you love it." Jenny put the paper on the last desk, then strolled toward the front of the classroom. "How is work going?"

Sully nodded. "It's slowly picking up. I have a delivery in the car for the diner, and it looks like the mayor's wife wants a new set of cutlery for their anniversary."

"Cutlery? For an anniversary?"

"Twenty-five years, silver." Sully shrugged. "Hey, it's an order, so I'm happy." Being a cutler was a dying art. There were so many cheaper options for pretty cutlery in a home, but Sully's reputation as a master cutler was finally beginning to bring in some new business, and now that she had a website, she was getting orders coming in from all over the place. She glanced at her watch and winced. "I'd better get going. I want to get Lucy in between the lunch and dinner rush."

She picked up her satchel, and the not-so-subtle

clink reminded her of the unofficial delivery in her bag. "Oops, nearly forgot."

She pulled the heavy cloth bag out of her satchel, and set it down on Jenny's desk with a dull chink. "Better find a good place for this lot."

Jenny's eyebrows rose as she undid the drawstring and peered inside. She whistled. "Wow. That is a lot of silver dollars. That will help quite a few families," she said quietly. She lifted her gaze to Sully's. "You take a big risk, you know."

Sully shrugged. "Hey, every little bit counts, right? It's not much, but if it helps, than that's the main thing." She was satisfied with this particular delivery. She'd counterfeited over two thousand dollars, this time, and that bag contained only about half that. Jenny would make sure it got to those who most needed it. This null community was struggling, more so than most, and if the offcuts from the pieces she made could help put food on the table for some of these people, then the risk was worth it. She pulled her strap up over her shoulder as the school bell chimed outside, signaling the end of the lunch play period. "Now, hide it, or we'll both be in trouble."

Jenny opened her desk drawer and dropped the bag inside as the door to the classroom burst open, and her students swarmed inside. Their eyes brightened when they saw Sully, and she was nearly bowled over when the twenty or so seven-year-olds rushed to her. She hugged as many as she could as she made her way through the throng to the door.

"Hey, Sully, you want to join us next month for the school fete?" Jenny called.

The school fete was scheduled to coincide with the Harvest Moon Festival. Sully turned as the kids cheered, and she folded her arms and frowned. "I don't know. Is it worth it, Noah?" she looked at the young red-haired boy, who nodded, his blue eyes bright. Noah's mother, Susanne, was another of Sully's friends.

"It is, Sully. We've got rides and *donkeys*."

Sully's eyebrows rose. "Donkeys?" She glanced over at Jenny.

"Petting zoo," Jenny explained. She leaned closer. "Jacob will be there, too."

Sully shot her friend an exasperated look. Jenny had been trying to fix her up with her brother since she'd moved to Serenity Cove, and to date Sully had successfully avoided the hookup. Jacob was nice—good-looking, too, but she just wasn't interested. In anyone. She turned back to Noah.

"Donkeys, huh? Oh, well, I'll have to come for that." She winked at him. "Tell your mom hi from me." She waved to the kids as she closed the door behind her, grinning. A day surrounded by nulls? Yes, please.

She strode out of the two-story building that was elementary, middle and high school to the resident null community, and over to her beat-up sky blue station wagon. She sat in the driver's seat for a moment, enjoying the peace, the quiet. All the kids were back in class, but she was still close enough she was affected by their presence.

She closed her eyes. She was surrounded by…nothing. It was so beautiful. Dark. Silent. Peaceful. It was the absence, the void, that embraced her, and she loved it. She knew most witches avoided nulls like a hex, but she found there was a tranquility in their presence that she couldn't find anywhere else.

She opened her eyes, and shored up her shields, making sure that there were no cracks, no fractures in her defenses. When she was satisfied her mental walls were strong, and no light could cut through, she started her engine and drove the ten minutes into Serenity Cove.

She pulled the box out from the back of her car, lifting the tailgate with her hip. She didn't bother winding up the window or locking it. Anybody with half a mind to steal her car must be desperate, and welcome to it. Besides, everyone in town knew this was her car, and you didn't steal from a witch. The resulting curse wasn't worth it.

She walked up the steps to the Brewhaus Diner, and her flip-flops made a smacking sound on the veranda. She pushed through the door and the tinkling sound of the bell above the door brought an almost instinctive response as she stepped inside. She put a smile on her face as she ignored muffled emotions knocking at her protective walls.

Cheryl Conners, the waitress, was hiding her hurt that Sheriff Clinton was absorbed in his phone and not her. Sheriff Clinton was worried—but that seemed to be his default setting. Harold's gout was troubling him, Graham, the cook, was tired and his feet hurt, Mrs. Peterson was fighting off a strong cold, and Lucy—

Sully halted at the diner counter. Lucy wasn't happy. No, she was...heartbroken. She couldn't see the woman, but she could feel her pain—and that was with her shields up.

She placed the box on the counter and looked over at Cheryl as the waitress walked over to her.

"I'm here to see Lucy," Sully said softly. She glanced toward the swing door that led to the kitchen and the office beyond. "Is she okay?"

Cheryl shook her head. "She got some bad news."

She lifted her chin in the direction of the sheriff. "They found Gary's body last night."

Sully gasped, then lifted her hand to cover her mouth. "Oh, no."

Gary Adler was the coach over at the null comprehensive school, and Lucy's longtime boyfriend. No wonder the woman emitted the feel of devastation.

Sully patted the box on the counter. "Look, I'll leave these here, we can talk about sorting stuff out later. She's got enough on her plate, tell her not to worry about this. We can talk when she's ready, but don't stress over it." She adjusted the strap of her bag on her shoulder. "When is the funeral?"

"Won't be for a few days, yet," Sheriff Clinton said, glancing up from his phone. "We've got to wait for the autopsy."

Sully nodded. Gary had watched what he ate, exercised regularly, and apart from that one Christmas festival, didn't drink much. She wasn't aware of him suffering from any illness. They'd have to do an autopsy to find out what had made a relatively healthy man drop dead.

"Any ideas what the cause was?" she asked the sheriff.

He grimaced. "We're guessing it was the stab wound to the heart that did it."

Cheryl's jaw dropped. "What?"

Sully's eyes widened. "Are you saying he was murdered?"

"Well, it didn't look like he fell on the knife, or stabbed himself," the sheriff commented dryly.

"Oh, no, poor Lucy," Sully murmured. "I'll go home and put together a tea for her." She nodded to herself. "I should go visit with Gary's mother, too." Gary's mother lived in a tiny cottage on the northern tip of the sea-side town, along with the bulk of the null community. "She'll be devastated."

Sheriff Clinton nodded. "Yeah. I'm sure Mary Anne would appreciate a visit, but I don't think a tea will help her."

Sully smiled sadly. "Not in the usual way, but herbs can still affect a Null, just like any other person, and there's always a little comfort to be found in a shared brew."

She waved briefly to the sheriff and Cheryl, and was nearly at the door when she snapped her fingers. She walked back over to Mrs. Peterson, and gently placed her hand over the older woman's.

"How are you, Mrs. Peterson?" she asked loudly so the woman could hear.

"What's that, dear?" Mrs. Peterson leaned forward.

"I said, how are you?" Sully said as loud as she could without shouting at the woman.

She opened her shield a crack and pulled in some of the pain she could sense in the swollen knuckles, and fed some warmth through in return, laced with a little calm.

The older woman's face creased like a scrunched-up piece of paper when she smiled up at Sully.

"I'm doing well, Sully," she said in her wavery voice.

"You're looking nice today. I like your dress," Sully said, gently patting the back of the woman's hand. She could already sense the easing of tension in the old woman as her arthritic pain subsided.

"What mess?" Mrs. Peterson glanced down in confusion at the table.

"Your *dress*," Sully repeated. "I like your dress." Pity

she couldn't do anything about the woman's hearing—but she was an empath witch, not a god.

"Oh, thank you, dear," Mrs. Peterson said, and her face scrunched up even further as her smile broadened.

Sully nodded and winked, then turned in the direction of the door, cradling her hand on the top of her satchel. She closed her mental walls, ensuring nothing else leaked in she wasn't ready for. She walked on toward the door and waved at Harold when he signaled her. "Don't worry, I'll bring you something back later, too, Harold." She wagged a finger at him. "But you really do need to lay off the shellfish."

She pushed through the door, her smile tightening as the pain in her hand throbbed. Poor Mrs. Peterson. That really was a painful condition.

She skipped down the steps and dusted her hands as she walked to her car. To anyone else it looked like she was shaking black pepper off her hands as she discarded the pain she'd drawn in from Mrs. Peterson.

She considered the teas she'd make for Lucy and Mary Anne Adler as she climbed into her car. Lemon balm, linden and motherwort, she decided. They each had a calming effect, and the motherwort would be especially helpful with the heartache and grief. She waited for a motorcycle to turn across the intersection in front of her, and then pulled out. She sighed. Poor Gary. Murdered. Who would do such a thing?

Chapter 2

Dave pulled his motorbike into a spot on Main Street, and slid his helmet off his head. He looked around. So this was Serenity Cove, huh? The town was picture-postcard quaint. Victorian cottages, cute little boutiques and stores, and lots of white picket fences and ornate trim. Lots and lots. This place looked so damned sweet, he could feel a toothache coming on.

There were a few people wandering around. Admittedly, he thought there'd be more. It was summer and Serenity Cove had a fishing marina, nice little beaches—if his online searches could be trusted—but for some reason there wasn't the usual vacationers drifting around with beet-red sunburns and sarongs. A local bar also seemed to be missing from the scene. He eyed the diner across the street. In lieu of a bar to visit and source information, this place would have to do. Maybe someone in there could tell him where the bar was—after he got some intel on Sullivan Timmerman.

He swung his leg over the bike and placed his helmet over the dash and ignition, uttering a simple security spell. It never paid to mess with a witch's stuff.

It had been surprisingly easy to track down the witch. The guy had a website, for crying out loud. It was obviously a front, though. A cutler? He'd never heard of the trade. Most people just went to the store and bought their cutlery. Who would have a set made?

He crossed the street and entered the diner, the tinkling of the bell over the door causing the patrons to look up. He didn't remove his sunglasses, but then he didn't have a problem seeing inside An older man, an even older lady and—oh, good. A sheriff. Dave sighed. He wasn't sure if it was the bike leathers, or the tattoos, but the law always seemed to w nt to chat with him.

He strolled down to the opposite end of the diner counter and slid onto a stool. The solitary waitress bustled over to him, a smile on her face. Dave smiled back. He read her name tag. Cheryl.

"Hey, stranger, can I get you something?" She leaned a hand on the counter and gave him a wink.

He grinned as he removed his gloves. "That depends, Cheryl." Her smile broadened at his use of her name. "What can you recommend?" He kept his tone light and flirtatious, and out of the corner of his eye he saw the sheriff lift his gaze from his phone.

She folded her arms on the counter and leaned forward. "Well," she said, drawing the word out slowly. "I've just put a fresh pot of coffee on, so I haven't had a chance to burn it, yet, and the peach pie is pretty good."

He nodded. "I'll take that. For starters," He winked

back at her. She was pretty, she was nice and liked to flirt. Serenity Cove might be all right, after all.

"What brings you to Serenity Cove?" The sheriff put his phone away and directed his full attention to him. His tone was casual, conversational, but the look in the man's eyes was anything but.

"I'm looking for someone," Dave replied as Cheryl placed a plate in front of him. She reached for the coffee carafe and poured him a cup, and he took care not to touch anything until she was finished. He waved away the cream and sugar she offered.

"Who?" the sheriff asked. This time his tone wasn't so casual or conversational.

"Tyler," Cheryl chided. "Be nice to our visitor."

"No, it's okay," Dave said. If there had been a murder, this officer would know about it—had to, in a place as small as Serenity Cove. He needed information from the man, and he didn't want to seem threatening or dangerous, because that would lead to an entirely different conversation.

"I'm looking for a friend," Dave said, flashing a smile at the sheriff in an effort to appear friendly. "I was in the area, so I thought I'd catch up."

"You have a friend?" the older man sitting at a booth near the door piped up. "Here?"

Dave kept his face impassive. Was the guy surprised at the idea of him having a friend in Serenity Cove or having a friend at all? "Yeah."

"Who?" Cheryl asked as she leaned against the counter. She didn't bother to hide her curiosity.

"Sullivan Timmerman."

Cheryl's eyes widened. "You know Sully?" her expression was incredulous as she looked him up and down.

"How do you know Sully?" the sheriff asked, his brow dipping.

Sully, huh? Dave took a moment to slip a bit of the peach pie into his mouth as he thought about his response. He always had an explanation ready for barflies, but talking with law enforcement required finesse and strategy. He swallowed the mouthful of pie—and Cheryl was right, it was pretty good.

"Are you an old boyfriend?" the older guy in the booth asked.

Dave coughed into the coffee mug he held to his lips. Boyfriend? Sullivan Timmerman had boyfriends?

"We went to school together," he responded cautiously once he'd cleared his throat. He hoped to hell Timmerman hadn't gone to school around here, although the information he'd found online suggested probably not. Timmerman had set up his business four years ago, but he hadn't been able to find any mention of the guy in the local schools' hall of fame lists for athletics or other clubs.

"Did you date?" Cheryl asked, waggling her eyebrows.

"Uh…" He ate some more pie as he thought of an appropriate response.

"What's that about Sully?" the old lady called out, cupping her hand to her ear.

"This guy used to date Sully," the guy in the booth yelled back.

"Why do you hate Sully?" the woman asked, horrified.

Dave blinked as Cheryl leaned over the counter. "Date, Mrs. Peterson. *Date.*"

"Oh." The old woman looked him up and down, then raised her eyebrows. "You don't say."

"You just missed her," Cheryl told him, then waved toward the door. "She left about five minutes ago."

Her. *Her.* He dipped his head for a moment. Phew. Then he frowned. He'd somehow felt a masculine energy in his vision and had assumed he was looking for a man. In his line of work, he couldn't rest on assumptions. The radio on the sheriff's hip squawked, and the man sighed as he levered himself off the chair.

"Gotta go." He grabbed his hat off the seat next to him and put it on his head. "How long are you intending to stay in Serenity Cove?" he asked Dave.

Dave waved a hand. "Oh, I'm only passing through." This kind of job never took long.

The sheriff nodded, satisfied, then turned to walk out the door.

"Bye, Tyler," Cheryl called. The sheriff didn't turn back, but lifted his hand in a casual wave of farewell. Dave caught the fleeting look of disappointment on her face before she masked it with a smile. "So, you used to date Sully, huh?"

Wow. These people were good. He bet that by the time he got back to his bike, he and this Sully would be in a serious, angst-ridden relationship. Which could work for him, really.

"Yeah," he said, folding his arms on the table and leaning forward conspiratorially. "I want to surprise her, though. Uh, do you know where I can find her?" He sent a compulsion spell in Cheryl's direction.

"She lives out at Crescent Head, north end, overlooking Driftwood Beach," Cheryl responded automatically, then blinked.

"Thanks." Dave scooped up the last of his pie, and nodded farewell as he rose from his seat. He donned his gloves and waved politely to the older patrons as he passed them.

He halted outside the diner. Two youths were checking out his bike. One of them even had the audacity to reach for the handlebars and pretend to steer. He frowned. His security spell should have knocked the kid off his feet. He flicked his fingers at him, but encountered...nothing. He frowned and tried to again.

Nothing.

He grimaced. Great. Nulls. He glanced about. Where there was one—or in this case, two—there were always more. Hopefully, though, it wouldn't interfere with what he had to do.

He sauntered across the street, and the teens took off as soon as they noticed him. He might not be able to cast a spell on them, but at least he could still look fierce.

Good. Because he had a witch to hunt.

Sully ignored the sparks as she ground the steel against the wheel. She turned the arrowhead slowly, shifting now and then to avoid smoothing the sharp angles she'd hammered into the steel. She pulled back, lifting the arrowhead to the light. Just a little more off there...

She held it back to the wheel and evened out the side, sliding the steel across the spinning wheel. When she was satisfied, she took her foot off the pedal and switched off the grinder.

She crossed over to the forge she'd made out of a soup can, sand and plaster. She'd turned the torch on a little while ago, so it was now ready for her. Using pliers, she carefully placed the arrowhead inside the forge, and then waited for it to glow. She stepped back and lifted her mask to take a sip of water from the glass on the shed sill. It was hot in the shed, and she was sweating profusely.

It didn't take too long before the arrowhead was glowing. She reached in with the pliers, and carefully dunked it into her bucket of oil, pausing for a long moment before withdrawing it.

Sully smiled. The arrowhead was in the square-headed bodkin style. Sure, the broadhead arrows were sharper and caused more damage, but every now and then it was a nice change to go for a classic shape. Besides, it had worked for the Vikings, so it wasn't completely useless. And it was exactly what Trey Mackie wanted—he wanted to try hunting just like his computer game avatar did. When the set of arrows were completed, she'd have to have a word with him about aiming at folks. She didn't make weapons for "fun". Weapons weren't toys. She'd bespell them, but she also wanted to make sure the youth used them responsibly.

She placed the arrowhead on the bench next to the other four she'd made that day. Damn, she must reek. She'd go for a quick dip before heading out to see Mary Anne. She shut down the torch on the forge and cleaned up, then quickly strode across her back garden to her cottage. Within minutes she'd donned a bikini, then threw on a peasant-style top and her long, flowing skirt. She didn't bother to fasten the belt that already twined through the loops on her skirt. The loose clothes were her stock standard wardrobe, especially for summer. She grabbed a ratty old towel, slipped her feet into her flip-flops and trotted to the end of her street. A path led from there to the stairs at the top of the cliff, and then down to the beach below. She paused at the grassy verge at the top of the stairs and took a moment to tilt her head back and let the sun shine down on her. This

was one of her favorite spots, offering a one-hundred-
and-eighty-degree view of the ocean. She could feel the
kiss of a breeze against her skin, the heat of the sun as
it beat down on her. The smell of salt and grass and the
summer blossoms in her garden… The waves crashing
on the beach below. This was one of her recharge places,
where she could give herself up to elements of nature
and restore her own energy. She gazed out at the vista.
Dark clouds were gathering on the horizon. Whether a
storm was coming, or about to pass, she couldn't tell.
She sighed and then headed for the stairs.

Driftwood Beach was pretty much deserted. She
saw a man walking his dog down the other end, but it
looked like he was at the end of his walk, rather than
the start. She was the only other person to walk across
the sands. Most folks preferred the more sheltered Crescent Beach for a swim, just on the other side of the
headland. Occasionally surfers would venture this far
north out of town, but the surf at Caves' Beach was
much better. She hadn't necessarily been looking for a
private beach when she settled here at Crescent Head,
it had just worked out that way. And she loved it. The
less people she had to deal with, the better.

The surf was crisp and cool, exactly what she needed.
The water embraced her, shielded her. She couldn't feel
when she was fully immersed in the water. It was just
her and the deep void, the occasional sea creature and
strands of seaweed that always startled her into thinking
it was a shark. For some reason, though, she was never
bothered by the predators of the sea. No matter how
far she swam out, it was like the sea provided a shelter
for her. Buoyant, enveloping…peaceful. She let herself
go, relaxed her mental shields and surrendered to utter

unguarded enjoyment. This was as good as being surrounded by nulls, and the void their presence created.

After diving beneath a couple of waves she strode
out of the water, lifting her knees so she could walk
faster. Within minutes she'd patted herself dry, pulled
her clothes on over the top of her swimsuit and fastened
her belt. She stood on the beach, looking out over the
water. By now it was late afternoon. She'd like to stay a
little longer, maybe watch the sunset, but she'd promised
teas for Lucy and Mrs. Peterson, and Harold something
for his gout. She decided she'd take a double-prong attack with Harold. Something to rub on his toe for in-
stant comfort and a tea to start working from the inside.

She remained where she was and closed her eyes. She
mentally pictured her shutters rolling down to shield
her mind. As she was going to be visiting grief-stricken
women, she added a couple of extra layers to ensure she
was protected from the waves of heartbreak she'd en-
counter. Once Sully was sure she could stand calmly
in a room with them both and not crumble to the floor,
curl into the fetal position and sob at the overwhelming pain, she opened her eyes.

A movement in the corner of her vision made her
turn her head. A guy was walking along the beach.
No, walking was too gentle a word. He was striding
purposefully, his gait even and rhythmic. His broad
shoulders moved with each step he took, like the slinky
stalk of a predatory big cat. Graceful. That's what it
was. Little puffs of sand rose at each step, catching in
the breeze to dance a little before falling back to the
beach. The man moved with a physical grace that suggested he was used to moving, with an added strength
that made him look dangerous.

And way sexy. Sully took a moment to enjoy the

view. He was built. Like, stripper-at-a-bachelorette-party built, with broad shoulders and lean hips, and thighs that looked… Her lips curled inward. Strong. Despite the heat, the man wore leather pants, boots and a black leather jacket over what she hoped was a T-shirt, for his sake. His hair was cropped short, and the sunglasses hid his eyes. She briefly wondered if he looked just as good out of them as in them. She'd once dated a guy, Marty, who looked hot in his shades, but when he'd removed them he'd revealed his sunken eyes, the dark shadows beneath and the enlarged pupils of a drug addict—which was never a good combination when mixed with his witch talents—such as they were.

Sully shook her head as she turned her back on the leather-clad man. Cute, but she wasn't interested. She sure knew how to pick 'em, as her grandmother would say. Marty was the reason she'd moved clear across the country and settled herself in a Null-saturated area. Never trust a guy who hides his eyes.

She scooped up her flip-flops and started to trudge along the waterline in the opposite direction, toward the timber stairs that hugged the cliff and led to the cliff-top walk.

She normally cut her herbs at either sunrise or sunset, when they were most potent. She'd have to hurry so she could collect all the ingredients for the teas she planned to make for her patients. Clients. Whatever you wanted to call them.

A soft breeze, warm and whispery, teased at the hem of her skirt. She grasped some of the fabric in her hand, lifting the skirt as she waded through the shallows, her lips curving at the rhythmic, refreshing chill of the waves washing over her feet.

"Sullivan Timmerman!"

Sully frowned at the sound of her name and glanced over her shoulder. The man in black was closer to her, his expression—well, it didn't look flirty or friendly. No, he looked determined.

"What?"

"Are you Sullivan Timmerman?" the man asked again, and Sully nodded, although the movement was more a cautious dip of her head. She halted, but still looked over her shoulder at him, ready to bolt if need be. At this distance, though, she could see more of his face. He was unshaven, but not unkempt. The dusting of a beard along his jawline was closely trimmed, but it didn't hide the strong line of his jaw, or the sculpted shape of his lips. His cheekbones were balanced, his sunglasses revealing tiny lines at the corners of his eyes that could be from laughter, or scowling, she had no idea. Although she couldn't see his eyes, she could feel his stare boring into her.

There was an intensity about this man, a focus, that sparked a flare of attraction, yet the overwhelming impression she got was one of danger. She instinctively bolstered her shields with more protection. Whatever this guy was going through, she didn't want to feel it.

And yet…she knew she'd never seen this man, but there was something familiar about him, something she couldn't quite put her finger on, but it was intuitive, a bone-deep recognition she couldn't quite fathom.

"Uh, yes," she answered. She turned to face him warily. "Who wants to know?"

The man raised both of his arms out from his sides, palms up, fingers curled slightly. He started to murmur in a low voice, and it took Sully a moment to realize he was talking in the Old Language. She frowned as she struggled to decipher his words.

"…for your dark crimes, and the Ancestors call upon your return to the Other Realm, to a place of execution—"

Sully's eyes widened in shock. Holy crap. A memory, lessons long since learned and nearly forgotten, fluttered in her mind, but it was dread that hit her, followed by comprehension.

"—until you are dead. May the Ancestors have mercy upon your soul."

His wrists rolled as he brought his arms around in front, toward her, and still clutching her flip-flops, she brought her own arms up, crossing them in front of her chest to brace against the magical blast that rolled over her.

Her feet created long burrows in the sand as she was pushed back under the force—a force that should have crushed her, but was mostly deflected by her shields.

The man blinked when he realized she remained standing.

"What the—?" Sully gaped at him, stunned dismay warring with anger. The Witch Hunter. He was here. Now. For *her*.

The man tilted his head. "Hmm." He raised his arms again, and Sully narrowed her eyes.

"Oh, no you don't." She refused to be at another man's mercy. She summoned her own magic, drawing from deep within and hurling her own cloud of badassery in his direction. Their powers met with a thunderous clap. Sully's shields coalesced into swirling colors as his magic rolled over her safeguards, and she twisted, guiding the force around and beyond her. Away from her.

Holy capital H.C. Crap. The Witch Hunter. One of the most powerful witches in existence, and he wanted to return her to the Other Realm.

She sidestepped another supernatural blast, de-flecting it right back at him. He grunted as it hit him, sending him stumbling for a few steps. It gave her enough of a respite to bolster up her shields. She didn't have the juice to kill him—and she couldn't begin to fathom the karma that would come from killing the Witch Hunter—but she might be able hold him off long enough to—*oh, crap.*

It seemed he'd figured he couldn't pierce her shields, and had decided a more direct approach was in order. He roared something that could have been a battle cry in the Old Language—or perhaps a curse word—then lowered his head and charged straight at her.

Sully dipped to the side and started to run, but he flung out his arm and caught her around the knees. She hit the sand hard. She tried to wriggle away as he pulled her toward him.

Chapter 3

Dave swore as the witch flung a handful of sand in his face. What the—how the hell was Timmerman so damn strong? She'd shaken off his initial blast like a dog shaking off water.

She muttered something, and then her bare foot connected with his chest, sending him flying. A percussion incantation. Damn it. He flung another blast in her direction, but saw the sparks as it rolled over the armor she'd shielded herself with. Any other time he'd admit to being impressed, but right now he was annoyed. He had a duty to perform, and her impressive damn barriers were preventing him from doing it.

He murmured a spell, raising his hands, fingers splayed, satisfied when he felt the erosion spell spread over her shield like a wave of acid, eroding her safeguards.

She flinched, her face paling, and she murmured

something. A wall of sand rose around him, enclosing him. He uttered a quick spell, and the sand erupted away from him.

A flip-flop slapped him in the face. His head whipped back at the sting. He blinked, shaking his head, then focused on his—where the hell did she go?

The beach was empty. He narrowed his eyes, scanning the sand. There. His lips curved. The damn witch had covered herself with an unseen spell, but that didn't mean she didn't leave tracks.

He saw the footprints and the little puffs of sand as she ran up the beach. He took off after her. He gritted his teeth. He hated running in sand. It always felt like it was clawing at you, pulling you back, slowing you down. He angled across the wet sand, where it was firmer under foot, then growled. *Screw it.*

He raised his hand toward her, murmuring a restraining spell, and a lariat of power lashed from his hand, encircling his target. He heard her surprised cry when he yanked her back. The sand was forming thrashing mounds, until finally she couldn't hold her invisibility *and* fight off his magical restraint, and her concealment gave way to show the struggling woman as he dragged her toward him.

A wave of water edged around his boots. Damn it. His favorite boots were getting a bath in salt water.

He grasped her thighs, and she roared—*roared* at him, her fist connecting with his jaw. His teeth snapped, and he blinked, then jerked to avoid the feet that kicked uncomfortably close to his groin. He tugged her farther along the sand.

"Sullivan Timmerman," he panted, straddling her thighs to keep her from turning him into a eunuch. "You have been found guilty of—"

He closed his eyes instinctively as her hand flashed toward him, catching him on the cheek in an open-handed, stinging slap. By the time he focused again, she held a short but wickedly sharp blade in each hand, one pointed at his groin, the other against his throat.

He froze, and his eyebrows rose. "Well, aren't you full of surprises?" That was an understatement. The woman had deflected his power with a skill he hadn't seen before, and now had him at a slight disadvantage. Only slight, though. He outweighed, outmuscled and outpowered her. If outpowered was a thing.

"This is a little extreme for some coins, don't you think?" she panted up at him.

He frowned. "What?" Coins? What? The memory of her victim, the man in the alley with the *X* carved in his flesh…the draining of his blood. The blade in his chest…he didn't recall seeing any money. What the hell did all that have to do with coins?

"What the hell do the Ancestors have against the nulls?" she demanded.

His frown deepened. What the—? He was having trouble keeping up with the conversation. And why were they even having this conversation? Was she completely mad? Did she seriously not comprehend the damage she'd done—to an innocent, to the balance of nature itself? He'd never really had a witch withstand justice before, at least, not long enough to challenge the Ancestors. The blade at his neck pressed against his skin just a little harder.

"Get off me. Now." Her blue eyes glared at him, and her slightly lopsided mouth formed a tight pout. Her hair hung in a tangled curtain behind her, dark and wet and…okay, maybe a little bit more than mildly sexy. She was attractive, slim yet curvy beneath him. Her cotton top clung to the wet triangles of her red bikini, and despite the toned strength of her arms and the thighs he straddled, she still had a softness about her that would have had him buying her a drink in a bar under different circumstances. Very different. Like, without the execution directive.

Maybe that was one of the reasons this woman was so damn dangerous. She looked like some sexy beach goddess, but he'd seen the blade in the man's heart, the carving on his wrist, and…ugh. His eyes flicked to those pouty little lips. She'd drunk his blood. She'd killed a human. And it hadn't been in self-defense. It hadn't been to protect others. It had been calculated and cruel. It was intentional harm to an innocent, to the personal benefit of the witch. He had no idea *why* she'd killed the man, or why she'd murdered in the manner she had, but he was the enforcer, his authority was recognized by Reform society and by the witch population. No matter how damn smoking hot sexy the witch was, she'd committed a crime against nature, against all of witchery, and she had to be punished.

He held up his hands, palms out, in a nonthreatening manner as he rose. She shuffled out from beneath him, her daggers still held in a guarded, defensive position. He eyed her outfit. Loose sleeves, loose skirt—where the hell had she hidden those blades?

He let her back up a little. She thought she now had the upper hand. She was so wrong, but for now he'd let her go with it.

"This is not fair," she hissed at him as she took another step backward.

His eyebrows rose. "Not fair? Do you think I haven't heard that before?"

She shook her head, frowning at him. "What I did—

sure, some might consider it a crime, but I was doing it for the greater good."

He shook his head. "Yeah, I've heard that before, too."

"Damn it, I mean it. There was no harm done!"

"No harm?" he repeated, incredulous. His brows dipped. "Are you kidding me? You think that what you did was *harmless*?"

"I was doing a service for the community," she snapped back at him.

"A service." His lips tightened, and he had to look away for a brief moment. Her words sparked a flare of anger in him that he didn't normally let himself feel. "You want to talk service? I live my life in service, and what you did—" he wagged a finger at her. "You should be ashamed. You've brought darkness to all of witchery for your actions."

Her eyebrows rose. "Darkness? To all of witchery? Wow. They've really set the bar low, then, haven't they? What I did, and how it affects others, should have no bearing whatsoever on all of witchery. For the Ancestors to call upon the Witch Hunter over such a trifling matter—that's extreme."

He gaped at her. She talked about murder so callously, as though it was of such little consequence. He couldn't begin to imagine the damage this woman could do if she wasn't stopped.

He took a step forward, and she shifted, angling the blades toward him. "I can defend every damn thing I've done," she said in a low voice.

Disappointment, hot and sickening, roiled through him. "You defend the indefensible," he said. "And for that, the Ancestors call you to—"

He dived for her, thigh muscles bunching as he

launched himself at her. He caught her hands and raised them above her head as he tackled her to the ground. Her breath left her in a grunt as she hit the sand. He spread his body over hers, using his weight to anchor her beneath him.

That's when it hit him. It was as though their powers met and coalesced in a sensory explosion. Her scent, salty and sweet, clouded his mind, as though blanketing him in an awareness of the woman beneath him. Her hair, wet and dark, still showed the odd strand of burnished gold. Her skin, smooth and warm, her eyes so blue and stormy, and her mouth—a delicate, lopsided pout that drew his attention.

For a moment, they both halted, staring at each other. Her mouth opened, and her expression showed her confusion, her surprise. His gaze dropped down to her lips, and he could hear his heartbeat throbbing in his ears—or was it her heartbeat? He couldn't tell. He lifted his stare to hers, dazed. He blinked—and time snapped its fingers, speeding up through the last few moments, folding itself over so that he felt a little unbalanced, a little bereft and a whole lot shaken.

She was supposed to be a hit, damn it. As though she was also catching up to speed—or perhaps she hadn't felt whatever the hell that was—the woman beneath him frowned up at him and started to struggle again.

She was surprisingly strong, and tried to free her arms, those blades glinting in the light from the setting sun. His grasp tightened on her wrists until she whimpered slightly and released her hold on the short daggers.

He stared down at her. Her cheeks were flushed, her blue eyes bright with outrage and perhaps a tiny bit of fear. Her chest was heaving beneath his, her breasts

brushing against his pecs. His legs were tangled with
hers, and as his gaze drifted down her body, he saw the
fabric of her skirt had hiked up in the struggle, revealing a shapely calf and toned thigh. He'd have to be a
dead man not to find the woman attractive, and it was
with a heavy heart that he returned his gaze to hers.

She was young. Passionate. Highly skilled. What a
waste of a witch. She could have done so much good,
and yet she'd acted against nature, against humanity—
the vulnerable people they were charged to protect from
the shadow breeds.

"Please, don't," she whispered, shaking her head.

"I have to," he told her quietly. "This brings me no
joy."

Her pouty lips trembled, and she nodded. "I know."

He blinked at the unexpected concession from the
witch he was about to kill. He eyed her face, the resig-
nation in her expression, despite the resistance in her
eyes. He wished… He shut that thought down. That way
led to madness. Wishes were for fools. His lips firmed,
and he sucked in a breath.

"The Ancestors call upon your return to—"

"The Other Realm, yeah, I know the drill," she said.
"I remember the First Degree classes. Why don't we
skip the speech and get to it?"

He frowned. She had just fought him off with skill
and power of an elder, she'd almost gotten away from
him, had pulled a knife—two, actually—on him, and
now she wanted him to hurry up and kill her. This
woman was doing his head in.

"Why are you suddenly so eager to die?" He dipped
his head to gaze directly into her eyes, despite his sunglasses. Admittedly, this was possibly the most conver-

sation he'd ever had with one of his hits, but he couldn't help it. She was an intriguing package of contradictions.

"I just realized that death isn't all bad," she said softly, lifting her chin.

He tilted his head, surprised. "You do realize that being summoned to the Other Realm is kind of...*bad*." It was hell—at least, a witch's version of it. Being summoned by the Ancestors who watched from beyond the veil was most definitely not good. The Ancestors had been there long enough to know how to tailor punishment to an excruciating degree for the individual witch who dared to act contrary to the beliefs and morality of the universal covens.

Her expression softened into one of sadness, a weariness that was a stark contrast to the young, vibrant woman she'd seemed just a short while ago as she'd tried to kick his ass.

"I'm ready."

He hesitated. He didn't often come across a target resigned and accepting of their fate. This particular hit was proving a first on many fronts. He nodded. "Okay, then." His frown deepened. After holding a blade to his balls, this witch was proving to be quite civil.

He moved back, just a little bit, one hand still grasping both of her wrists as he pulled his other hand back, almost as though to strike. "May the Ancestors have mercy upon your soul."

He summoned his inherited powers and sparks flickered at his fingertips.

Heat blazed across his chest. He cried out in pain and grasped his left pec as he rolled off her. He blinked furiously, trying to catch his breath.

What was happening? What the *hell* was—?

"Argh," he growled as the name branded on his chest

flared to life. He shook his head. No. No, this can't be happening. She's here, he was about—

He winced as the wound blistered anew, and pulled at his T-shirt, tearing the fabric from neck to hem. He grunted when the cloth pulled away from the burn.

The witch on the ground next to him rolled, grabbing one of the blades in the sand before she scrambled to his side. She clasped the dagger in both hands and raised it above her head, poised to bring it down on him.

The pain was blinding, all-consuming, and he couldn't do anything to defend himself. When the ancestral fire was branded into his skin, he was powerless. He stared up at the woman above him, confused. She was here, and yet her name was being rebranded into his flesh.

Another innocent had been killed.

But not by this witch.

The woman started to bring the blade down, but she gasped when she looked down at his body.

Sully dropped the knife, her gaze locked on the Witch Hunter's chest. His T-shirt hung in tatters at his side. His chest was broadly muscled, his skin a light golden tan, his toned torso lined with dark tattoos that looked both beautiful and dangerous, but it was the glowing mark that drew her gaze, and made the sweat break out on her brow as she tried resurrect her shields.

Sullivan Timmerman.

It was written in the Old Language, but she couldn't mistake it.

Her name radiated on his chest, searing through his skin as though borne from a fire within, and the cords of his neck stuck out in stark relief as he tilted his head, growling in pain.

Holy capital H.C. Crap. She was too late.

She sucked in a breath at the hot wave that flashed through her, over her. It was *everywhere*. Pain. Tormented heat. Searing agony. Guilt. Self-loathing. Confusion. Loyalty. So many more emotions, too fast, too ferocious to name, bombarded her. The sensations were excruciating.

The Witch Hunter writhed on the ground, his teeth gritted, until she felt the pain drop from excruciating agony to aggravating throb. He gasped as he rolled over and onto his knees, wheezing slightly.

Sully looked away, mustering all the strength she could from within to shakily layer up some protections, although they were weak and tattered. Holy f—

"Sullivan Timmerman," the man at her side gasped, turning away from her as he removed his sunglasses to stare at the sea.

She eyed him warily. She tried to swallow, but couldn't quite get past the lump in her throat. Her arms hung limply by her side and she trembled all over. It didn't seem to matter, though. The Witch Hunter didn't look like he was talking to her, though. He was on his knees, hands fisted in the sand, and she stared at the back of his head as his chest rose and fell with deep, shuddering breaths. How the hell could the man still be conscious after that experience? Her gut twisted, and she felt shaky and nauseous, and quite frankly wanted to curl up on the sand and pass out.

After a moment he dipped his head, then he slid his sunglasses on. Sully rose to her feet, stumbled on her shaky knees and almost face-planted in the sand when she bent over to scoop up her blades. If he was coming for her again, she was going to fight. He'd obliterated her shields, and it would take her some time to rebuild them, but she could still hit.

Right now, though, all she could feel was him. His pain, his shock, his confusion.

He glanced over his shoulder to her, his brows drawn. "Sullivan Timmerman...?"

This time, his tone was uncertain, and she raised her arms in front of her in a defensive block, blades ready. She didn't bother to answer him. She'd almost gotten herself killed the last time she'd responded.

He shook his head as he rose to his feet. "You're not the right one." Even if she couldn't hear it in his tone, or see it in his face, she could feel the shock reverberating through him, the dismay. The guilt.

Her eyes widened, and she gaped at him. "Are you—? What the—? Holy—." She blinked at him. He'd just attacked her. Nearly killed her. And she wasn't the *right one*? She'd almost *died*. For the briefest of moments, she'd *wanted* to die. She squished that thought down deep, buried it under a fragile barrier.

He drew himself up to his full height, and she could see his wound was already beginning to heal, the lettering darkening to a semblance of what she'd assume would become a tattoo that matched the rest of the markings on his body.

He touched his abdomen and dipped his head. "I have made a grave mistake. My duty is not with you. Please forgive me, Sullivan Timmerman."

His apology was sincere, his gestures faintly noble. Courtly. His earnestness was almost tangible, along with a profound sense of guilt, of sadness and of dismayed shock. And pain.

"For—forgive you?" she responded, her mouth slack. She'd practically begged him to kill her.

Her lips tightened, her eyes narrowed. "Screw you, Witch Hunter."

She backed away from him, then turned and headed toward the cliff stairs. He'd tried to kill her, and normally she wouldn't be turning her back on a man who'd just tried to kill her, but she'd felt his remorse, his guilt. His exhaustion. He wouldn't come after her again.

"I'm so sorry," he called after her. She didn't look back as she flipped him the bird, then realized she still carried her blades. She slid them into the slim-line sheath that formed part of her belt, and it wasn't until she put her foot on the bottom step that she realized she'd left her flip-flops behind.

She glanced back at the beach in frustration, just in time to see the Witch Hunter drop to his knees, then collapse on the sand, his unconscious body an inert dark form on the sand.

Chapter 4

Dave's eyes fluttered open. He frowned. Stars? He blinked. Yep. Stars. A cool breeze—not unpleasant—brushed across him, and he could hear the rhythmic roar of waves. He shifted and groaned. His neck was supported by a mound of sand, but it felt like he'd been lying there for hours. He moved his arms and realized a light cloth covered him. He glanced down. Despite it being sometime in the night, the stars and a glimmer of the moon gave enough light to see a little. He picked at the cloth. A towel?

He sat up, hissing at the pull of skin on his chest. He flicked off the towel. A white patch was taped to his chest. What the—? He peeled back a corner of the bandage and caught a whiff of something disgusting. He scrunched his nose up. Ew. He could smell marigold, aloe vera, maybe jasmine and something else he couldn't quite put his finger on, but whatever it was, it smelled gross. He patted the tape back down. Someone had made him an herbal poultice to help heal his wound and limit infection and inflammation. He could think of only one person in the area that would have the plant knowledge for it, yet he couldn't quite believe she'd do that for him, not after what he'd attempted to do to her. Where was she? He glanced around. He was alone on the beach, with just the waves to keep him company.

He rolled to his knees, then his feet, groaning as the kinks in his neck and back straightened themselves out. He shook out his shoulders. Sleeping on the beach worked only if you were drunk and in the company of a woman. Here, he was neither.

His tattered T-shirt fluttered in the breeze, and he shrugged out of his jacket so he could discard the ruined garment. His mouth tightened. Damn. He'd almost killed her.

He dragged his thumb across his forehead. What the hell happened? He'd struggled to comprehend when his chest had started to burn again. He'd had Sullivan Timmerman right where he wanted her, and had been about to send her across the veil, but then…

It was still so hard to accept, to make sense of. Another innocent had died at the hands of Sullivan Timmerman, yet the woman had been right in front of him at the time, ready to accept her fate. When he'd uttered the name and channeled the killer's vision, he'd seen the latest victim. An older woman, tears running down her face as she'd stared up at him with confusion, horror and pain, and then with shock as the blade had pierced her heart. Once again, the killer had carved that mark on her wrist and used that same horn to capture the woman's blood. And once again, Dave had been booted out

of the vision when the killer had consumed the blood
and uttered his spell—whatever that damn spell was.

He placed his hand over the dressing. He'd had the
wrong person. His stomach clenched, and he had to suck
in some deep breaths to stop from throwing up. He'd almost killed an innocent—a crime that would send *him*
across the veil to the Ancestors. How could that be?

Sullivan Timmerman wasn't a common name. How
could he have gotten it so damn wrong? Guilt, hot and
sickening, wrung his gut. The woman had answered
his call, and had confirmed her identity—she'd even
mentioned something about coins, as though she knew
she was guilty of some wrongdoing... He looked down
as the towel fluttered in the breeze, then rolled a little
along the sand. He reached down and picked it up.

Death isn't all bad.

What the hell did she mean? She was so young, so
full of life, so full of power when she'd fought him—
the first witch to be able to maintain a defense against
him...ever. She was also the first witch to halt him in
his tracks, midhit. What the hell was that all about?
And yet, when he'd had her down on the sand, it was as
if all her fight had left her, and she was ready to cross
the veil. He'd nearly killed an innocent witch. How...?
What...?

He started to walk across the beach toward the trail
at the edge of the dunes that would lead him to where
he'd parked his bike. He ducked his head as he trudged
through the sand. He'd fought with a woman, for God's
sake. He—the guy who inked up women with protective spells against their abusers, who was committed to
never hurting an innocent, who believed the women in
his life, however fiery and frustrating they could be—

and his mother and sister could be plenty of both—
should be safeguarded, whatever the cost.

He stumbled. Hell. He'd tackled the woman. He'd
threatened her, dominated her. He was no better than
the monsters he hunted.

His toe hit something, and he glanced down. A white
flip-flop lay half-buried in the sand.

Hers.

He scooped it up, turning it over to look at it. It was
well worn, with dents in the rubber from her heel and
the ball of her foot. He sighed as he continued along
the beach. He'd have to make it up to her. Somehow. He
didn't apologize very often, but words couldn't make up
for his transgressions against her. Part of his job as the
Witch Hunter was to redress the balance, wherever possible—especially by counteracting the misdeeds of the
malefactors. What he'd done today with this Sullivan
Timmerman—well, he had some counteracting to do.

After he caught the real Sullivan Timmerman and
put an end to these murders.

He crested the last rise and walked over to his bike.
He slipped the flip-flop and towel into one of his panniers. He wasn't quite sure where to start. All he'd managed to see was the female victim, an older woman, and
what looked like a wooden floor beneath her, and the
claw foot of a threadbare sofa.

He straddled his bike, started it and flicked up the
kickstand with his heel.

Kill one Sullivan Timmerman, then make it up to
the other Sullivan Timmerman. He'd better get busy.

Sully boxed up the teas she'd cut for Lucy and Mary
Anne Adler. She realized her hands were trembling, and

she curled her fingers over. Tears formed in her eyes. She'd been ready to die.

She blinked, sniffing, as she gathered the boxes and grabbed her satchel. She wasn't going to think about it. Nope. She was going to be a good little witch and completely ignore the ramifications of this afternoon's incident. She wasn't going to think about that moment when his body lay across hers. She should have felt threatened, frightened, but she felt—nope. Not going there.

She hesitated at the front door, gazing out at the sea that reflected the light of the moon and stars. From this point she couldn't see directly down to the beach. She'd have to walk to the edge of the headland to be able to do that.

She wasn't going to walk anywhere near the headland at the moment. What if he was still there?

Well, it would serve him right. She slammed the door closed behind her and stalked over to her car. The guy had tried to kill her.

He was just doing his duty.

Screw duty. The man was the Witch Hunter. She climbed into her car and started the engine, reversing out of the drive. All coven children were taught about the Witch Hunter. Much like the bogeyman, the Witch Hunter was someone to fear, someone who would come after you if you did something wrong. You never knew what the Witch Hunter looked like—only that he was out there, and ready to hunt you down if you so much as hinted at violating the universal laws of the covens. Witchery lore claimed there were Witch Hunters in every generation, chosen by the Ancestors, and assigned with the duty of preserving nature's balance. Only a hunted witch could recognize the Witch Hunter for who he—or she—was.

No wonder he'd seemed "familiar".

She drove down the dark road. Her cottage was the last one in a street of four, with a considerable distance between neighbors. They had no streetlights, and the real estate agent who'd handled the sale had told her to be thankful she had indoor plumbing, a landline and electricity. Cell phone reception kind of sucked, though. With the expanse of the ocean on three sides, the nearest cell tower was quite a distance away. She had to go into town to her shop to get access to the internet, and even there connectivity was a little spotty.

She still couldn't believe it. The Witch Hunter had come after *her*. She shook her head as she turned left onto the coast road. The only crime she committed was a pesky little Reform one, and not one against an individual, a coven, or nature. Why the hell were the Ancestors upset by a little coin-making? Sure, counterfeiting was *slightly* illegal, but it was all to help others, so really they should be proud of her, right? Witches blurred the legal lines often, with the making of potions and toxins, and spells designed to reveal or conceal... but she'd never used nature's power to provoke another to an unlawful act, nor had she sought power through the suffering of others, or personal or financial gain at the risk of another. Those were pretty much the deal breakers with the Ancestors, and as far as she was concerned, she'd done neither.

You're not the right one.

She frowned. The Ancestors had gotten it wrong... she grimaced at the memory of the lettering blazing across the man's chest. That had looked painful. Oh, not the chest. No, the chest had looked damn fine, actually. All those glorious muscles... She shook her head. She was lusting after a guy who'd tried to kill her. She thought she was better than that, now. That she'd grown some insight, maybe even some self-respect and dignity. She needed her head examined. Or to get laid. She preferred...neither. She hadn't had a companion since she'd left the West Coast and arrived in Serenity Cove four years ago. If she thought the Witch Hunter was a long drink of sex on the beach, it was either too long between lovers, or she really hadn't experienced the personal growth she'd fooled herself into thinking she had.

No, damn it. She'd learned her lesson, and wasn't prepared to make those same disastrous mistakes again. Ever.

She wound down the driver's window, trying to get some fresh air, some snap to reality. Her car was so old it didn't have air-conditioning. She lifted her chin as the wind ruffled her hair. The warm breeze carried the scent of salt and brine, and almost as though he had a homing device in her brain, her thoughts returned to the man on the beach.

She'd been shocked to see him collapse, and had reluctantly, cautiously approached him. She'd lightly kicked him, but he hadn't stirred. She'd tentatively relaxed her shields and discovered he truly was unconscious. She couldn't blame him. That branding—damn, that had stung like the bejeebus.

She should have left him there for the crabs, or for the tide. Her mouth tightened. When he'd been poised above her, ready to deliver the death strike, she'd sensed him.

He'd been fighting his own reluctance to kill her. She'd felt the burden of his duty, his responsibility to the Ancestors, to the covens. She'd sensed—of all things— his honor that gave him a core of steel. She'd felt his pain, too, over the killing, and his absolute commitment to delivering her to the Ancestors for her crimes, and his determination to save the vulnerable from her actions. Having all these emotions, the true metal of his character, she'd glimpsed something she wasn't expecting. She'd seen beyond his actions, beyond his awareness, and she'd seen through the veil. She'd sensed the nothingness. No dark, no light, no pain…no emotion. She'd seen a glimpse of…peace. No emotions to dodge or defend herself from. No effort required to constantly shore up her defenses, to protect her own heart and mind from the pain of others. And for the briefest of moments, that oblivion seemed heaven-sent.

She'd spent so much energy shielding herself, the constant effort to mute the emotions of others on a daily basis was tiring. At that moment, when the veil parted, and time stood still for her, offering her a glimpse of what could be, she'd realized how alone she was, and how tired she was of playing at being someone else for those who thought they were closest to her, yet knew her not.

For that briefest of moments, she was ready to step through the veil into the Other Realm, and accept the solace it offered.

And then he'd received that bodyline text from the Ancestors, and she'd snapped out of it, thank goodness.

She was such a *sucker*. The guy had passed out on her after expending all that cosmic energy fighting her, and then enduring some epic pain, and what had she done? Checked on him. What a sap. She'd gone and made him a darn poultice for his wound. She'd even packed the sand into a pillow for him. She told herself it was to get back on the good side of the Ancestors, by looking after their Witch Hunter.

But she was an empath witch, and she didn't have the luxury of being able to walk away from a person in pain without making some effort to help. That, and he was the *Witch Hunter*, for crying out loud. She couldn't begin to imagine how pissed off the Ancestors would be if she turned her back on their warrior.

She sighed as she rounded a bend in the road. He certainly looked the part. Hard muscles, skin that was warm and smooth, and strong, handsome facial features. She was surprised the Ancestors had chosen such a hunk for their most difficult job. She'd always expected the Witch Hunter to be some twisted, not-so-attractive guy who looked on the outside as mean and harsh as she thought he'd have to be on the inside.

Only he hadn't been mean and harsh on the inside. He'd been determined, yes, and ruthless to boot, but she'd sensed a surprising hint of fairness in him, and a heavy dose of honor. Surprising as she hadn't expected to find either in the Ancestors' assassin.

She turned off the highway, and after a short drive turned onto the street where Mary Anne Adler lived. She frowned at the flashing red-and-blue lights, and slowed to a stop when a county deputy held up his hand.

A man emerged from Mary Anne's house, his hat in his hands, and the sheriff nodded when he saw Sully's car. He trotted down the stairs and over to her car, and she propped her elbow on the window frame. She leaned her head out slightly to look up at him.

"Evening, Tyler."

"Sully. I'm afraid I'm going to have to ask you to move on," he said, resting his hand on the roof of her car.

She frowned, and picked up the boxes that sat on the passenger seat. "I'm here with some tea for Lucy and Mary Anne." She knew Lucy and Gary had moved in with Mary Anne for a little while, to help her get her house ready for sale so that the older woman could downsize and move to a place closer to town.

The sheriff grimaced. "Well, Lucy's in the back of an ambulance on her way to St. Michael's Hospital," he told her.

"Is she all right?" Sully asked, concerned, then realized what a stupid question that was. Of course the woman wasn't all right. She was on her way to the hospital.

Tyler nodded. "She will be."

"Uh, well, do you want me to stay with Mary Anne until she gets back home?" Sully offered. The poor woman had to be devastated by her son's murder, and probably just a little anxious with her daughter-in-law being rushed to hospital.

Tyler's face grew grim. "Mary Anne isn't going to be needing your tea anymore, Sully. She died earlier tonight."

Sully gaped, and sorrow pierced her from within. Mary Anne was a sweet lady. "Oh, no. That's so sad. Gary's death was too much for her, huh?"

Tyler shrugged. "We'll never know. She was murdered."

Sully blanched, stunned. "No."

"Well, we're still investigating, obviously, but from what I saw, I'm pretty sure it wasn't a suicide or an accident."

Sully tilted her head against the backrest. "How— how did it…?" she couldn't quite finish the sentence. How did Mary Anne die?

Tyler glanced back at the house. "I can't say. Not yet." He looked down at Sully. "But I will say this—go home and lock your doors. Stay safe."

He tapped the roof of her car, then turned back to

the Adler house. A deputy was unravelling yellow tape along the front veranda railing, and Sully's blood cooled in her veins at the sight, and what it meant.

The Adler house was a crime scene. Sweet little Mary Anne had been murdered in her home. That woman was so lovely, Sully couldn't imagine anyone having enough animosity, enough rage, to want to kill the older woman. And so soon after her son's murder. Were they connected? She couldn't quite believe that one murder had been committed in their sleepy little cove, let alone two. What were the odds that they were two separate, random acts? What were the odds they were connected? Poor Mary Anne. Sully shifted gears and reversed down the street until she could do a U-turn. It wasn't until she was pulling into her darkened yard, with only the moonlight and the stars to illuminate her garden, that Tyler's words really sank in.

Lock the doors. Stay safe.

What the hell kind of danger was out there? And why did he think it could visit her?

Chapter 5

Dave frowned at the Closed sign on the shop door. There was a lot of that going around Serenity Cove, today. He'd just tried to get some breakfast at the diner in town, only to find it was temporarily closed for business. He'd managed to find a burger joint down near Crescent Beach. He'd also found a bar, but it was too early to open.

He had not found a certain witch, though. He'd checked the beach he'd first seen her on, and then had taken the walk up the stairs to the top of the cliff. He'd found a cleared area at the top, and then a little road that led back to the highway. He'd found her home—her garden was very impressive, along with a little shed out the back. He hadn't been able to find her, though.

And he needed to find her. He needed to…seek forgiveness. Redemption, maybe. His gut tightened inside him, like a corkscrew twisting into a cork. What he did, killing witches, it was a crap job that someone had to do. He was there to stop witches from abusing power, abusing the vulnerable. It was an ordained vocation, and he was *supposed* to be doing *good*. He had a witch to hunt, but he'd found he couldn't concentrate until he made it right with the witch he'd wronged. His shoulders tensed. He didn't want to think about what he'd nearly done, but he didn't usually shy away from the difficult—that's why the Ancestors had picked him in the first place. Still, he felt like a heel for what he'd done, how close he'd come to really hurting her.

He glanced down at the flip-flop he gripped. He'd used it to perform a locator spell, and even now it was tugging away from him, toward the door that was closed to customers. He glanced about. Sullivan Timmerman's shop was on the edge of town. It was set back a little from the road, with a parking area in front. Just like the rest of the stores in the area, it had a sweet facade of Victorian wood trim, painted white, and a soft pastel blue on the clapboards. It gave an impression of welcome and charm, the kind of thing he'd associate with a sweet little grandmother—only the witch inside was no grandma, and after seeing her defense against him, he'd say sweet wasn't his first descriptor for her. Fiery, maybe. Sweet, not so much.

He was trying to ignore the towel, the sand pillow and the dressing that had soothed the pain in his chest.

He knocked on the door, then peered through the glass pane. For a moment all he could see was his reflection, his sunglasses glinting in the sunshine. He had to cup his hands around his eyes and press up against the window to see inside. The shop interior was dark. A little on the small side, and devoid of anyone, including the witch he sought. She was in here, somewhere, damn it. The flip-flop told him. He glanced carefully about in the gloom and finally noticed the flickering light through a transom window above a door that led from the shop room into an area behind.

He knew it. She was here. He shrugged out of his leather jacket and draped carefully, silently, over the glass-topped counter display. The garment was great on a bike, lousy in the summer, and creaky when he wanted to be quiet.

He muttered a quick yield spell, and the door unlocked, swinging inward. He shook his head. She hadn't bespelled her property at all, from the looks of it. He stepped inside and closed the door behind him. He hesitated, then flicked the lock. He had to apologize, and he'd prefer no interruptions, and no witnesses.

He stepped up to the door that led out back, and tested the doorknob. He shook his head when it twisted at his touch. Security was not a priority for this witch. He opened the door a little and peered through it. It opened into some sort of workshop. There was large machinery, grinding wheels, anvils and sharpening blocks. There was an artist's desk, with a number of sketches pinned to the corkboard above it. His eyes widened when he saw the wicked-looking blades lined up on a magnetic knife rack on one wall. Different lengths—hell, was that a *sword*?

He could hear a regular thump, thump, thump, accompanied with a faint grinding sound. It took a moment, but he finally narrowed down the source of the sounds. She sat at a machine, and every time she pressed her foot on the pedal, a weight would descend, making the thump, thump noise he could hear. He realized it was a press of some sort. She'd place a metal prong into the press, and the weight would descend, and then she'd remove and slide into another chute, and thump again. When she removed the prong, he could see tines had been cut into the metal end.

Forks. She was making…forks? He watched her for a moment. Her blond hair was tied back into a thick braid, and she wore a loose-fitting blouse over a long patterned skirt. She was so intent on her work, her head and shoulders dipped each time she set the prongs in the chutes. At one point she arched her back, and his gaze was drawn to the long line of her body as she tilted her head back and rubbed her neck. The flowing clothes made her look willowy and lithe, but he could see the strength in her arms as she placed the newly formed forks onto a tray next to her. Then she returned to her task, inserting the metal prongs into the chutes and cutting tines in the ends.

He stepped inside the room, and the floorboard creaked beneath his feet. She whirled, and he ducked, hearing the thud as the fork hit the timber door behind him. He glanced over his shoulder. The fork had impaled in the wood, quivering, at roughly the same position his head had been mere seconds before. Yeah, he guessed he deserved that reaction—and a whole lot more.

He turned, and she'd already picked up another fork and held it poised to throw again.

"Whoa, whoa," he said, hands up as he straightened. "I come in peace."

"Then go in peace—or pieces. Your choice."

Okay, so he could understand her…resistance to meeting with him. Fair enough. "Please," he said. He tried to send her some calming waves, only he could sense the block between them. Damn, she was good.

"Why are you here?" she asked, slowly rising from

her stool to face him properly, her movement fluid and graceful. She'd lowered her hand, but he noticed she still retained her throwing grip on the fork. She had dark circles beneath her eyes, as though she was tired. He couldn't blame her.

He held up her flip-flop. "I've come to return this. And to say thank you…" He took a cautious step toward her, offering her the footwear. He cleared his throat. "I also came to apologize," he said in a quiet voice.

She tilted her head, as though assessing him, then stepped forward, accepting her flip-flop. "That's okay." She dropped the fork into the tray.

Dave frowned. That's…okay? It was that easy? He was expecting shouting, ranting, at least a remonstrative finger waggle. "You're not—you're not angry?"

She nodded. "Oh, I'm angry, but I know you had good reasons, and you're already beating yourself up about it way more than I could."

He gaped for a moment, then his eyes narrowed. This didn't make sense. He'd expected her to react explosively—okay, and maybe the fork still buried in the door behind him went a little in that direction, but… "You're awfully Zen about this."

She stepped closer to him, her eyes dark with emotions he couldn't name. "It's not every day the Witch Hunter comes after me," she admitted. "And it's not every day the Witch Hunter admits to making a mistake."

He winced, then nodded. "It was a mistake. A big mistake. A mistake of epic proportions. What happened…shouldn't have."

She tilted her head, and her honey-blond braid slid over her shoulder. She gazed at him in open curiosity. "Who are you?"

"You know who I am."

"No, I know you're the Witch Hunter. What's your name, though?"

"Ah, that's right. We haven't been formally introduced." He inclined his head. "My name is Dave Carter."

Her brow dipped. "Oh."

"Oh?" She sounded…disappointed.

"I just thought your name would be more…exotic."

His eyebrows rose. "More exotic?"

She nodded. "Yeah. Not so plain."

"Plain."

"Uh, normal," she tried to clarify. Dave pursed his lips. Normal. His name was probably the only normal thing about him.

She looked at him carefully. "So, how does it work?"

He shifted. He'd never talked about it. He wasn't supposed to. The Witch Hunter was the blind justice of the Ancestors of witchcraft. His mother knew—he'd *had* to tell her. She'd been his elder, and needed to know why he wasn't going through the Degrees for their coven. He should have guessed his sister, Melissa, was eavesdropping at the time—or maybe he did and he'd still wanted her to overhear so that she would understand, and there was at least one person he could talk to. Some of the other covens in Irondell knew—the witch community wasn't as big as the werewolf or vampire tribes, so news got around. People were wary of him, though, and his occupation didn't inspire shared confidences. Most witches avoided him like the plague. But other than that, he mentioned it only when he was performing a hit, as he recited the ritualistic words that would send the witch beyond the veil.

"It's…complicated."

She arched an eyebrow. Well, he guess she at least deserved a little bit of an explanation.

"I receive the name when a crime is committed, and I go hunt." Simple, really.

She frowned as she glanced at his chest. "I saw... how." Her voice was soft, confused. "I haven't committed any of those crimes, though."

His eyes narrowed at her word selection. *Those* crimes. Did that mean there were other crimes she *had* committed? He was getting curious about those coins she'd mentioned on the beach.

"It's never happened before," he admitted.

She frowned. "How can you be certain?"

Cold horror washed over him at the prospect. "Because I wouldn't be able to continue," he said roughly. The thought he could have killed other innocents...it would crush him. Cripple him. He shook his head. No. If that had been the case, the Ancestors would have yanked his ass into the Other Realm. The punishment for a Witch Hunter to break the laws they've sworn to uphold would be extreme, to say the least.

She folded her arms and strolled over toward another door he only just noticed. "Soooo," she said slowly, "when a witch breaks one of the Three, they...brand you with that witch's name, and you go hunt? Like a guard dog? Sic 'em, Rex?"

He tilted his head. "Kind of..." he said slowly, hating the analogy, no matter how apt it seemed. She opened the door and entered what was a small kitchen, with a door leading to the backyard, and another that led to a small bathroom, and a door that led to what looked like an addition to the back of the house. Shop. Factory. Whatever the hell this place was. She crossed over to the stove and lit the stove, then placed a kettle on it.

"But how do you know you're going after a witch for something serious? I mean, what if the Ancestors want you to just warn someone?" She reached up to a cupboard, and Dave's gaze flicked down to where her loose blouse rose above the belt of her skirt. He wanted to focus on the gold skin of her back and side, but his eyes widened when he saw the decorative panel at the back of her belt, with two metal prongs that looked suspiciously like the hilts of the blades she'd used on him. How about that.

He forced himself to concentrate on the conversation, and he narrowed his eyes at her words. "Do you feel like you've needed to be warned about something, Sullivan?" *What* was this chick into?

"Sully," she corrected him, then shook her head, her expression forced into something that almost looked innocent. "Uh, no. Not really. I just—I guess I never thought I'd ever have the opportunity to talk with the Witch Hunter, and I want to understand…how do you know you're doing the right thing?"

Wow. She cut straight to the heart of his current doubts. He wanted to shrug it off with some sort of general comment, but Sullivan—no, *Sully*—deserved at least the truth from him, in all its unadorned, vicious glory.

"When a witch breaks one of the Three," he said, referring to the Three Immutable Laws of Witchcraft— never draw on nature's power to provoke another to an unlawful act—never seek power through the suffering of others, and never draw on nature's power for personal gain at the expense of another's well-being, "I am delivered their name, and I see their crime."

She frowned. "You *see* the crime?" Her face relaxed into something he could only call sympathy. "That's got to be hard." She turned as the kettle whistled, and lifted it off the stove. She pulled down a tin and spooned tea into two strainers and popped them into the ceramic mugs she'd pulled from the cupboard.

He was glad he was wearing his sunglasses, and could hide is surprise as she made the tea. He hadn't told anyone about that before, and it was difficult to broach such a personal subject. He'd never expected to feel sympathy directed toward him over it, but she was right. It *was* hard. There were some things you just couldn't unsee. Some crimes—especially the kids, damn it. He swallowed as he shut down that line of memory. He'd seen his own kind do terrible, horrible, heinous things. He'd seen them do great things, too, but when dealing with the dregs, you started to feel like you were covered in the muck, and it was all you generally got to see.

He cleared his throat. "I see the crimes, so I know what they've done, and generally where I can find them."

Her hands halted, and she slowly turned to face him, her face showing her confusion, and perhaps a hint of nervousness. "What did you see me do?"

He reached for one of the mugs—he couldn't quite believe the woman he'd tried to kill the day before was calmly making him tea in her kitchen.

His lips quirked. Sully Timmerman was proving to be an unexpected intrigue, on so many levels. "I didn't see you."

She frowned, confused. "Then why come after me?"

He sighed. "Usually, I see the crime through the killer's eyes, and can be with them for as long as it takes to identify them, or their whereabouts. This time I got neither."

Her frown deepened as her confusion did, and he

leaned against the doorjamb. "I saw what Sullivan Timmerman did. Not you, this…monster. I saw—" he hesitated. It was one thing for him to witness these horrendous acts, he didn't need to spread that taint to this woman.

Her brow eased. "It's okay. You can't surprise me."

His mouth tightened. "Oh, I think I can."

"I think I have a right to know what I was accused of, don't you?" Her tone was gentle, yet with a core of steel-like implacability. She wasn't about to be fobbed off with half-truths and generalizations. She wanted—and deserved—the facts.

"I see through the witch's eyes," he explained. "So I see what they do. I saw someone get stabbed, and some ritualistic markings, the drinking of blood…"

She shuddered. "Yeah, well, I didn't do any of that. What did this witch look like?"

Dave grimaced, then sipped his tea. "That's the problem. Usually I can stay with the witch until he or she looks in the mirror, or passes a window, and I can see their reflection. Usually I get to see the neighborhood, some more of the crime scene, enough to establish their location… This time I got bumped."

"Bumped?"

He took another sip, nodding. Once the dam broke, it felt easier to talk, easier to explain. There was something surprisingly relaxing about Sully Timmerman. "Bumped. He—or she—drank the blood, said a spell and bam, I was out of there."

"So you didn't get to see this witch's face, or where they were?"

"I saw an alley, I saw a sign on a building—Mack's Gym, by the way—and I had the name."

Sully's mouth pouted as she mulled over his words.

"Mack's Gym is in the next town..." Then she shook her head. "But I don't understand. My name?"

He nodded. "Yep. Sullivan Timmerman." He frowned, then glanced down at the tea. "What's in this?" He was finding it too easy to talk.

"Oh, it's just a little lavender, lemon balm, a tidge of nutmeg..."

His eyes narrowed. "Antianxiety?" Most of those ingredients were relaxants.

She shrugged. "A calmative. I thought you could use it."

He had to admit, it worked. He'd come here with his gut roiling, concerned about how she'd receive him, whether she'd hear him out...whether she'd forgive him. But...how did she know? Realization dawned, and he put the mug down.

"You're an empath." It wasn't a question. Everything added up. She'd made him a poultice to ease his pain and help him heal, had made him as comfortable as possible on his bed of sand and had displayed an unexpected insight to his turmoil—accepting he had a job to do.

She stepped back, her skirt moving around her legs as she did so, her movement was so sudden. "What—what makes you say that?" she asked cautiously. Warily.

He eyed the increased distance that now separated them. He'd spooked her, somehow. He shrugged, trying to keep it casual. "Oh, just putting the pieces together. I don't know how many witches would patch me up, hear me out and make me tea after I've tried to kill them." She was a sweetheart. She'd tried to ease his pain, and ease his guilt.

She frowned as she crossed to the sink—putting even

more distance between them. "That's quite a stretch. Maybe I'm just a sucker for a bad boy."

His lips quirked. As tempting as the suggestion was, he doubted it. He edged a little closer, and put his own mug in the sink, managing to hem her in at the same time. Sully paused, her gaze on the mug he still clasped. "Ah, now that's where you're wrong, Sully," he said in a low voice, leaning forward. "I can be very, very good."

Sully lifted her gaze from the large hand that made her mug look like a kid's tea party toy, up the corded forearm, over the bulging bicep, the edge of the dark tattoo peeking out from beneath the sleeve of his fresh black T-shirt, and across the broad shoulder and torso to the strong column of his throat. She swallowed, hesitating, before lifting it farther. The man had a great jaw. Strong, defined, with just the right dusting of hair that made you want to reach and stroke it. Was he—was the Witch Hunter *flirting* with her? His lips curled up at one end, a sexy little smile that made heat bloom tight and low in her stomach. She couldn't see his eyes behind the dark lenses of his sunglasses, couldn't see whether he was flirting, teasing, or just making an observation. And she desperately wanted to see his eyes.

The fact that she couldn't was frustrating, and just a little unnerving. She could relax her shields, get a sense of what he was feeling, but that method was fraught with risks. Risks she'd learned long ago weren't worth it, and she should have the sense to know better.

She stepped back, clearing her throat. "I'll take that under advisement," she said softly.

He tilted his head, and she tried to keep her expression impassive. Aloof. That's what she was going for, here. Distant. Cool. He was the Witch Hunter, tracking down a murderous wi—she frowned.

"I want to help," she blurted.

His eyebrows rose over his sunglasses. "What?"

"There is a witch out there murdering in my name. I want to help you catch him. Her. Whatever."

He shook his head, backing up a little. "Sorry, sweetness. No can do."

Funny. He didn't sound apologetic at all. She put her hands on her hips. "I insist. You said Mack's Gym. That's local. You'll need someone with local knowledge to help you. I can do that."

He shook his head. "I work alone."

"And look where it got you," she said, gesturing to herself.

"Hey, that was an honest mistake," he said in faint protest.

"One that you should avoid making again," she said primly. "Let me help."

"Not happening."

She stepped closer. "Someone is using my name—"

"It could be just as much his as it is yours," he pointed out.

"I can tell you now, there is no other person in the county with my name," she informed him. "But this person even has the Ancestors confused," she told him, her tone serious.

This time Dave stepped closer toward her, and she had to tilt her head back to meet his gaze through his sunglasses. "The term is Witch Hunter—not hunters," he told her roughly. "We don't buddy up on a job. This is something I've got to do on my own, Sully. You haven't seen what this person is capable of. I have. I don't want you anywhere near him."

"But this is *my* name, Dave," she protested.

"And I will get him," he assured her, "and you will stay far away from this matter, and be safe."

She opened her mouth to protest further, then halted when he stepped closer and cupped her cheek. Sensation. Heat. Desire. Protectiveness. Everything bombarded her, leaving her trying to catch her balance. Her shields. It was like he could pierce her shields with just a touch, invading both her personal and mental spaces. She tried to shore them up, but no matter how many times she tried erecting them, his presence kept swamping her.

"I owe you one, Sully," he told her seriously, his voice low. "What I did, I have to make it up to you. I'm granting you a favor."

A flare of forthrightness, a heavy dose of resolve, washed over her. "A favor," she repeated.

He nodded. "I happen to take debts very seriously. I owe you."

Well, she didn't think he owed her anything, but if this was important to him, she wasn't above using it. Warm promise. Integrity.

"Great. Let me—"

He placed a finger on her lips, and again, sensations rolled through her, her senses awakening to him, overriding her personal shields. She could feel his determination, his dedication—and his resistance. And something else. Something... Oh. Desire. She trembled, feeling a reciprocal flare of attraction.

"I have to find this witch," he murmured, "and I will not endanger you. This favor I grant you is for your use, at a time of your choosing, but I will never let you use it to put yourself in danger. Do you understand?"

His voice was so deep, so low. His expression was

grim, intent. She stared up at his sunglasses, stunned by the sincerity, the commitment behind his words. "Uh, yes." She whispered the words against his finger.

"You need anything, you call for me."

She nodded slowly.

"I'll come for you. This is my promise to you." He said the words like a vow, conveying a determination that was…well, knee-weakening.

He dipped his head once in acknowledgment. His finger trailed across her lips. It was as though every cell in her body awakened and paused in anticipation. He brushed his finger first over her top lip, then across the bottom, pressing it down gently. Her mouth parted, and he lowered his head, removing his finger as his lips pressed against hers.

Chapter 6

Oh. My. God. She closed her eyes as he kissed her. His kiss was sweet, tender, capturing her lips in a firm yet delicate kiss. She sighed against his mouth, and then his other hand rose until both of his hands cupped her cheeks, and he deepened the kiss.

Warmth, slow and seductive, curled inside her. She could taste him. Coffee and male, a sweet and savory concoction that had her tilting her head back, wanting more. He smelled magnificent, all woodsy—sage, juniper and neroli. His lips were soft, yet firm. Supple. His mouth moved over hers, dancing almost, with a grace and skill that stole her breath along with her caution.

He slowly raised his head, and he was so close she could see his eyes behind the dark lenses of his sunglasses. It was too dark to see any detail, but his gaze swept across her face, and then he stepped back.

"Uh, I'd best be going," he rasped, jerking his thumb in the direction of the door.

She nodded. She would have said something—anything, only her brain forgot to kick-start again from the sensory overload.

He backed toward the door. "I'll keep in touch," he said, his voice husky.

She nodded. Yep. She would have said it, too, but she got only as far as opening her mouth.

He walked back through her workroom, then paused at the door that led to her shop floor. He gestured beyond to the front door, his brow dipping. "You should beef up your security," he told her. "Maybe a perimeter spell."

She blinked. Uh, maybe...? Only it wouldn't be much use. Nulls. She half nodded, then shook her head as he departed. What?

She heard a motorbike start up outside, then sagged against her kitchen bench as she heard it roar away. She lifted her right hand and gently pressed her fingers against her lips.

The Witch Hunter had kissed her.

He'd kissed her.

Dave shifted on his bike as he rode through town. He was sitting just a mite uncomfortably. What the hell had possessed him to kiss her?

Well, she was attractive, in a fresh, girl-next-door kind of way. Sexy girl-next-door, though. And she was sweet. Too sweet for her own good, really. He shook his head. Tea. She'd given him a calmative tea because she'd sensed his turmoil at what he'd done to her. Who *does* that?

She was such a fascinating mix, though. Back on the

beach, she'd given as good as she'd got. She'd matched him with her powers, and had fought him with a skilled strength that was impressive. And she was armed. He'd seen her belt. She seemed so sweet, so trusting, yet she carried twin blades, and had made him concerned for his ability to bear children. Sweet, but spicy. A contradiction of lethal innocence.

And he'd granted her a favor. He *never* granted favors. He was the collector of debts, and had a bank of favors owed to him from a number of members of Reform society, from vampire or werewolf primes—to light warriors. And he'd granted this witch a debt.

Maybe it was because every time he touched her, he lost time, lost awareness of everything save her. The scent of her, all floral and summery, her warmth, her gentleness—when she wasn't trying to unman him—her...care. She'd minimized his effect on her, because she could see, feel, sense—however it worked with an empath—the effect of his job on him, and sympathized, putting his needs above her own.

That humbled him. He sensed her shields, though. They were impressive, almost tangible blocks to getting to know the woman inside—and he really wanted to get to know that woman. He could usually get a sense of people when he touched them...good, bad, past, present and future—he saw some of each. He was selective with his clients for that very reason. He didn't ink up anyone with one of his spells unless they deserved it, or desperately needed it, needed his special brand of protection. Sully, though, well she consumed his senses at a touch, but those messages, those visions he normally received about a person were missing with her. The protective walls she'd erected within herself were stunningly effective, and it made him wonder why she felt the need to close herself off so thoroughly from those around her. It had to be exhausting, maintaining those protections.

He glanced about the town square as he rode around it. The diner still hadn't opened, but there was a cluster of people at the bottom of the steps. Even when the place wasn't open, it seemed to be the hub for the town people to gather and gossip. He recognized the waitress, Cheryl, who lifted her hand at him as he rode by. He gave her a brief salute in return, then turned at the end of the block. There was a bar at the far end of the marina, he'd discovered. He glanced at the docks. Most of the boats were out. He'd learned Serenity Cove wasn't so much a vacation spot for cruisers, but a working fishing port. The salt and brine was distinctive, and he drove around the weighing station and the fishermen's co-op, to the small parking lot of the bar at the end.

He parked his bike and set his helmet on the dash, uttering his security spell as he did so. That was one more thing he didn't understand about Sully. Her store was poorly secured. One flimsy lock on the front door that a teenager with a penknife could pass. When he'd visited her home, he hadn't sensed any blocks or shields there, either. As though she couldn't be bothered. He didn't know a witch who didn't layer their security with any number of spells. Some were innocuous, some had painful elements invoked for trespassers. Personally, he preferred the painful variety. He didn't have any patience for those who tried to steal or damage his property.

He walked into the bar, pausing when he stepped into the dim interior. At this time of day a couple of patrons sat in a booth, a couple more at the bar. A game of college baseball was playing on the television above the bar, and the thickset, middle-aged bartender leaned his palm on the bar, watching it.

Dave walked up to the bar and sat on a stool two down from another patron. The bartender looked over at him, an eyebrow raised in query.

"Beer, please," Dave said.

The bartender lumbered over to the under-the-counter fridge and pulled out the first beer his hand grasped. He grabbed a bottle opener from the counter, then slapped a coaster down and thunked the beer onto it.

"Thanks," Dave muttered.

"Well, if it isn't Sully's friend," a tired voice muttered from the stool two down from his.

Dave turned, then frowned at the familiar man until he recognized him. The sheriff, out of uniform. No wonder he hadn't recognized him immediately. It was like seeing your elementary school principal sitting at your dinner table. Out of place and damn uncomfortable.

"Tyler, right?" That was what Cheryl, the waitress, had called him, wasn't it? He purposely didn't address him by his title. The man was out of uniform, and Dave hoped this was an opportunity to get the man to open up about the murders he'd seen.

He gestured to the sheriff's nearly empty bottle. "Another one for my friend," he told the bartender.

Tyler's eyebrows rose, but Dave noticed he didn't decline the beer.

"How'd it go with Sully?" Tyler asked idly, although Dave suspected the man wasn't as nonchalant as he appeared to be.

The bartender clunked the new bottle down on the bar. "You know Sully?" he asked, and Dave almost saw curiosity flare, but then the crowd roared on the TV, and he turned his attention back to the game.

"Didn't quite go the way I expected," Dave admitted to the sheriff.

"Oh? No more spark?"

"Oh, there were plenty of sparks," Dave said, thinking of their power struggle on the beach. "I had this meeting all thought out in my head, and it didn't go at all to plan."

Tyler chuckled. "Hell, been there. But you're still here?" His expression was friendly, but Dave could see the interest in his eyes at figuring out the new stranger in town.

Dave nodded. "Yeah. I thought I'd stay a couple of days. Hey, what's with the diner? I went for breakfast, but it's closed, even though the sign says it's usually open today."

Tyler moved his now-empty bottle aside and reached for the new one. "Yeah, well, Lucy, the owner, isn't well."

Dave's eyes narrowed. He sensed there was more to that than the sheriff was letting on. The game on the TV hit a lull, with the teams changing over, and a news broadcast filled the ad break. Dave watched as the announcer read about the murder of a local woman. His arms muscles tightened when he saw a photo of the deceased woman. It was the elderly woman from his vision.

The bartender sighed, then looked at the sheriff. "Mary Anne? What sick bastard would go after an elderly woman in her home?"

Tyler nodded, his gaze flitting to the screen momentarily before dropping back down to the bottle of beer he held. "Well, Tony, you got the sick bastard part right."

Dave frowned. "Isn't that the second murder in the area in what, a week?"

Tony, the bartender, nodded. "Yeah. First one was her son." He shook his head. "Seems like the family pissed off someone."

"So, the murders are related?" Dave asked casually.

Tyler tilted his head to stare at him for a moment. "Yeah, looks that way." He lifted his beer to his lips and drained the bottle, then stood. "Thanks for the beer."

Dave realized the sheriff was shutting down any further conversation on the topic. He smiled, masking his frustration. He knew the law weren't supposed to talk about open cases, but he'd hoped he could make the sheriff crack.

"Good luck with your investigation," he said.

Tyler hesitated, glancing over his shoulder. "We're going to get this sick bastard," he said quietly, his gaze meeting Dave's. Dave's eyes narrowed. Was that—was the sheriff warning him?

Tyler pulled at the door and disappeared into the daylight.

Dave turned back to the bar, his attention now on the bartender. "So, mother and son, huh?"

Tony tore his gaze away from the game that had now resumed on the TV. His gaze flitted to the door, then around the bar, and then he nodded, folding his arms on the bar.

"Yeah. Pretty sad. Gary was a great guy. Didn't come in here all that often, wasn't much of a drinker, but he was the kind of guy who'd always stop and say hi, or give you a hand if you needed one. He and Lucy were going to be married in June."

Dave winced. That woman was going to need some time to heal. He added her name to the list of folks affected by this witch's actions. "And the mom?"

Tony grimaced. "Well, I didn't have too much to deal with her. She was a great crocheter, though. She'd make beanies for all the newborns at the hospital. My sister got one when her daughter was born. Meant a lot, to her, that kindness from a woman she barely knew."

Dave frowned. "It doesn't sound like they were the kind of people to have any enemies."

Tony snorted as he straightened from the bar. "Nulls always have enemies."

Dave's eyebrows rose. "They were nulls?"

Tony looked at him, surprised. "Well, yeah. They're all over the north end. That's why we're so into fishing, here. Tourism blows."

"Huh." Dave drained his beer, than pulled some cash out of his wallet, placing it on the bar. "Thanks."

Tony nodded, picking up the cash and strolling over to the cashier. "Anytime."

Dave strolled to the door, then hesitated. "Say, do you know a Sullivan Timmerman?"

Tony frowned. "Sully? Sure. Everyone knows Sully. Sweet lady."

"Uh, no, I mean another Sullivan Timmerman," Dave clarified.

Tony shook his head. "Nope. That would be weird."

Dave nodded. "Yeah, I guess it would be."

He left the bar, and straddled his bike. He frowned as he gazed out at the tiny harbor. Nulls. Why the *hell* would a witch want to kill *nulls*? The very nature of a null meant that the witch's powers were nullified in their presence. No werewolf could shift in their presence, no vampire could get their fangs on, no witches could cast spells...

He kick-started his bike and eased open the throttle as he rode out of the parking lot. Maybe it had nothing to do with nulls, and everything to do with the victims?

He needed to find out more about Gary and Mary Anne Adler.

* * *

Sully stood next to Jenny as the preacher gave his graveyard sermon. She glanced across the open grave to Lucy. The woman leaned heavily on Cheryl, her face streaked with tears and pale with exhaustion. Even from this distance, Sully could see the deep bruise on her chin and along her cheek. Cheryl had told her the previous day that Lucy had been attacked from behind and had fallen heavily on the wooden floor. She hadn't seen her attacker, hadn't witnessed Mary Anne's murder, but had found the older woman's body when she'd regained consciousness.

Sully returned her gaze to the open grave, Gary Adler's coffin poised above it. His mother would be interred at the end of the week, as her body was still at the county coroner's, her autopsy only just recently completed.

"This is so sad," Jenny whispered. "A family wiped out."

Sully nodded. It was beyond sad, really. "It doesn't make any sense, does it?"

Jenny shrugged. "Depends which side of the fence you're sitting on. Some of the older folk remember the Reformation, and what happened with us. They say it's happening again."

Sully flicked a glance at her friend. "Seriously?"

Jenny nodded, just once.

Sully frowned as she watched Gary's coffin lowered into the grave. The late afternoon was fiercely hot, and bottles of water had been handed out among the small crowd. The funeral directors had erected a tent, and Sully wasn't sure whether it was better to stay under the tent and out of the sun, or to get some distance from all the hot, sweaty bodies and brave the furnace beyond the shade. And of course, everyone wore black.

She glanced at Jenny. Her friend had a point. Nulls had experienced a varied history. On the one hand they were reviled by the shadow breeds. Any shifter or vampire, or even witch, was reduced to being powerless and vulnerable in the presence of a null, which meant ordinary humans had seen the benefit in protecting them, and using them as a barrier against the breeds. They lived in the gray area between natural and supernatural. Not quite a shadow breed, but not an ordinary human, either. As a result, they were hunted by the shadow breeds in well-planned, ruthless skirmishes. During Reformation, they were given no territory, being classed as a subcategory of the human race. As such, they were often not treated as equal to any other race, shadow breed or not. Some of the crimes that had been committed against them were horrific, but with the recognition of a new hybrid breed just outside Irondell, there was renewed action to also recognize nulls as a race of their own.

In the meantime, no shadow breed would willingly go near a null community. That meant a lot of trade and tourism was restricted in the null-saturated areas. Humans walked the fine edge of losing business among the shadow breeds, and having protection from being prey to the breeds if nulls were about. To hear that the murder of two nulls—the first murders in the area since Sully had moved there—was possibly race-based was... disheartening.

Sully had gotten to know many of the nulls. They'd initially viewed her with mistrust. Why would she want to associate with them? She'd learned that apart from the block on her powers, there was something familiar about the nulls. They loved family. They had a tight-knit community, where each looked out for the other. They worked hard and partied harder, but they were just like any other human community—or witch, vampire or shifter, with one major difference. They just didn't get into power plays.

And that was probably one of the most attractive qualities, in her mind.

"Tyler will find whoever did this," she whispered to Jenny.

Jenny turned to her, her eyebrow raised. "We're not going to wait for the humans to help."

Her friend turned to walk over to Lucy, and Sully caught up with her. "What do you mean?" Sully whispered.

"Tyler's a good guy," Jenny whispered back, "but these crimes have targeted nulls. We have our own ways of dealing with this."

"Really?" Sully glanced around the mourners.

Jenny smiled. "I keep forgetting you're not a born null."

"Thanks." Sully frowned. "I think."

Jenny halted, scanning over Sully's shoulder. "Oh, hey, I see my brother. You go ahead, I need to go see him. Gary was one of his close friends."

Sully nodded. Lucy crossed over to the group of nulls that had stepped away from the grave to have a quiet talk. She turned back to approach Lucy, and it was as she was stepping up to hug her that she felt the little scratching at her shields. She was out of null range. But no, she should be able to manage.

She smiled sadly at Lucy and held out her arms.

Lucy stepped into them, sobbing softly, and Sully

held her. She smiled briefly at Cheryl over Lucy's shoulder. The waitress looked almost as miserable as Lucy.

"I'm so sorry," Sully whispered into the crying woman's ear.

"Thank you for being here," Lucy said softly, hiccuping into her shoulder. "I'm so sorry about the cutl—"

"Shh," Sully hushed her. "There's nothing to apologize for. This is more important."

Lucy squeezed her tight, and Sully could feel the woman trembling in her arms. She could sense the grief, the heartrending sorrow in her. It was muted, like an annoying pain knocking at her shields. Sully hesitated, then heard Lucy sob anew. She couldn't leave her like this. Nobody should have to go through this heartfelt agony. Lucy had lost two members of her family in quick succession in the most violent way. Sully could feel the woman fracturing in her arms. Her trembling increased, her breath grew ragged as her sobs grew harsher. Sully closed her eyes, then opened her shields a crack. She sucked in the pain, trying to absorb only some of Lucy's pain, but she could feel the grief of the fellow mourners clawing at her shields, peeling them back. She fought, trying to shed the talons that were shredding her walls. She slammed a barrier down, and Lucy's head lifted, surprise on her face. The woman hiccupped, then patted Sully on the shoulder as she turned to the next person lining up to offer their condolences, her composure once more slipping into place as she brushed away her tears.

Sully stepped back, and would have staggered if Jenny hadn't caught her arm. Her friend eyed her curiously. "Are you okay, Sully?"

Sully nodded, smiling tightly as the pain screamed inside her head like a banshee with her finger in an elec-

trical socket. The nulls could stop her using her powers, but once she absorbed pain, they couldn't stop her
from feeling what was already inside. And with them
around, she couldn't dispel it.

Oh, God, so much pain. It was unbearable. Sully
could feel it eating at her mental walls, coursing through
her brain like a hot wash of acid. Even now, her vision
was beginning to darken at the edges. She had to dispel the energy, but had to get away from the nulls to
do it—and you never did a discharge of this magnitude
where other humans might pick up some of the spill.

"I have to go," she rasped to her friend, and started
to walk between the gravestones toward the parking
lot. She had to get out of here. She was going to lose it.
Even now, bile rose within her, burning her throat. She
swallowed, trying to contain everything.

"Oh, hey, there's your boyfriend," Cheryl said.

It took Sully a moment to realize Cheryl was talking to her. She tightened her lips as she glanced about.
Boyfriend? What? Sully saw Dave in the shaded corner
of the parking lot, leaning against his bike.

He frowned, straightening from his bike as she hurried toward her car.

"Sully."

She braced her hand against the car, bending over
as her stomach muscles clamped as though a vise was
trying to squeeze her gut in half. Her hands shook as
she delved into her satchel and finally found her keys.
They jangled in her hand like a wind chime in a tornado.

Two hands clasped hers, removing the keys from her
grasp, and then she felt a strong arm guiding her into
the passenger seat.

"I'll drive."

Chapter 7

The voice sounded like it was echoing down a long tunnel. She blinked furiously, trying to see beyond the darkness that was now bleeding into her vision. Perspiration broke out on her upper lip and lower back, and she winced, bending low in her seat. She felt rather than saw Dave slide into the driver's seat, and within seconds the car was in motion, driving out of the cemetery and headed wherever the hell they were going—she couldn't see, and quite frankly didn't care.

She groaned, her jaw clenching as she rode another wave of intense pain. As though from a distance she could hear the scream of wheels as Dave sped along the coast road.

They'd been on the road for only a few minutes—maybe. She was beginning to lose track of time, but she thought—hoped—they were far enough away from the crowd.

"Pull over," she gasped. Oh, God, this was intense. The pain—she panted as she tried to ride the hot wash of agony.

"What? Are you sure?

"*Pull over.*" Her voice emerged as something low and guttural and quite unnatural. The car jolted and bumped as he steered it onto the shoulder, slowing down.

She opened the door before he'd quite stopped.

"Sully!"

She tumbled out of the car, falling to her knees on the gravel. Her fingers clawed over, and she dug her nails into the earth, trying to ground herself.

"Sully—"

She held up her hand in warning. *Don't come near me.* She couldn't speak, couldn't communicate other than that one abrupt, urgent movement. She crawled a foot, her stomach muscles wrenching, and she screamed at the excruciating heat that rose up from within, as though a ball of fire was exploding inside her—inside her gut, inside her brain. It was blinding light and suffocating darkness, it was fiercely hot and blisteringly cold, it was nothing and it was everything, all at once. She released the pathetic hold she had on her mental barrier, opened her mouth and retched up all that heartache, all that crushing sadness and consuming sorrow.

Over and over, the hot tide of negative energy roiled through her, and her stomach heaved, her throat burned and her eyes watered as she expelled Lucy's and the other mourners' grief in a hot black sludge that splashed on the ground and ran to rivulets, steaming as it soaked into the ground.

When she had no more to expel, when the last drops had left her body, she wiped a shaky hand across her chin. She straightened on her knees and started to sag.

Strong arms caught her, and this time she was too weak to fight that coalescence of power, that collision of energies. His scent, sage, juniper and neroli, his warmth, and then an overwhelming tide of tenderness, concern and just a hint of awe. It embraced her.

"Come on, sweetness. Let's get you home."

Dave pulled into Sully's driveway and cut the engine. The sun was setting, streaking the sky with fiery pinks and tangerines as dusk crept in. He climbed out and walked around the back of Sully's car—a sky blue station wagon throwback that should have visited a wrecking yard years ago, from the looks of it. The gears had been a little clunky, too. He'd have to look at them for her. He opened the passenger door, and Sully's eyelids slowly rose.

She hadn't quite passed out, but she was close. Whatever the hell she'd done had clearly drained her. He didn't question the relief that she was still conscious, still breathing, after what he'd seen her do.

She grasped the upper frame of the door, as though getting ready to haul herself out. "Thanks for the ride—" her voice trailed off as he leaned in and scooped her up.

"Relax," he told her. She needed sleep. She felt so limp in his arms, so…spent.

"No, I can—" her head bumped against his shoulder "—walk."

He snorted. "Please. You can't even keep your head straight."

He cradled her as he strode up the steps and uttered a yield spell. The lock clicked and the door swung open. Dave walked into her house, glancing about. A hallway ran from the front door of the house and doglegged at

what he assumed was the kitchen. There was a room
on either side, neither of which looked like a suitable
place to set her down.

"Bedroom?"

Her head lolled forward, and she waved her arm
down the hall. "Back."

He walked down and around the corner. The hallway had a small bathroom at the very end, a doorway
that led to the kitchen on the right and a closed door on
his left. He muttered a few words, and the door swung
open as he approached.

Yeah, this looked exactly like what he'd imagine her
bedroom would look like—if he'd wondered about it.
There was a bay window that overlooked her garden,
and sheer, gauzy white curtains that blew in the breeze
coming in from the open sash windows. There was a
window seat beneath the bay window that looked well
cushioned, with pillows in what looked like delicate
blue flowers that matched the other cushions with blue
or green striped panels, and a navy knit blanket hap-
hazardly draped on the end.

Her bed was queen-size, with an ornate white iron
bedframe that surprisingly didn't look overwhelmingly
feminine. He flicked his fingers beneath her knees and
the powder blue coverlet pulled back enough that he
could lay her on the crisp white cotton sheets. She subsided against the pillows, and she struggled against the
heavy weight of her eyelids.

"Thank you," she whispered, as though she didn't
have the energy for her full voice.

He smiled as he drew the coverlet over her body. So
polite. "My pleasure."

She snuggled down, rolling over a little and sliding her hand beneath her cheek. She frowned, and he leaned closer.

"Sully, are you okay?" he asked softly, concerned by her expression. Was she in pain?

"Why are you my boyfriend?" she murmured drowsily. Her tone was breathy, but there was no mistaking the confusion.

"Uh…" Dave hesitated. Oops. He hadn't expected that rumor to still have legs. "Well—" His eyebrows rose at the faint snore. "Sully?" he said gently. Her eyelids didn't even flutter.

She gave another delicate snore. He tucked the coverlet in around her, knowing he'd dodged a conversational bullet, then leaned forward and kissed her forehead, a little surprised at the tenderness he felt. That was a first. "Sleep well, sweetness."

He stood over her for a moment, his brows pulled down in a frown. What the hell had she done? She'd hugged that woman, and then couldn't seem to walk or see straight. He reached out and lightly cupped her cheek. He couldn't see, damn it. No past, no future and certainly no clue as to what had happened to her at the funeral. She was like a vault, closed off to his visions. He removed his hand, his fingers trailing across her smooth skin in a gentle caress. He curled his fingers into a fist. He liked touching her.

He stared at her thoughtfully. He couldn't afford to like touching her. His hands—they'd hit. They'd hurt. They'd killed. Sully was—well, she was different. She was… His brow dipped in a slight frown. She was too interesting for his own good. She was sweet—when she wasn't throwing forks at his head—she was gentle and caring. He'd seen how she'd embraced that woman at the funeral. Just walked right on up and opened her arms to the woman. She'd supported her when the woman looked on the verge of collapsing. She'd seemed so strong, so calm—until she'd turned and walked away. And then he'd seen her face when her mask had slipped. He'd seen the pain, seen how her face had drained of color, and how her legs had seemed to wobble. But she'd kept that hidden from her friends. She was open and genuine, and yet impressively well guarded and cautious. So strong for her friends, and conversely, so vulnerable away from them. And yet, he didn't mistake this vulnerability for weakness. And that brought him back to where he'd started. She was too damn interesting for his own good.

He couldn't afford to explore the mystery that was Sully Timmerman. Not with what he did—and what he'd done... He was a ghost. Once he'd figured out what was going on here, and resolved it to the satisfaction of the Ancestors, he'd be going back to Irondell—until the next trip, the next hit. He had no business getting interested in Sully.

Dave crossed over to the window seat and toed off his boots. He made a nest among the pillows, and drew the throw blanket at the end over his legs. He leaned his head back against the inset wall, and gazed at the woman sleeping so soundly in the bed. It took a while, but eventually he fell asleep, too, watching over her.

"You told them we *dated*?"

Dave jolted awake, slightly disorientated. Coffee. Bacon. He hadn't had dinner. God, that smelled amazing. He straightened the sunglasses that had slipped a little in his sleep. He looked around, blinking when he saw Sully standing next to him, arms akimbo, a frown on her face as she glared down at him. His gaze swept over her. Her hair was unbound, falling in loose waves around her head and shoulders, all shiny honey and totally appealing. She wore an off-the-shoulder peasant-style white top. He couldn't see any bra straps. Was she wearing one? His gaze drifted down. That thought had him waking up fast, along with the realization that she was not in a happy mood. His gaze snapped back up to hers.

But she was obviously back to her usual spitfire setting, which was a good thing to see. A damn good thing to see, actually. His gaze started to drift south to her chest again, and he forced himself to blink, look away. *Don't perv, you perv.*

"What?" he asked, then yawned, mentally scrambling to think past the bra situation and the bacon in the next room.

"You told Cheryl we dated in high school. I've just got off the phone from Jenny."

Dave blinked as he rose from the window seat. Ouch. Apparently the window seat wasn't much better than the sand the night before.

"Jenny? Who's Jenny?" He needed coffee to jumpstart this conversation properly.

"My friend, Jenny, who had an interesting chat with Cheryl yesterday at Gary's funeral."

He closed one eye as he looked at her. "Cheryl is the waitress at the diner, right?"

Sully nodded, her eyes narrowing.

He blinked again, then nodded. "Oh, yeah. She's nice. Got a thing for the sheriff, I see."

Sully pursed her lips. "Everybody knows that except for the sheriff." Then she went back to frowning. "You told them I was an old girlfriend."

He stretched, then smiled as he started to walk to the door. "Don't sell yourself short, you're not *that* old."

She thumped him in the arm. Ouch. Okay, so she wasn't in the mood to be teased. Sully strode across the hall and into the kitchen, and made a beeline for the kettle that was beginning to whisper on the stove. She was barefoot, and he caught a glimpse of tanned calves and pink polish on her toenails. Her skirt flowed with each movement, but he was pretty sure she didn't know how it skimmed her hips and butt in a way that couldn't help but draw a guy's attention. Damn, he had no idea domesticity could look so damn sexy in the morning.

He settled himself on a stool at her kitchen counter and watched as she moved through the kitchen. Her clothing might be loose, but it still draped over her limbs, and he could make out the shape of her thigh, the indent of her waist, the swell of her breast... And he shouldn't be noticing that. Not with this woman. And right now she was upset with him.

"I told her that so I could find out where you were," he told her truthfully. "Back when I thought you were murdering people."

"The whole town is talking about it," she hissed. She pulled out two mugs and started pouring the coffee.

He tilted his head. She sure was fired up about this. She was so Zen about him trying to kill her, but having her name connected with his seemed to really tick her off. "Shelving the fact I may have told a little fib to find you, what's so bad about people thinking we used to date?" he asked conversationally. The more he thought about it, the more the concept interested him. Heck, when was the last time he'd *dated* a woman? Not a hookup, not a one-night stand, or a spontaneous, fun-minded bed-buddy, but a *date*, with planning, and a full meal, real conversation, aftershave...

She slammed the mug down next to him on the counter. "Because I would never date someone like you," she snapped.

He blinked, surprised by the little flash of hurt at the words. He schooled his features into calm disinterest. "Someone...like me?" he asked conversationally. His gut tightened with tension as he waited for her response.

Her mouth tightened, then she nodded. "Yeah. Someone like you." She grabbed a plate at the side of the stove and started serving up some scrambled eggs and bacon.

"What is that supposed to mean?" He abandoned all attempts at remaining casual as she thunked the plate down in front of him, followed by the cutlery she pulled from a jar at the end of the counter.

She turned back to serve up her own plate. "You're physically dominating, and you'll do or say whatever you need to in order to get what you want."

She walked around the other side of the bench and sat on the stool next to him.

He stared down at his plate. *Uh, wow.* He slid some scrambled eggs on his fork and shoved it in his mouth, even though he'd lost his appetite.

It wasn't like he could argue with her. He did use his body to dominate others, particularly when doing a job. And after what had happened on the beach, Sully would know that better than anybody. Problem was, he had to. No witch he ever faced *wanted* to cross the veil to the Other Realm. These people were criminals, murderers...psychopaths. If he didn't dominate them, they'd kill him—and many others.

And yeah, he would say or do whatever he needed

to if it meant dispatching a witch in order to protect the vulnerable.

He swallowed his scrambled eggs, and reached for his mug. "Fair call." And he hated it.

She sighed. "It's just—I don't date, and now they think I do."

Dave frowned. "You don't date...ever?"

"Never."

"Why not?" She was attractive, sweet-natured, smart, strong—she'd held her own against him. Mostly. She had the body of a siren. His gaze drifted over the creamy skin revealed by her top, and again wondered about her underwear—or, hopefully, lack of it. She was gorgeous. Why didn't she date?

She shrugged. "It's a lifestyle choice. I have my work to concentrate on."

He cut up some bacon and chewed it thoughtfully. He could relate to that. Kind of. There was no way he, as a Witch Hunter, could have a significant other. He'd known that from the start, and had accepted that. But he couldn't deny it—every now and then he'd feel lonely, and would seek out company. Not as a *date*, though. But Sully—Sully wasn't a Witch Hunter. She didn't have to up and leave in the middle of the night, didn't have to fight to the death every time she went to "work", didn't have to try to give the impression of being normal instead of being all torn up inside, hating what had to be done. He didn't know why she didn't date, why she wasn't available for a relationship, why she wasn't looking for company, or just plain fun... and yes, he was very curious, but was in no position to be allowed to care. Either way, though, his story at the diner had unintended consequences, which is the last thing he wanted for her.

"I'm sorry. I'll clear it up with Cheryl when I see her." He looked at her briefly. Her cheeks were still a little pale, and there was the faintest of shadows under her eyes. "How are you?"

She met his gaze as she sipped her coffee. She placed her mug on the counter. "Better, thank you."

He turned to face her on the stool. "What happened?"

She averted her eyes. "Uh, not sure. Probably sunstroke." She nodded. "Yeah. It was really hot." She finished her breakfast quickly.

He frowned. "That's the first time I've seen someone with sunstroke throw up black gunk."

"Really? Oh, I've seen it happen," she murmured as she rose from the bench. He watched her as she walked around to the sink, concentrating fiercely on navigating her way through her kitchen. Sully Timmerman sucked at lying.

"Sully."

She halted at the sink, head down, then turned to face him. "Yes?"

"Is it because you're an empath?" he asked softly. He'd heard of them, but had never encountered one, before. Empaths were considered the witch version of truth seekers, those individuals occasionally born across the shadow breeds with the uncanny ability to sense emotion, and to gauge honesty and subterfuge. They were highly sought after in some cases—fantastic to use in civil litigation or high-value deals. In other cases, they were considered a threat, particularly by those who were trying to keep secrets or maintain lies. He knew one, Vassi Galen, but she'd always kept her truth-seeking talents a secret. Maybe that's what Sully did, to avoid the risk of folks wanting to shut down the walking lie detector. He held up a hand. "It's okay, you don't need—"

"Yes." She nodded slowly. "Yes, it's part of being an empath." She shrugged, palms up. "When you do your stuff, you get a name branded across your body. When I do my stuff, I draw in other people's pain, and it can sometimes make me…ill."

"Are you sure you're okay?" He couldn't help his concern. She'd coughed up a bucket-load of steaming black goop, and practically passed out.

"Yeah. Once I get rid of it, I'm generally fine. Yesterday was hard to control, though. There was so much grief and heartbreak."

"And you drew it all in?" Hell, no wonder it looked like she was barfing up toxic tar.

She shook her head. "No. Not all of it. Lucy lost the love of her life, as well as the woman who pretty much adopted her as her daughter. She will feel sorrow, and she'll feel grief, and I can't take that away from her, because that's based in the love she has for those people, and I'd have to take away that, too. I took away some of the pain of it, that's all." Sully grimaced. "Only I can't necessarily cherry-pick who I help in that kind of situation. Once I crack the wall, anything can come through."

"Crack the wall?" His eyebrows rose as he looked down at her. "Is that what it's like?"

She thought about it for a moment. "Yeah, I guess it is. When you open that gate, the emotions come in. In a situation like that, it's like a…flood. With claws." She shuddered, then waved her hand. "But that's gone now." She took a deep breath. "Thank you so much for driving me home." She frowned. "Why were you there?"

Dave looked at her for a moment. "Actually, that's

a really good question," he said slowly. "I wasn't expecting to see you there." Over the past few days he'd
tried talking to the first victim's neighbors, his work
colleagues, people at the gym, but they were all pretty
noncommittal, and for the first time he couldn't just bespell these people to tell him what he wanted to know.
Darn nulls.

"I knew Gary, and Lucy is a friend. Naturally I'd go
to his funeral. What about you?"

Dave frowned. "You knew Gary Adler?"

Sully frowned back at him. "Yeah. How do you—
?" Her eyes rounded. "Oh. Good. Grief. You saw Gary
die."

Chapter 8

Sully leaned back against the counter and looked up at him in horror. "Mack's Gym. Gary was a member. I didn't know where he'd died—Tyler didn't tell me that, but that would make sense." She closed her eyes briefly. Another realization dawned.

"Oh, heck. On the beach—you saw Mary Anne die." She felt the itch of tears in her eyes. Whoever had killed that nice little lady had done it in a way to bring a Witch Hunter down on him. She blinked, then looked up at him. "When I went to visit her that night—"

Dave frowned. "You went to visit her?" His voice was low and harsh.

"Yes, I'd heard about Gary, and thought I'd take Mary Anne and Lucy some tea—"

"You could have walked in on the killer," Dave exclaimed.

"No, her body had already been discovered, the sheriff was there—and why are you angry with *me*? It's not like I went looking for a killer—like you," she said, glaring at him.

Dave took a deep breath, then nodded. "You're right. You weren't to know, I just—I just don't want you hurt."

She blinked. "Oh." He sounded so…protective. He was taller than she, and his shoulders…she eyed his shoulders. There was so much strength there, in his broad chest, his muscled arms. His short hair was rumpled, his T-shirt a little wrinkled and the sunglasses shielded his eyes, yet for once she had no trouble reading his expression. He looked rough and sexy and just a little dangerous, with the soft curve of his lips when he let his witchy protective side out.

But she'd seen how protectiveness could be used to disguise control, and she wasn't going to be sucked in again. "But I'm an empath," she told him firmly. "I constantly feel hurt, and I know how to handle it. You don't need to worry about me."

His lips firmed. "I can't let anything happen to you."

"Anything else," she said, giving him pointed look. Then she sighed at the obstinate lift to his chin. "Look, it's very sweet, but I don't need a protector. What I do need is to figure out what's going on, here."

"*I'll* figure it out," he growled.

"Dave, please," she said, clasping her hands together. "Whoever did this, did it in *my name*."

Dave walked back a little and leaned back against the fridge, shaking his head. He folded his arms, and his biceps bulged with the movement. He'd caught some of the fabric of T-shirt with the movement, and it pulled out from his jeans, exposing just a little bit of skin, that fascinating marking framing his navel—oh, good lord, she was staring at his navel. She snapped her gaze back to those sunglasses. He looked sexy and strong and more than a little stubborn.

"Nope."

"Lucy was one of the first people I met when I moved to Serenity Cove," Sully argued. "She introduced me to a lot of the folks here, including Gary, who introduced me to my best friend, Jenny. He and his mother were super sweet to me. They brought me into their community, and that's where I—" Sully shut her mouth. Uh. That's where she met more of the nulls, and learned how they were all battling poverty, and how she came upon the idea to use the offcuts of her cutlery and weaponry to produce counterfeit coins. Gary had even helped her build the coin press.

Dave arched an eyebrow at her hesitation. "That's where you...what?"

"Really got to know these people," she said, then cleared her throat. "Uh, these people, they gave me a safe place, Dave, and now someone is killing them in my name."

Dave frowned. "What do you mean by safe place, Sully?"

She'd said too much. She bit her lip. She never talked about...before. Dave straightened from the fridge, his face grim as he walked a little closer. He dipped his head so that he was on eye level with her. She saw her reflection in his sunglasses—did he ever take them off?

"What are you running from?" His voice was low, and she could hear the curiosity tinged with concern in his tone.

She frowned. "No. I don't run from anything." She didn't try to delude herself anymore, either. She'd worked damn hard over the last four years, and felt stronger than she ever had before. Hell, she'd been strong enough to hold off a Witch Hunter. No. She didn't run from anything, not anymore.

"When I said safe place, I mean for an empath. They shut everything down. With these people, I don't have to shield myself so much, I don't have to protect myself. *They* become my wall." She trailed her finger along the sink. "You have no idea what that is like, for someone like me. To not have to constantly watch for emotion, to always guard against everyone around you." Sully lifted her gaze to meet his. "So when someone starts killing these very special friends of mine, I want to help stop that. And you can't do this on your own."

Dave lifted his chin. "Of course I can."

Sully's eyebrow rose. "Really? How many nulls have talked to you about Gary? About his mother?"

Dave's lips pursed, and Sully's gaze was drawn to them. They looked…soft. Just a little plump—not stung-by-a-bee plump, but kissy-plump.

And here she was again, getting all woozy-doozy over the wrong kind of man. She cleared her throat. Focus. Think of Gary, and Mary Anne…

"Please, tell me what happened to them. Let me *help* you. What did you see?"

Dave sighed, his breath gusting over her bare shoulder. She trembled. She couldn't deny it, the sensation was…nice.

He held up a finger. "Fine. I'll tell you, but this is my gig. We're not partners, you're not doing any investigating, you're—" He hesitated, as though trying to find the right word. "You're a consultant."

A consultant? That wasn't going to work for her, but she knew when to pick her battles. She gave him a nod. Just one. Enough to make him think she actually agreed.

He reached past her and started to run some water

into the sink, then reached for the detergent on the windowsill. "I see a blade in the heart, which is the kill action that gets the Ancestors involved," he told her. He started washing the breakfast dishes, and she grabbed a tea towel from the oven handle, and started to dry as he handed her the cleaned dishes.

"Then he—or she," he added, "removes the knife from the chest, and carves some sort of symbol into their wrist, squeezes some of their blood out—"

Sully looked up at him when he stopped talking. His mouth was curled in distaste. "Go on," she urged him. "I'm no shrinking violet."

He turned his head to look at her. This close, she could see the light of his eyes behind the lenses, maybe even his eyelashes. She saw his gaze drift over her. "You're not, are you?" He was making a comment, more than asking a question. He washed the frying pan and set it on the drainer next to the sink, and pulled the plug.

"He squeezes some of their blood out and drinks it."

Sully scrunched up her face. "Ew, gross."

"He—or she—says a few words, and then I get bumped."

Sully wiped up the frying pan and bent down to put in her pot cupboard. "And that's not normal?"

"No."

She frowned in puzzlement. "I wonder if he—or she…?" She looked at Dave. "You really don't know whether it's a man or a woman?"

Dave shook his head. "I really don't, and I'm an equal opportunity hunter. The killer wears gloves and whispers the spell. Can't tell whether it's a guy or a chick, and I know chicks can be just as psycho-crazy as guys."

"Oh," Sully said faintly. "Good to know."

He turned to face her, and folded those big, beautiful arms of his again. She shook her head slightly. Stop staring at those arms. "Uh, so, we have a witch who has killed nulls. *Nulls.*" She shook her head again. "I don't get it."

"Neither do I." Dave sighed.

"Maybe the witch didn't realize Gary and Mary Anne were nulls," she thought aloud. "Maybe the witch thought they were ordinary humans. I can't see what benefit he'd get out of killing a null—" She frowned, and tapped the sink. "Drinking null blood—that's going to reduce his powers. I don't get it. He must not have known."

"I need to find out more about the guy, and his mother. Who they came into contact with, who might have held a grudge—who stands to gain from their deaths…"

"We can talk to Jenny," Sully said, turning toward the door. Dave caught hold of her arm.

Fierce protectiveness, warm and snug, curled around her. Exasperation. Frustration. Curiosity. Damn it, he was doing it again, plowing through her shields as if they were made of tissue. Why couldn't she block this guy?

"Whoa, sweetness. *I'll* go talk to Jenny. I'll do it subtly. I don't want to go around announcing I'm a Witch Hunter, here to kill a witch. One—it would be around this town before I got out the door, and two—that's a conversation I really don't want to have with your sheriff."

Sully glanced down at his hand. "She won't talk to you," she told him.

Dave's lip's curled in a lazy smile. "I'll have you know some women find me charming."

She just bet they did. Smoking hot muscles, sexy

smile, a handsome face and an overall impression of...
experience.

"I told her we broke up because you cheated on me.
My best friend won't give you the time of day unless
I'm with you. And this *is* a small town. How many nulls
do you think know about you now?"

His grip slackened, but not before she felt the flash of
surprise. She continued on her way to the door. "You're
not the only one who can tell a fib."

Dave shoved his hands in his jeans' rear pockets and
tried to make himself comfortable against the wall. He
hadn't even bothered to try the tiny little seats attached
to the tiny little desks. Had he ever been that small as
a kid? The kids were outside on a short break, and it
was surprisingly relaxing, hearing the kids' chatter and
laughter outside, a little muted, while he stood in the
silence inside the room.

Okay, maybe not *that* relaxing. He lifted his gaze
from the students' desks to realize Sully's friend was
still staring at him. Coldly.

Well played, Sully. There was no way he'd be able
to get this woman, or any of the nulls they'd passed
on the way in who'd given him similar death stares, to
give him the time of day, let alone any solid information on the victims.

"So you want to find out more about Gary and Mary
Anne, huh? Why?" Jenny definitely wasn't sounding
cooperative. He pursed his lips as he looked over at his
new "partner".

Sully nodded, seemingly oblivious to the tension in
the room. "We want to find out who did this."

Jenny frowned. "Why?"

Sully frowned back at her. "Why not?"

Jenny's eyebrows rose. "We're not used to others being interested in what happens to us."

Dave watched as Sully folded her arms. "Jenny, this affects all of us. A murder is a murder, no matter who the victim is."

Jenny tilted her head. "Sully, you have no idea how many nulls have been murdered in the past where it's been treated as though they were dogs being put down. Heck, Reform doesn't even recognize us as a breed of our own. We are a *subset*."

Dave winced. Sully's friend had a valid and sobering point.

Sully's frown deepened. "Have you ever felt like I've treated you like a subset?"

Jenny's eyes widened. "Of course not," she said hurriedly. "No, you've been so generous and helpful with all of us, especially with—"

"Nothing," Sully interjected, and Dave's eyebrow rose.

"Uh, nothing that I wouldn't do again," Sully quickly supplied, her cheeks blooming with heat. Dave's eyes narrowed behind his sunglasses. What had she done for them? What had she done that she didn't want him to know about?

Jenny's gaze slid quickly between Dave and Sully, then back to Dave, and she nodded. "Exactly." She tried to mask the confusion and curiosity about them, but apparently Sully's friend was about as good as Sully when it came to lying.

So Sully's friend knew whatever it was his sweet little partner was into. He shelved that observation for later.

"When someone hurts you guys," Sully said quietly,

stepping up to Jenny's desk, "I hurt, because you guys are my friends. You're my family."

Dave found himself wondering what had happened with Sully's original family. She'd made comments about her First Degree classes, so she'd been brought up in a coven, but where were they now? And why had she left them?

Jenny smiled, although there was a tinge of sadness to it. "Thanks, Sully. That's so lovely to hear." The young woman turned to face him, and her eyes narrowed. "So why do *you* want to help?"

"Uh..." He wasn't quite sure what to say to that. Sully had shut down his one plausible excuse for being in town. He needed to set the record straight. "Look, about Sully and me—"

"He's trying to make it up to me." Sully's quick interruption made his mouth slack. What was she doing?

"Don't you think that's too little, too late?" Jenny commented.

Dave looked at Sully. What happened to setting folks straight? For right now, though, it would work for him. He could adapt. "I made a mistake," he said, and this time it wasn't so much a lie but a variation of the truth. "I need to make things right between us."

"So you're going to do that by...looking into a couple of null murders?"

"He's also got skills in this area," Sully added. "He's an investigator."

This time Jenny eyed him shrewdly, and he felt like he was being measured carefully.

"You mean, like a cop?"

Dave shuddered. "Not quite." Not at all.

"A private dick, or something?"

Hell, this was getting worse. He frowned. "Or something."

"Seems apt," Jenny muttered, and Dave noticed that Sully was trying not to smile and failing spectacularly.

Great. "Uh, Gary and Mary Anne—did they have any enemies? Did they owe money? Did Gary...cheat?"

Both women frowned at him. "No," they said in unison.

Jenny rose from her seat. "Gary loved Lucy. There was nobody else for him. Mary Anne—she was well respected in our community. Loved, even. Gary really tried to help with these kids, and everyone could see that. He was a nice guy, and didn't deserve what he got."

She glanced out toward the kids lining up in the schoolyard. "Look, I can't talk now, I have to go." She smiled at Sully. "Come over to Mom and Dad's for dinner. A few of us are getting together to remember the Adlers. We can talk, then." Her gaze slid to Dave. "You may as well come, too."

He nodded. "Fine." He would have loved to have talked more, but maybe this way he'd get a chance to talk with more of the nulls, and get a better sense of what these Adler folk were really like—and how they became the target of a murderous witch. He followed Jenny out to the door, but halted when she paused.

"If you hurt Sully again, I'm going to pulverize your nuts," she said in a low voice, then smiled brightly at the kids lining up outside the door. "Hey, guys!"

Dave's eyebrows rose as the fierce woman of less than a second ago morphed into a sweet kindergarten teacher as she walked out to the students. Sully stepped up behind him, and he turned to glance briefly at her. What was it with the women in this area? So nice, so...he kept coming back to the word, but he couldn't find one that fit better than *sweet*. So damn sweet. And so dangerous you had to guard your life, your gonads and your heart.

Sully raised her eyebrows when she saw him looking at her. "Is everything all right?"

He nodded as they stepped down toward the parking lot. Sully turned and waved as her name was called, and then stopped to catch a little red-haired boy who literally threw himself at her. She laughed as she set him down.

"Hey, Noah. How are you doing?"

"Good! Are you still coming to the festival?"

"I sure am! Don't want to miss those donkeys. Hey, how are your mom and dad?"

"Dad says he's going to catch you a big tuna!"

"And what does your mom say?" Sully asked with a knowing glint in her eye.

"Mom says we're having mac and cheese, then."

Dave's eyebrows rose at the comment, and Sully grinned. "Well, you tell your dad that if he does catch that tuna, I'll have to make you all my tuna and rice bake."

"Noah! Come on, we have to get back to work," Jenny called from hallway.

Noah sighed. "I have to go," he said, and Sully nodded.

"Yeah, but I'm pretty sure Miss Forsyth has some art planned."

Noah's face brightened, and he waved as he ran back to his class.

Dave watched the pupils wave at Sully as they walked back into the building. There was no hiding from the fact that these kids adored her. Her friend, Jenny, seemed decent, once you got past her frosty defenses and painful threats, and she was protective of Sully—like any good, loyal friend. The nulls respected Sully. That was...unusual.

He slid into the passenger seat of her beat-up car, and glanced over as she climbed into the driver's seat. "How did you get so cozy with the nulls?" he asked, curious.

She frowned as she started her car. "What do you mean? They're people. They're nice people."

"Yeah, but they're also a fairly closed community. They don't like outsiders."

"I guess they don't see me as an outsider then," she said simply as she drove away from the school.

"Hmm." He leaned back in his seat and watched the scenery flash by. How was it that a witch was able to be accepted by a null community? They normally avoided everyone with supernatural abilities, and the practitioners of magic did the same. He frowned.

"They don't know you're a witch, do they?"

She kept her gaze on the road. "I can't be a witch around them, so it doesn't really come into the conversation. I can't do spells, I can't do rituals, I can't practice magic near them, so when I'm with them, I'm not really a witch, am I?"

His eyebrows rose. "Wow. That's an interesting defense."

She frowned. "Defense? Defense for what?"

"You're lying to them."

She shook her head, flashing him a brief but pointed glare. "No. I'm not. I've never said I'm not a witch. In their presence, I'm just plain old me. Normal." She held up a finger as he opened his mouth to argue. "And that's me without any shields or artifice, so in reality, I'm more me when I'm with them, than when I'm not. Totally authentic."

He pinched the bridge of his nose, raising his sunglasses just a little. "Your logic is giving me a headache." He positioned his shades and stared out the window. She'd mentioned something similar before, about how she didn't have to block herself when she was with the nulls. And yet, she kept this one important, innate detail about herself from the community she said she trusted. But if she couldn't be a witch around them, like she said—was she really lying to them? Or just omitting a detail about herself that had no impact on them?

"Where to now?" Sully asked, interrupting his thoughts.

"The graveyard, please," he said. "I need to pick up my bike."

Sully nodded, then flicked him a quick glance. "Then what are we doing?"

"Well, I have to find a place to sleep," he told her. "I wasn't expecting to stay in town this long." He shifted in his seat. No, he'd fully expected to roll into town, kill Sullivan Timmerman and then roll on out again. "Can you recommend any places to stay?"

Sully frowned. "There's a motel down south, about thirty minutes' drive. Nothing much up north. We're not really a tourist mecca."

He frowned. Thirty minutes away. That was a little too far from the action. "Nothing closer?"

Sully drove carefully around the bends of the coastal road, then looked at him briefly. "I have a foldout couch," she offered.

His eyebrows rose. Staying with Sully…he could feel his body throb at the prospect, and tried to hose it down with rational thought. Sully was nice. And she didn't date—she wasn't the love-'em-and-leave-'em type of woman. She was a lady, and deserved so much more than the frolic-in-the-bedsheets that he was limited to offering.

But…she could give him access to the nulls, provide some local information in the tracking down of this killer.

And it would be pure hell living in the same house and not touching her. He eyed her hands on the steering wheel. Her skin was covered in small marks, a legacy of the craft she worked. They weren't the soft hands of a woman who did office work. They revealed a delicate strength, and a capacity for pain and perseverance. Almost like the dainty hands of a warrior, if that was possible. He wondered what it would feel like to have her hands on his body. He could feel himself growing hard at the prospect.

And that was exactly why he should stay the hell away from Sully, and her foldout couch. He couldn't afford to be distracted from his duty.

"Thanks, that would be great," he said, then glanced back out the passenger window. *Hell, here I come.* He tried to distract himself, and thought about what they'd learned from Jenny—pretty much nothing. He frowned.

"Why didn't you let me set Jenny straight about us?"

Sully's lips pursed as she focused on the road. "You heard her. There is a real us and them attitude there. If you don't want people to know who you really are, tell them something they'll believe. I couldn't think of another way for us to get them to talk."

He looked at her carefully. *If you don't want people to know who you really are, tell them something they'll believe.* That had just rolled off her tongue, as though she was talking from experience. She was talking about convincing people, not about telling them the truth. What other "omissions" was she guilty of? The difference between what he knew about his new "consultant", and what he didn't know, just got greater.

Sully Timmerman just got a whole lot more interesting.

Chapter 9

"A toast to Gary."

Sully sipped from the cup of ale she'd been handed. She was leaning against the wall near the living room door inside Jenny's parents' home, and the house was packed. People were still arriving, mainly men who'd just come in off the boats, and had done a quick shower and change before heading over. Food was set out on the kitchen table, and people were helping themselves, piling up plates before they sat or leaned against any available surface.

Sully peered around the doorjamb. Dave was just outside the back door, talking to some of the younger fishermen as they smoked cigarettes outside. They'd been wary of him, at first, but she could see they were beginning to relax around him. Even if he still wore his sunglasses at night.

She turned back to those gathered in the living room.

Sully was content to listen to the stories the gathered folks wanted to share. Some were funny, some were poignant, but all showed the deep respect and love this community had for the murdered victims.

"So, you have a boyfriend, huh?"

The deep voice whispering in her ear made her jump, and she turned.

"Jacob," she said, half laughing in relief when she recognized Jenny's older brother.

He grinned. "Sorry, didn't mean to startle you."

He stepped back into the hallway, and she followed him, so that they could talk without intruding on the memories being shared within the room.

"How are you, Sully?" The tall fisherman tilted his head to the side as he looked down at her. "I didn't get a chance to talk to you at the funeral."

She waved a casual hand. "I think it was something I ate, combined with being in the hot sun. I'm fine now." And she was. She'd tried to bolster her shields before coming, but the null effect made her work unnecessary. Surrounded by nulls, none of her empath powers worked, and she didn't have to worry too much about shielding herself, even if she could. "How are you?"

"Dealing with the fact you've got a boyfriend," Jacob teased, although there was a slightly serious light to his eyes.

"It was quite the surprise to see him," she said truthfully, although she felt a little discomfort at perpetrating an untruth. "How's the fish?" she asked in an effort to distract.

Jacob shrugged, his blond hair glinting in the light. "Biting, but not busy."

Sully winced. The community were doing it tough, and were hoping the fishing loads would increase.

They'd implemented a sustainable fishing program, but that didn't seem to be paying off just yet. "Sorry to hear that."

Jacob glanced around, then leaned down toward her. "Hey, I hear Leo Campi is doing it tough. Dislocated his shoulder in a netting accident and can't work for several weeks. We're passing the boot around tonight," he said, pointing to the leather boot that Jacob's father, Jack, just passed to the person next to him, after stuffing some paper money into it.

Sully nodded. "I'll see what I can do," she said quietly. She had some silver that had been delivered the day before at the shop, and had some cheaper metals she could melt and press into coins. "They'll have to travel into Irondell to spend it, though. Too many coins circulating here will draw attention."

Jacob nodded, patting her on the shoulder. "Thanks, Sully. You're all right, you know?"

"She is, isn't she?"

Sully turned at the sound of Dave's voice. He stood just behind them in the hallway. The Witch Hunter smiled at her friend, and stuck his hand out. He hadn't removed his leather gloves. Sully's brow dipped. Huh. Funny, she'd only just noticed that. This man always wore his sunglasses, and with the exception of eating, he pretty much always wore his gloves.

"Hey, I'm Dave, the ex."

Jacob eyed the gloved hand for a moment, then shook it. He smiled grimly. "I'm Jacob, the current…friend."

Sully looked at both men who seemed to be engaged in some sort of staring contest. Both men were tall, with broad shoulders and an impressive physical presence, yet they looked as different as night and day. Dave, with his neat beard and dusty blond hair, and Jacob with his dark hair and hazel brown eyes. And both looked like they were sizing each other up.

"Hey, Jacob, I wanted to ask you—this is the first time I've been invited to this sort of thing," she said, trying to distract them both. "It's really powerful. Is this how you normally handle someone's passing?"

Jacob finally relinquished Dave's hand. "No, but Gary and Mary Anne were PBs, so it's a special night. For both of them to go..." He shook his head, his expression a mixture of sadness and concern. Then he frowned. "Jenny mentioned you two were wanting to help, somehow...?"

"Uh, Dave has some experience with this sort of thing," Sully explained.

Jacob's eyebrow rose. "With null murders?"

Dave shrugged. "Murder is blind," he said. "Shouldn't matter what breed, it should just matter."

Laughter rose from inside the living room. Another story had been shared about the Adlers. Sully could hear the clink of glasses and mugs as people toasted their departed.

Jacob looked at him thoughtfully, then folded his arms. He dipped his chin in the direction of Dave's sunglasses. "Do you have a vision problem?"

Dave smiled. "I think I see pretty good. Hey, you said the Adlers were PBs—what does that mean?"

Jacob glanced at Sully, and she shrugged. She hadn't heard of the term, either.

"PBs are purebloods," Jacob informed them. "They can trace their lineage back to before The Troubles." The man shrugged. "Shape-shifters have their alphas, vampires have their primes, covens have their regents and everyone has elders—we have our purebloods. Their lineage hasn't been tainted with shadow breed blood, or diluted by ordinary humans."

Sully blinked. It was interesting. The shadow breeds took a similar view of null blood tainting their bloodline, and muting their supernatural abilities…but there were many mixed-bloods throughout all communities. Still, this was a surprise. What else did she not know about these people she'd just spent the last four years with? "Huh. I never knew there was a hierarchy within the null community."

Jacob grimaced. "Meh. We respect them, and the purebloods definitely get a voice at the council, but we like to think it's your actions that define you as a person, not your ancestors."

"Interesting," Dave said grimly. Sully realized he was thinking about his own actions, and how closely linked it was to the Ancestors. For Dave, it really was a case of ancestors defining him as a Witch Hunter.

"Are there a lot of purebloods around?" Sully asked, curious about this new facet of the community she'd adopted.

"Some. There's more over on Stoke Island—it has the highest population of purebloods in the country."

"How is it that the rest of the breeds don't know about this?" Dave asked.

"In case you haven't noticed, the rest of the breeds don't give two hoots about us," Jacob said. "Besides, it doesn't really mean much. PBs are still normal like the rest of us. There's no added strength or ability. Just inherited blood."

Sully met Dave's gaze. "Interesting," they said in unison.

Dave followed Sully into her home. He'd driven his bike out to the null area, and Sully had taken her car, so they hadn't had a chance to talk on the way home.

Now her expression was thoughtful as she turned on the lights in her living room. He glanced inside the room. There was an impressive bookcase on one wall with— he squinted—gardening books? Mathematical theory? Reform politics? Yeesh. He definitely wouldn't be borrowing a book from her. He looked away from the bookcase. She'd already pulled out the sofa and covered it in sheets and a blanket. She must have done it in the afternoon when he'd been out at the library, looking up any stories he could find that mentioned the Adlers. All the articles he'd located had been complimentary. His lips quirked as he stared at the made-up sofa. There was even a neatly folded towel on the pillow.

He looked over at Sully. "So, are you and Jacob an item?"

He could see his question surprised her. He didn't know why it did—he'd seen the way Forsyth looked at Sully, and the almost protective, possessive glare he'd sent in Dave's direction. You didn't need any magical powers to see the guy had feelings for her.

"No, just friends," she told him. She scratched her temple. "Did you think Gary's and Mary Anne's murders have something to do with the fact they're PBs?"

He looked away as he set his backpack down on the floor. Her answer had pleased him, and he didn't want to think too much on the why. He focused on what they'd learned. "I don't know. Why would a witch want pure null blood? It's not like they can do anything with it." *Ugh.* He'd just spent the last two hours with a bunch of nulls, and the knowing, the awareness, the darkness that surrounded his natural ability like a cloak… Well, it was enough to give a witch the heebie-jeebies.

Except for Sully. She seemed to enjoy it. Go figure.

"But it could explain why you get bumped out of your visions…?"

He thought about it for a moment, then nodded slowly. "Possibly." He frowned. "But it's *null* blood. Why consume it? What possible benefit would that have for a witch?" Just the thought made him want to gag.

Sully crossed over to the small end table that held her phone and a notepad and pen. "Can you remember what the witch drew on their wrists?"

"Yes," he said slowly, watching as she brought the notepad and pen over to him. "Why?"

"Can you draw it?"

He nodded. In two strokes of the pen he'd drawn the symbol he'd seen carved into Gary's and Mary Anne Adler's wrists. *X*. He showed it to Sully, who frowned when she glanced down at it.

"It's from the Old Language?"

Dave's eyebrows rose. "I'm impressed. You're familiar with the Old Language."

Sully gestured toward his chest, her cheeks heating. "I saw my name…"

"And you were able to translate it?" Okay, he was more than impressed. For all intents and purposes, the original language of the witches was dead. Learning it, deciphering it, was usually down to Witch Hunters and bored scholars wanting to challenge themselves. But the language was one thing. Learning the symbols, the ancient runes—that was another thing entirely. "How did you learn it?"

Her shrug was noncommittal. "Oh, it was just something I was interested in at one time."

A general interest didn't explain being able to decipher without a key, or instantly recognizing a rune for what it was. His sweet little cutler seemed to hide some pretty big secrets.

"Do you know what this rune means?" he asked her. She frowned, her attention caught by the symbol on the notepad.

"No, I don't. I might be able to look it up, though."

Dave's eyes rounded. "Look it up? How?" There were no computer databases for this sort of thing. No text books to consult. No dial-a-friend service. She would have to have—

Sully walked over to the bookcase, arms out. She closed her eyes, murmuring something so softly he couldn't hear it. The books on the shelves began to glow and shimmer, the defined edges blurring as they transformed into an entirely different library. Damn, she'd hidden it behind a camouflage spell—a damn good one if it fooled another witch. He'd had no intention of going anywhere near her books.

She held out her palm, and again murmured something. This time, though, he recognized the ancient language. She was asking for information on runes. His brow quirked. Who was she asking? He could feel the crackle in the air, the weight of power in the room.

A tome flew from a shelf, and she caught it, staggering back under the force. Her eyebrows rose. "Uh, thanks," she muttered.

"Who are you talking to?" He gazed around the room, then looked back at the bookcase.

She glanced up at him as she walked over to the end table. "The books, of course."

He nodded. "Of course." He looked down at the book she held in her arms. It looked remarkably like—his heart thudded in his chest.

"Is that what I think it is?" he asked hoarsely, stepping closer.

"What do you think it is?" she asked as she set the tome down on the table. He looked down at it. No. It couldn't be.

"A coven grimoire."

Sully glanced at him for a moment. "Yes, it is." She tilted her head, her brows drawing together. "You act like you've never seen one before."

"I haven't. I'm not allied with a coven." Only those in the third level of a coven could even view their coven spellbooks. As a Witch Hunter, he had heard of them, but never seen one. Until now. Dave felt like his eyes were going to pop from his head.

"You have your coven's spellbook?" He had to ask again. It was incredible. These things were passed down from generation to generation, added to through the years... They were the living resource of a coven's history, their power, their alliances and enemies, the spells they'd devised and recorded.

"Not the current one. This is an old version," she said. "We had to make a copy to allow for new spellwork."

"And you have your coven's original? I thought these were protected, that a coven never let any of them go?"

She frowned. "This *is* protected," she told him. "It's with me."

"This is your coven's archive?" he asked in disbelief. A coven's archive was sacrosanct. It held the history, the good and the bad, the strengths and weaknesses, of a coven. The coven protected those references, and they were always honored as deeply private and confidential material. If you accessed a coven's archive, you could access and then exploit those weaknesses, or sabotage their strengths, or worse, steal from them. A coven protected their archive just like a werewolf pack or vampire colony protected their territory. Accessing a coven's archive without permission or supervision was a serious crime among the witches.

And only the most loyal and powerful witch within a coven was entrusted with the security and care of an archive.

Mind. Blown.

He looked down at the volume she held in her hands. "How old is it?"

Sully blew her cheeks out. "Well, that's a good question. This one's been handed down for several generations, it's hard to date it."

His jaw dropped. No. It—it couldn't be. The pages were made of vellum and what looked like—Dave clutched his chest. Honest-to-God papyrus. He pulled his leather gloves off and reached for the codex. Halted. Then took a deep breath and touched it.

Images swam through his mind, of a man painstakingly writing in the book, of passing it to his son, of a ritual within a ring of monolithic stones, of a woman clutching the tome to her chest as the howls of werewolves echoed through the forest, along with the screams of her coven. A young man stumbling along a riverbed, ducking and weaving as vampires chased him, while hundreds fought in the fields behind him. The Troubles.

That same man handing it to a pregnant woman, his face twisted in pain and anguish, an arrow sticking out of his gut. The woman sobbing as she bent to kiss him. "Gabriel…" she cried as he died.

Holy fu—. Dave whipped his hand away. He swallowed, then wagged his finger at the ancient book.

"That—that's not possible," he said, despite the visions he'd seen that proved it was, indeed, possible. "That is not supposed to exist." Gabriel. Gabriel, a legend of The Troubles, who'd saved so many lives with his magic, who'd unlocked many of the secrets of the shadow breeds during the wars, and had helped devise spells and weapons to fight against them. This—this was Gabriel's grimoire.

"You're right. It's not supposed to exist."

Dave lifted his gaze to Sully. She looked remarkably calm for having the oldest book of witchcraft in modern times here in her living room. "Who *are* you?"

She frowned at him, perplexed. "You know who I am. My name is branded onto your chest, for crying out loud."

He tried to think. He really did, but the ramifications of this, of the very existence of this book long thought destroyed before the dust had settled on a new world order…

"Gabriel's grimoire. It was believed to have died, along with his line, during The Troubles."

"He had a family."

Dave held up a hand as he subsided onto the sofa bed. "Whoa. Stop. My brain is exploding. Are you telling me that his wife managed to pass it on to someone?"

Sully shook her head. "No, I'm saying that young woman passed it on down the line."

Dave took a deep breath. *Okay. Settle. This* will *make sense.* "What coven are you from?" he asked quietly.

Sully hesitated, then dropped her gaze to the codex on the table. "I'm from the Alder Coven." Her voice was so low, he barely heard the words.

"The Alder—" Dave closed his mouth. The Alder Coven. Conspiracy theories abound about the infamous coven. It died out in the Roman invasion. They all perished with Atlantis. Pompeii. Or the Minoans, with the first reported shape-shifter. Hell, there was even the story of them being swallowed by flames in a city that burned after an earthquake. Then of course, came The Troubles. He didn't think anyone had connected Gabriel to the Adler Coven, though. Wow. He would have thought she was crazy. Crazy beautiful, but definitely a few sandwiches short of a picnic. Now, though, with the evidence right in front of him, he couldn't deny it.

"Man, you guys are good." He moved from stunned amazement to full acceptance and realization in the blink of an eye.

He rose, picked up the grimoire and gently but hurriedly placed on the shelf. "What the *hell*? You can't just whip something like this out whenever you like," he whispered furiously.

"Dave, this book is so protected—"

"You brought this book into a null area," he whispered harshly. "You bring a null into the house, and all of your protections don't mean diddly."

"No, this is different," she whispered, then frowned. "Why are we whispering?"

"Because you have Gabriel's grimoire in your living room," he whispered back as he turned to face her.

"Dave, relax."

"You can't tell me to relax," he exclaimed softly. "You have a mammoth book of ancient spells, Sully. Do you know how many people would *kill* for this?"

She frowned at him, then straightened her shoulders as she glared at him. "I am a member of the Alder Coven. I have sworn to protect this book with my life. Of *course* I know how many people would kill for this," she said, her voice low and fierce.

"Then why show me this?" he asked, gesturing at the shelves. Now he would have to keep this secret to his dying day, and if his sister ever found out he knew and hadn't told her, well, she'd make sure his death was slow and painful. Hell, his mother—God, she'd have a field day with this. And then would plot until she held the tome in her own hands. Every witch he knew would want to get their hands on this, and every shadow breed in existence would want to destroy it.

This book was the source of modern-day spells, but covens only worked from bits of it. Nobody had the full resource.

Until now.

"How can you just pull this out, like it's so damn ordinary and mundane?" he asked, and had to shove his hands in his jacket, otherwise he'd act exactly like his coven elder mother on a rant at his rebellious sister, and gesture wildly.

"Because I trust you, Dave," Sully said.

He thought a blood vessel popped in his brain. "You *trust* me?" Okay, he hadn't meant to yell that at her, or make her flinch, but her words had surprised him. Stunned him. "You *can't* trust me. I tried to kill you, remember?"

"You apologized for that."

He clutched his temples. "You have to stop defending that," he told her. "You—you're so—so—" his brain scrambled for the right word.

Sully lifted her chin. "So what, Dave?" She arched an eyebrow.

He flung his arms out. "I'm trying to think up the right word, but all I'm getting is gullible."

Her blue eyes widened in surprise, then darkened with anger. "Gullible? You think I'm *gullible*?"

"No, but I can't think of the right—ah!" he snapped his fingers. "Naive. You're naive."

Sully blinked, as though trying to marshal her thoughts into a logical sequence. Good, because he'd hate to think he was the only one losing his mind over this.

"You trust too easily. I came up to you on the sand— a stranger, and you stopped and talked to me," he said, his thumbs pressing against his chest. "You were going to let me kill you, you've invited me into your home and you barely know me—" his eyes widened as a thought occurred to him. "What would have happened to the grimoire if I'd killed you?" he breathed, as the slow chill of horror crept over him.

"The grimoire would have gone to its new owner," she stated calmly. "There is a built-in hereditary spell."

For a moment he was distracted by all the protections and wards this book must have on it, but then brought his gaze back to the woman in front of him— the woman who could get herself into serious trouble for trusting too easily.

"You have to protect yourself better," he told her. God, the more he learned about this woman, the more he wanted to shield her. And that totally wasn't what he was used to. He was used to annihilating witches, not protecting them.

"Dave, you're the Witch Hunter. Our own version of law enforcement. Why shouldn't I trust you?"

"I kill people, Sully," he rasped, pain burning his throat. "I kill witches. Like you."

She shook her head. "No, not like me. You kill the evil among us, Dave."

He shook his head at the blind faith, the respect in her voice. He deserved neither. And that hurt. It hurt how much he wanted it to be true, and how far away from the truth it was.

"You don't get it. The Ancestors picked me because I can kill my kin and walk way," he told her. "I've had to, in the past." He shrugged out of his jacket, and then pulled his black T-shirt over his head. "Look at me, Sully."

He held his arms out, and then slowly turned around. "Every single one of these names belongs to a witch I've killed." His back was covered in the black tattoos. His biceps. And now the spot over his heart. It was getting so that he barely recognized himself in the mirror anymore. He sometimes had to force himself to stare at his reflection. Those names…each kill was burned into his memory. Those who had begged for mercy… those who had resisted and fought to live, or tried to kill him instead. He lifted his gaze to hers, and it was one of the hardest things he'd had to do. "You can't trust a monster like me, Sully," he rasped.

Her eyes were bright and luminous, as though she was fighting back tears. She took a tentative step forward, her hand out. She paused, then laid her hand on his chest.

There it was again, that clash of energy, that tidal wave of sensation, and then there was her touch. He closed his eyes at the contact, so light, so gentle and warm. He hadn't realized how much he'd craved a woman's touch—*her* touch. It was soothing, it was arousing, it was the very essence of a complex and complicated woman, and he wanted more—and hated himself for it.

"You may be a Witch Hunter," she whispered, and took a deep breath. "But I know you're not all bad."

He slowly opened his eyes. She stood so close, her honey-blond hair loose and luxurious around her shoulders, her blue eyes so full of sympathy, of tenderness. He felt like a brute next to her.

"I'm not all good, either."

She bit her lip, then moved her hand to cup his cheek. "You're good enough."

Her gaze dropped down to his lips, and his breath froze in his chest for a moment. She nodded. "You're good enough," she whispered. She rose up on her toes and pressed her lips against his.

He stood there for a moment, stunned.

Hell, if he wasn't a monster, he sure as hell wasn't a saint. He wrapped his arms around her waist, and slanted his lips across hers.

Chapter 10

She slid her arms around his neck as he gathered her close. So many messages, it made her dizzy trying to make sense of them all. Desire, so hot, so sharp, it took her breath away. Frustration. Loneliness. Self-recrimination. Arousal.

She'd meant to comfort him. She'd sensed his guilt and remorse, so heavy it was nearly suffocating. His gaze was hidden behind his sunglasses, but those lips, the set of his jaw… She'd wanted to reach out.

Now, though, there was no thought for comfort, for reassurance. Sully opened her lips to him, her breath hitching as his tongue slid against hers. His hands tightened on her hips, pulling her against him, and she could feel the hard ridge of his arousal pressing against her stomach.

Her hands trailed over his shoulders, his arms—oh, heavens, his arms. The man was magnificent. So strong and broad, so warm, so—

Dave flexed his hips against hers, and Sully thought she was going to combust. She slanted her head first one way, then the other, their tongues dueling, their breaths coming in shared, staccato pants.

His large hands slid beneath her loose top, and goose bumps rose on her ribs. She arched her back as his hands trailed up her back. She moaned. Heat, so much heat. Her heart thudded in her ears, and she could feel herself getting damp between her thighs. Her breasts swelled, and she pressed herself against him firmly. God, his chest was amazing. She ran her hands over the defined musculature of his torso. His skin was smooth, so sleek, so not what she expected. She could see some marks that weren't tattoos. Scars. But, astonishingly, the evidence of his strength, of his skill, just felt sexy against her fingertips as she caressed him.

Dave made a surprised sound against her lips when his fingers encountered the clasp of her strapless bra. She raised her eyebrows as she drew back, and he gave her a wicked smile. "I've been fantasizing about your underwear," he murmured, then took her lips again as his clever fingers undid the clasp.

He drew the garment away from her, and she shivered in his arms at the caress against her skin.

And then his hands covered her breasts beneath her top. She moaned, tearing her lips from his, her head tilting back as she surrendered to the sensation. He cupped the weight of her breasts in his hands, his thumbs strumming over her nipples.

So hot. Liquid heat slicked her thighs, and she pulled his head down, capturing his lips in a kiss that conveyed her own hunger. For him. For the Witch Hunter.

He growled softly into her mouth, then his hands glided down to her butt. He caressed her there, clasping the fabric of her skirt and inching it up her legs. She slid her tongue against his, her breath coming in pants. She could feel the heat of his body, the cool against her legs, her nipples tight with want. Dave bent his knees. His grip tightened, and he lifted her up. Sully swung her legs around his hips as he walked her back to rest her butt on a shelf of the bookcase. She ignored the clatter, the tumble of magical texts falling to the floor.

She lifted her head to take a quick breath, then closed her eyes as she tilted her head back. He was hard against her. Everywhere. Hard. Hot. His hips rolled against hers, and she shuddered. Her thighs tightened around his hips, and he moaned, low and sexy, as he trailed his lips down the line of her neck.

So much heat. She heard him hiss in her ear, felt him shudder. Heat. Like, burning. She pulled back, and his neck arched, the veins in stark relief against his skin. He leaned back, his hips holding her in place on the shelf.

The mark on his chest glowed. Her name.

Realization hit. *Oh, God, no.*

"Dave," she gasped.

The mark brightened, and Dave clasped the shelf on either side of her, gritting his teeth as he sucked in a breath. His biceps bulged, his knuckles whitened and his thighs tensed beneath hers.

He was in pain. She could feel it. Intense, burning. Consuming.

"Sullivan Timmerman," Dave gasped, tugging off his sunglasses.

Sully gaped as his light gray eyes turned silver, and his expression went slack as he stared sightlessly at the shelves above her head, entranced.

Instinctively, she reached out to give him comfort, to offer him support.

Red. Fire. Scalding. Darkness. Running. Panting. Determination. *A woman, scrambling down the side drive of a house. She pauses at the chain-link fence, fumbling with the gate's latch.* Satisfaction. Gotcha. *The woman turns to face her, her eyes wide with terror.*

"No! Please, no!" She holds up her arms to ward off blows, but the knife strikes fast. Not to kill, just to stop her from running. Triumph. *The woman clutches her stomach, her face twists in pain. She gasps as she falls to her knees, and she collapses, cradling her stomach as the stain blooms across her blouse.* Cold intent. End it. *The knife flashes again, plunging into her chest. The confusion, the shock, the terror, gently wanes as the light leaves her eyes.*

Dave lowered her to the floor and stumbled back, breaking their contact. Sully's vision snapped into focus once more. She was back in her living room, leaning back against her bookshelf, her skirt gently draping down to her calves as Dave grimaced. He shook his head once, still caught in the violence of his vision.

His lips tightened. Then his lips turned down, and for a brief moment sadness crossed his features, before it was removed by determination and that same ruthlessness she'd seen on the beach. He blinked, and the light in his eyes flickered down to a light silver.

"Are you okay?" she asked. His chest didn't glow anymore, and she could see him in his eyes again, not some vacant glaze.

His chest, though, looked painful. The mark that had healed a little was now rebranded onto his skin. Her name.

Sullivan Timmerman had killed again.

"I have to go," Dave muttered, wincing as he reached for his T-shirt.

Sully raised a shaky hand to her lips, trying to fight back the tears.

"Aman—Amanda Sinclair," she said, then clutched her stomach. Oh, God. Her family…

"What?"

"Amanda Sinclair. The woman he just killed. That's her name," she said, then covered her mouth. Deep breaths.

Dave frowned. "You—you saw?" he asked, his tone baffled as he took a step toward her.

She nodded. "Touch, we were touching. Oh, my God, Amanda," The tears fell, hot on her cheeks. Her gut clenched, and she could feel the bile rising in her throat.

Dave's eyes widened in shock, then his features showed his dismay. "Oh, Sully. I didn't know—I'd never want you to see—"

"He hunted her," she cried, her hands twisting in the cotton of her blouse.

Dave stilled. "What?"

"He—he was hunting her. I could—I could feel it."

Dave looked from her to the door, and back to her. He reached for her arm, gently pulling her away from the bookshelf, and then turned and guided her to sit on the foldout sofa.

"I'm sorry, I have to go, I have to find him—we'll talk later," he promised, his face filled with regret. "Where does Amanda live?"

"Lived," she corrected automatically, shock putting her into a numb autopilot. The woman was now dead. Oh, hell.

He nodded. "Yes. Lived. Sully, where did Amanda Sinclair live?" he asked gently.

"Two streets down from where we were tonight. Number 6." Her response was automatic, the words falling from her lips as she replayed what she'd seen in her mind. Amanda had been so terrified. Another tear fell on her cheek. She'd never felt so helpless, so useless, watching the woman's murder.

He cupped her cheek, and tilted his forehead against hers. "I'm so sorry, Sully." Intense guilt. Remorse. Grief. He was full of it. For Amanda—and for her.

"No, this isn't on you," she told him, blinking back her tears. "I'll come with you," she said, and braced herself to rise off the sofa. The Sinclairs…she had to go to them.

Dave's hand on her shoulder prevented her from moving. "No," he told her firmly. "You're staying right here."

"Dave, I know the family," she told him urgently.

He nodded. "I understand. But I'm going to the scene of a murder, Sully. This guy—he might still be there. I don't want you anywhere near this."

Her eyes narrowed. "I can take care of myself, Dave." She'd spent the last four years making sure that was true.

His lips firmed. "You're strong, I'll give you that. But this guy has now murdered three people. I'm not willing to take the chance that you could be the fourth."

She opened her mouth to protest, and he cut off her words with a quick kiss. "Please, Sully. I have to do this, and you being there—it will be a distraction. I'll be wanting to make sure you're safe, and not focusing on the job." Dave straightened. "I have to go. But we'll talk when I get back. I promise."

"Your chest," she said in protest. Dave was pulling his T-shirt on over his as head as he walked toward the door.

"I've got a first aid kit on my bike," he said brusquely, and then left.

Sully sagged back on the sofa, and stared around the room. Dave's suggestion was definitely the safest course. His job was to hunt the null killer. The witch killing the people she knew and loved in her name.

"Screw it," she muttered. Dave expected her to sit quietly at home. She hadn't let a man make her decisions for her for four years. She wasn't about to let that happen again. Her friends needed her. She trotted out to the shed in the back garden to gather some supplies.

Dave drove up to the makeshift barricade on the street and surveyed the scene. A crowd had gathered along the designated perimeter, and deputies were out to direct traffic and enforce the boundary. Red-and-blue lights flashed down the street, casting colored flickers into the darkness. The sheriff stood near the driveway gate and was talking to a man who Dave could only guess was Amanda Sinclair's husband, judging from his devastated, grief-stricken expression.

Darn. With the sheriff and his deputies traipsing all over the area, he couldn't get any closer to the scene. Couldn't witch his way past, couldn't bespell people to tell him what he needed to know, couldn't become invisible or forgettable—not in null territory, anyway. This was a novel experience, not being able to use his powers to get what he wanted. Which was exactly what Sully had said before, wasn't it? She wouldn't date him because he was the kind of guy who did and said whatever was needed to get what he wanted.

And yet, they'd kissed. So maybe dating was off the table, but other stuff wasn't...? He frowned. The burn in his chest had subsided, but was still an aching reminder of what he was in Serenity Cove for—and it wasn't to get up close and all kinds of personal with an empath witch who seemed to know him way too well for his liking.

He kicked out the stand for his bike and swung his leg over. He removed his helmet, wincing at the pull on his chest. He'd slapped a nonstick dressing over the wound and used tape to hold it in place, but it ached, and his skin was pinched by the tape with each movement. He hung the strap of his helmet over the handlebars, then strode a little farther along the edge of the perimeter. He eyed the front of the house. The door was closed. His lips tightened. No sign of forced entry. He glanced over toward the gate. A sheet was draped over the figure on the ground. He backed up a little. The drive had a five-foot-high wooden fence down one side. She wouldn't have been able to scale it, not with her killer right on her heels. House on one side, fence on the other, her only option would have been to run down the drive toward the street. He wondered if that had been the killer's plan, or whether he'd just been lucky.

"Excuse me, sir."

Dave turned as the deputy stepped around the roadblock, gesturing beyond him. Dave realized he was standing in the man's way and stepped aside, giving a casual wave of apology as the deputy passed him.

He turned back to the scene. Sully was right. Amanda Sinclair had been hunted down and killed. He glanced up at the night sky. The moon was a chunk of silver. A waxing gibbous moon. Enough light to stop you from tripping off the curb, but still kind of gloomy, especially in this neighborhood with no streetlights, he noticed, eyeing up and down the street.

A warm breeze ruffled his hair. He would have liked

to remove his jacket, but with the law already here, he didn't think he'd be sticking around for long. A hand thudded down on his shoulder, and he turned, hiding the wince at the resulting pull of muscle and scorched skin.

Jacob Forsyth. Sully's wannabe-boyfriend nodded grimly at him. "I thought you left?"

"I turned back when I saw all the police cars on the highway," he lied. He couldn't very well say he'd received a magical vision from the Ancestors. That wasn't something folks readily understood or accepted—except for Sully, it seemed.

Jacob nodded, accepting his excuse at face value. He looked over toward the cordoned-off house, his expression dark and grim. "This sucks. Ronald found her when he came home from the Adler farewell."

Dave looked over at him. "She wasn't at the farewell?"

Jacob shook his head. "Nope. She was home with the kids."

"Kids were in the house?" Dave looked back at the house in horror. He hadn't seen the kids in the vision.

Jacob nodded, his lips tight. "Yeah. They slept through the whole thing." His answer was short. Abrupt. The man was visibly upset—no, maybe angry was a better word—at what had happened.

"But they're safe?" Dave's gut clenched with apprehension at the risk to the kids.

"Yeah, they're safe."

"Thank God," Dave muttered in relief. Jacob watched him closely for a moment, then glanced back up the street.

"When did you say you arrived in Serenity?" Jacob's tone was conversational, but the words cut like hot steel.

Dave met his gaze. "I didn't." He should have expected this. "I arrived the morning of Mary Anne Adler's death." Which meant he wasn't in the area for Gary Adler's death, and he hoped that was enough to eliminate him from Jacob's obvious suspicions.

"Murder," Jacob corrected.

Dave inclined his head. "Murder."

"Where's Sully?"

"She's back home," Dave said.

Jacob nodded. "Good. She doesn't need to see this."

Dave turned back toward where the sheriff was talking quietly with the husband. Jacob sounded protective. Proprietary.

Not that he should care. He was here to hunt his witch. If the witch moved on, he moved on. If he managed to kill the witch, he moved on. If another witch committed a crime, he moved on. He couldn't see a scenario where he didn't move on. It shouldn't matter to him what Jacob and Sully did. He wasn't here to interfere with Sully's life—after what he'd done to her on the beach, he'd be ensuring that Sully's life was a long and happy one. If that meant a life with—*ugh*—Jacob, so be it.

Only, that idea was more irritating than the recurring brand on his chest, and just as painful, if he let himself follow that thought down the rabbit hole. He tried to tell himself he had no business feeling annoyed at this man trying to stake his claim on Sully.

But he was, especially when he still had the taste of her on his lips.

He tilted his head as he eyed the sheet-covered body. "Was Amanda Sinclair a pureblood?" he asked, curious.

Jacob stilled. He seemed to be considering his response. Then he leaned closer, and Dave lifted his chin to meet the null's gaze directly. "I know you're a friend of Sully's and all, and I know the noise you've made about helping us, but my bullshit radar is going full alert around you. You may have Sully convinced that you're here to help, but I don't know you, and I don't trust you. If you're wanting to get into Sully's good graces, figure out a different way, because this," the man said, gesturing between Dave and the Sinclair house, "is a pretty crap way of doing it."

Jacob turned and walked farther down the street, and Dave saw Jenny running up to her brother, her face distressed as she took in the scene.

Dave shoved his hands in his pockets, and turned to look at the few people nearby. Each time he made eye contact, they turned away. Jacob wasn't the only one who didn't seem to trust him. He wasn't going to get any answers from this crowd.

He sighed as he strode back to his bike. Tracking down this killer witch was getting more complicated by the day.

Sully quenched the blade in the tub of oil, watching as steam curled up from the surface. She withdrew it slightly, then dipped, repeating the process gently, moving her head out of the way of the small billowing flare-up when the vapors burned. When the blade had cooled, she placed it on the stone bench where the others lay, then raised her protective visor.

She surveyed her handiwork. Four blades. As soon as the metal blades were thoroughly cool, she'd do a hollow grind them on them, sharpen them and polish them, and then she'd cut out and fix the tangs inside the handles. She'd have four more close-combat weapons. When finished, these blades would have a forty-five-degree angle to the blade from the hilt that made it easy to draw them from whatever holster or sheath they occupied. She picked up one of the blades. The steel she'd used was composed of a greater iron alloy than usual, and then she'd give them decorative silver engraving along the blade. A kind of catchall against the shadow breeds. While the null's presence voided a shadow breed's supernatural abilities, it didn't stop the effect of injuries. With iron as the base metal, the blade had not only the physical aspects of creating damage, but any race sensitive to silver, or to iron, would still feel the effects of the metal. It was like a double-pronged attack by the wielder. Shadow breeds naturally had a greater muscle mass that put them at a slight advantage over ordinary human beings, whether they were nulls or not. This kind of blade did a little toward evening out the playing field.

Once the blades had cooled sufficiently and she didn't run the risk of shattering them, she'd engrave on them some simple spellwork, and bleed some molten silver into the designs. The spells would be voided if being wielded by a null, but if it was, say, a witch against a werewolf, or a human against a vampire, or even witch against witch, the spells would still engage—and cause significant damage. Her lips firmed. She wanted to get this witch, but if she couldn't, then she'd damn well protect her friends—protect them in a way she'd wished someone had protected her, all those years ago.

She rolled her shoulders, shaking off the tension, the dark memories. She'd worked through the night, and her neck and shoulder muscles were tired, her feet were sore and she'd definitely be feeling her biceps tomorrow. She reached over and turned off the burners for her forge. She'd added an extension to the back of her factory shop, creating a blacksmithing Shangri-la. It had taken her a few years, but she finally had a number of forges using different fuels, and anything she could think of in the creation of her cutlery…and weapons and coins. She could have made these blades at home. She eyed the other daggers, dirks and swords she'd also stockpiled that now were lined up neatly on one wall, weapons that she could create only here, in the bigger forge. In the past few days she'd made a whole bunch of arrowheads, and this time, she'd used her own unique broadhead style, with three blades angling out from the tip of the arrowhead. Excellent penetration, minimal deflection, maximum damage.

She removed her protective glasses, apron and gloves and started to clean up. She wrinkled her nose as she hung her leather apron up on a hook. Man, she was rank. She'd have to go home and shower before she did anything.

She put all her tools away, and then placed her new blades and their handles on a shelf running along the wall. She then pulled the sliding wall along its track until it settled into its position. She stood back and eyed the wall, then nodded, satisfied. It looked like a normal wall, and not the entry to her secret armory.

Once everything was cleared away, and the floor swept, she switched off the lights and locked the doors. She smiled as she turned to her car. Dave expected her to bespell her factory and shop. The problem was, in null territory, it didn't matter how many wards she layered over the access points, they were rendered useless here.

She yawned as she drove out of town and along the coast road toward her home. The ocean was on her right, and the sky was already lightening, the sun just beginning to edge its way over the horizon. It was early. Too early to call Jenny. She'd go home, have a quick shower and some breakfast and then—she yawned again. Okay, so it had been a while since she'd pulled an all-nighter in the forge.

She braked gently, eyeing the turnoff that would take her to the null neighborhood. She clenched the wheel. Poor Ronald. He and Amanda had just celebrated their four-year anniversary. She'd babysat their little darlings, Becky and Lily. She took the turn, and moments later was driving quietly down the main street. She stopped at the corner and looked down the street. Yellow crime scene ribbon fluttered in the warm morning breeze. Two deputies stood by their car, and another was using one of those wheely measure things as he walked along the driveway. The sheriff rose from where he'd squatted near the gate, camera in one hand as he rubbed his other over his face.

Sully eyed that gate. That's where it had happened. A flash of memory, Amanda's terror-filled eyes, her trembling hands. Sully blinked rapidly to dispel the vision.

A long night for the local law, too, by the looks of things. She eyed the house. Now was not the time to visit Ronald and express her condolences. She drove on down the street and took the next right, and then another right and then a left to head back out to toward the coastal road. A little while later she was pulling into her driveway and avoiding the motorcycle that was parked up near the side of the house.

She climbed out of the car, closing the door quietly, then climbed the stairs to her porch. She turned and gazed out over the headland. The sun was higher now, the sky bathed in fiery pinks, burning away the horrors of the night. Sully bit her lip as she again remembered seeing Amanda run down the driveway, only this time the memory morphed into her running, her stumbling along, trying to get away.

Of being caught.

Sully sniffed and turned her back on the beautiful view of a stunning sunrise over the ocean. She had stuff to do. Shower. Breakfast. Call Jenny.

She let herself inside the house, wincing as she tried to close the door silently, then cringing at the soft snick of the latch. Darn it. She hesitated. The house was quiet, save for a sonorous snore emanating from her living room. So Dave had returned. Her lips tightened as she remembered him commanding her to stay. That chafed. And she hadn't rebelled, either. She'd stayed away from the Sinclair home, from the null neighborhood. Damn it. She'd have to watch for that. She wasn't some guy's doormat anymore.

She slipped her flip-flops off and started to tiptoe across the foyer toward the hall. She peeked into the living room as she passed. Well, peeked and then stopped.

Dave lay sprawled out on her sofa, his feet dangling over the sofa arm at the end, one arm draped toward the floor. He made her lounge look like furniture from a dollhouse. The blanket laid pooled on the floor—it had been a warm night—and he lay there, with just the sheet covering him. Almost. His sunglasses were folded and placed on the end table by his head.

Her mouth grew slack. Holy mother of smoking hot men. His chest was bare, and she could see again all the Old Language lettering inked across his biceps, and down his rib cage and across his abdomen. A white square dressing was taped across his left pec, but it didn't quite cover his nipple. It was almost as if the Ancestors had used his musculature as a writing guide, and the markings enhanced the dips and bulges of his body. His sheet was—she swallowed—*just* covering his groin, and she could see his bare hip, and the curve of his butt cheek… She curled her fingers into a fist. *No touching.*

Warmth bloomed inside her. Damn, Dave Carter was one crazy hot Witch Hunter. She tried to look down the hall. She really did. Her lip caught between her teeth as she eyed his smooth skin, his broad chest with the—she frowned. Good grief. Had he used *duct tape* to stick his bandage down?

She shook her head. Men. She let her gaze travel down his body. The one leg outside the sheet revealed a strong thigh and muscular calf. Her heart thumped a little faster in her chest. She was perving on a guy who was sleeping, a guest in her home.

And she was not sorry at all. She eyed the sheet. It really was draped precariously. She tilted her head to the side. She wasn't sure if that was just a large rumple of the sheet or whether that was him…

She blinked. No. She should march herself down to the bathroom and jump into a nice cold shower. She nodded. Yep. That's exactly what she should do. She took a step back, and the floorboard creaked.

Her eyes widened.

Dave's eyes opened to slits, his silver-gray gaze meeting hers.

Chapter 11

Dave's lips quirked. Sully looked like she'd been caught with her hand in the cookie jar.

"Hey, good morning," he said, his voice husky as he started to sit up.

"No!" Sully said, her hand flashing up in that universal stop signal.

He froze. "What?" He glanced about, narrowing his eyes against the soft morning light. He couldn't see any threat. He looked back at her, bewildered. "What's wrong?"

"Uh, you might want to cover up," she whispered, gesturing in the general direction of his groin while keeping her gaze on the ceiling. Except for when she peeked at him. Twice.

His lips curved into a smile as he sat up. He didn't touch the sheet. Not that he was in any danger of losing it. His body had apparently recognized Sully before his brain kicked in, and his hard-on had hooked the sheet.

And then he realized she was wearing the same clothes he'd kissed her in. That loose billowy top with the strapless bra underneath. His eyebrows rose. "Are you just getting in?" He'd tiptoed in last night, thinking she was asleep down the hall in her bedroom.

Sully nodded as she glanced toward the end of the hall, then back at him. "Yeah. I couldn't just sit here, last night, so I went into the factory."

"The factory," he repeated, then frowned. "Your factory near town? With the lousy locks?"

She nodded. "Yep, that would be the one." Her gaze dropped to the sheet, and her cheeks grew rosy.

The room was gradually getting lighter, as the sun climbed higher, glinting through the bay windows, and he had to narrow his eyes against the glare.

"Sully, that could have been dangerous," he told her as he reached for his sunglasses.

She folded her arms, her flip-flops dangling from one hand. "You can't have it both ways, Dave. If it was too dangerous for me to go with you to Amanda's house because the killer may have been there, it should have been fine for me at my factory."

His lips tightened at her logic as he slid his glasses on. The dimming of the room gave him some relief, but he could still see Sully clearly. Too clearly. She was annoyed. Well, so was he. He'd slept here, knowing that he'd hear anyone entering through the house and could protect her. It was galling to realize he'd been protecting an empty bed.

"Sully, until I catch this guy, anywhere you go—"

She shook her head. "No, let's put this into perspective. So far, this witch has gone after nulls. I am not a null. There is no link between me and the victims, other than I know them, and in a town this size, so does pretty much everyone else. I'm going to go wherever I want, whenever I want—starting with visiting Jenny after breakfast."

"The guy kills in your name, Sully. The Ancestors gave me *your name*." He rose from the couch, frustration eating at him. He pulled the sheet with him to save embarrassment—not his, hers. Her eyes widened, but to her credit she kept her gaze fastened on his. "You say you only have a minor connection to these people, but we both know that's not right."

"You're right. My connection to these people is not minor. These people..." She gestured toward her front door, to the community beyond, "These people have become my family, my *home*." She turned to face him, and her expression was so sad, so frustrated, he took a step toward her before he realized what he was doing. He halted, clutching the sheet to his groin.

"I will do what I can to help them, to protect them," she said, her shoulders straightening. "So for the record, I will do everything within my power to stop this witch. Don't even think you can sideline me on this."

Her gaze had turned fierce, her blue eyes practically snapping fire at him.

This time he took that step, bringing him closer to her, and her gaze dropped to his chest. "Don't even think I'm going to let you risk your life here doing *my* job," he said, his voice low and rough. His job sucked. She had no idea the toll it took on a person, especially a witch, to kill another. It was that one little loophole— and every spell and rule had one. Witches were supposed to honor and protect nature and her creatures. Witches weren't supposed to harm another, but when they did, his ordained job was to harm them. And it sucked a little at his soul, each and every time.

She had to drag her gaze up from his chest, and he saw the moment his words sank in. Her eyes narrowed, and his chin jutted forward as he waited for her response, a response he could just see was going to be fiery.

"I am not about to let another man dictate what I can and can't do," she said, her voice sounding like it was pulled tight over sandpaper, all husky and coarse. "If you ever again tell me to sit and stay like a good dog, I will show you just how much of a bitch I can be."

He blinked. There was so much to unpack from those remarks, he was trying to figure out what to address first. Okay, the dog comment definitely had to be straightened out. He was horrified that's how she'd perceived his remarks, that he'd made a woman feel like that. "I'm sorry, Sully, I never meant to treat you, or make you feel like a—"

She smiled tightly. "I know you didn't, but when you command a strong, capable witch to stay at home and out of trouble, how do you expect it to sound?" She folded her arms, and he saw her breasts swell against the material of her top. He adjusted the sheet in front of him. They were having a serious conversation, for Pete's sake. He wasn't supposed to be distracted by her body.

Her gaze dropped to track his movement with the sheet, and a blush crept over her cheeks. So, he wasn't the only one battling distraction. Good to know.

She cleared her throat. "Would you have said it to me, if I was male?"

"Yes," he answered immediately. "Gender has nothing to do with this. If you were male or female, and I thought you were in danger from this witch, I would say the same thing—which is, let me handle this," he emphasized, leaning forward to meet her gaze. "If you're a witch, or a vamp or a shifter, this witch is capable of performing magic of some sort around a null. I've never seen that before—I didn't even know it was possible. We have no idea what this witch is capable of. We do know that he's killed two women as well as a strong, physically fit and capable man, so yes, guy or chick, I'm saying steer clear for your own safety."

He raised his hand to tuck a tendril behind her ear—and *pift*, there was that zing, that little clap of power that always happened between them, that awakened his senses on a cellular level, that heightened his awareness and made him feel like he was surrounded by a field of electricity with her. "Your safety is very, very important to me," he told her in a low voice.

Her gaze dropped from his eyes to his mouth, and her own mouth opened. She pressed her lips together. Swallowed. "It's just as well you're being sincere. A bit of a douche, but a sincere douche."

He smiled. "I've been called worse."

Sully nodded, then her gaze drifted down. He was tempted to lose the sheet, to sweep her up in his arms, step back to that damn sofa and make these sparks between them fly.

Sully gaped at him, then snapped her mouth shut. She jerked her thumb over her shoulder. "Shower. Me." She was looking at him. All of him. And there was a desire, a hunger in her eyes that was so naked, so blatant, he so damn wanted to reach for her then and there and finish what they'd started the night before.

He raised an eyebrow. "Is that an invitation?"

Her cheeks got rosier, and she shook her head. Just

a little nervous shake. "I mean, I'm going to take a shower." She hurried down the hall, and Dave smiled.

"Pity."

Sully pulled up in front of Jenny's drive, and glanced over at Dave. He'd opted to travel with her this time, instead of riding his motorbike. She wasn't sure if it was for the sake of convenience—they were both going to the same place, so it made sense—or whether it was to keep an eye on her.

Protect her.

She swallowed. She'd spent way too much time in the shower this morning, thinking about Dave and that sheet. Or rather, Dave without the sheet. Even now her cheeks heated with the images that had flashed through her mind as she'd washed away the sweat and grime from her night in the factory. His golden skin, those markings that followed the line of his sculpted muscles, those amazing silver-gray eyes.

The man was gorgeous. He oozed a dangerous sensuality that seemed to bypass any of her personal controls and call to something deep inside her, something she thought she'd gained control over.

She'd wanted him to join her in the shower. Heck, she'd wanted to join him on that sofa, just like she sensed he wanted. She couldn't remember ever having such an intense physical reaction to a man. Sure, things with Marty had been physical—way too physical, especially toward the end. She thought she was past all that, or at least wary of it, with a logical desire to steer clear of that kind of allure. Dave, though, was…more. More man. More muscle. More presence. More power. She should be running in the opposite direction, especially when he got his alpha witch on and demanded she stand down.

When he'd touched her, she'd sensed him—again. She couldn't mistake his need to protect her, and it was so genuine, so sincere, it touched her. He was frustrated, and he was worried—for her. She couldn't sense any darkness to his need to protect her. It was pure, it was light and it was so damn seductive, she'd wanted to jump into his arms and give him what they both wanted. Whatever that may be.

Which, in turn, annoyed her. She'd spent the past four years proving to herself she didn't need to be with a man… She didn't need permission, she didn't need approval, or assistance, or support, or any little tie that would anchor her to a guy. No. She'd learned she was more than capable of standing on her own two feet, of paying her own bills, of developing her own business, honing her craft—establishing her own damn identity.

She didn't need to be told where she could and couldn't go, who she could and couldn't see, what she could and couldn't wear, and what she could and couldn't think, feel, say, do.

There was something about Dave, though, something that snagged at her, drew her in. She had to shut that crap down right now. Before she got sucked into another nightmare.

Sully turned her head to eye him. He looked deep in thought, staring through the windshield. He'd showered after she had—which involved more fantasizing on her part about his naked body under the stream of hot water. Steam. Soap suds. Muscles.

She cleared her throat, and he turned to look at her, his eyes shielded by the dark lenses of his sunglasses. He was wearing a navy T-shirt, and she could see one of his markings peeking out from beneath the edge of his sleeve. Name, not marking, she corrected herself. The name of a witch he'd killed.

See, just that thought should give her chills. She'd been on the receiving end of his murderous intent, after all. Yet, it didn't. She'd seen him in action, seen his ruthlessness, his power turned on another—her—along with a physical dominance that should have her ducking for cover. But…it didn't. Why was that? What was it about this guy that made her ignore all her safeguards, all those red flags she'd warned herself to watch out for and steer away from?

"You might want to let me do the talking," she said to him. He'd told her the conversation he'd had with Jacob. She was mildly surprised the nice, friendly guy she knew had so abruptly shut Dave down, but she was beginning to find out a lot of mild surprises from the people she thought she'd gotten to know so well.

Dave's lips tightened, but he nodded. He didn't like it, she could tell, but, well, what could he do about it? Nulls didn't like outsiders. It was only because she'd been able to make teas and ointments that made them feel better that they had welcomed her in, initially. And Dave—well, Dave didn't look like the tea-drinking type, let alone the tea-making type.

They got out of the car, and Sully squinted against the bright sunlight as she closed her car door. She wore a loose cotton top with thin straps, and the sun beat down on her bare shoulders. Today was going to be a hot one.

She slid the strap of her tote up her arm to her shoulder as she waited for Dave to walk around the car, and they crossed the street together. They were walking up the garden path to Jenny's cottage front door when they heard the scream.

Chapter 12

Dave bolted up the steps and across the porch, hand out to thrust open the door. Heart hammering, he could feel the skin over his pec muscle beginning to warm. More screams.

No. God, no. Not again, not here. "Jenny!"

He heard a clatter in the kitchen. His arms pumped as he ran down the hall, scanning the rooms through the open doorways until he raced around the bend in the hall.

"Jenny!" He heard Sully's cry, the sound of her flip-flops smacking the floorboards as she raced along behind him.

The door to the kitchen was closed. Dave didn't slow down, just bent his right arm in front of him and shoulder-charged the door.

The door gave way, whipping open as he barreled through. Jenny was on the floor, screaming, legs kicking. A guy straddled her, but froze when he heard the door. Dave roared. Instinctively he summoned his powers, only to feel…nothing.

Damn it. Nulls. The guy didn't even turn to face him, but rose and raced through the back door. Dave's skin stopped itching.

His gaze met Jenny's wide-eyed fearful stare. She was crap-scared, but physically all right. He didn't stop, but darted through the back door. He hesitated briefly, scanning the yard. There. The back gate hung agape, as though it had been slammed closed but not latched, and was slowly swinging back open again.

Arms and legs pumping, he ran through the gate, and caught sight of a dark leg and shoe as his quarry raced down the narrow lane between rows of houses, and then around the corner. Dave took off again, hands straight, his stride lengthening. So close. Finally. So. Damn. Close.

He skidded around the corner. Damn it. Another lane. There. Farther up, the guy was hitting the gravel pretty damn hard. He wanted to send a blast toward him, level the bastard with a powerful shove of magic, yet being in the heart of the null neighborhood, it didn't matter how much he tried to draw on his powers, nothing would come forth. Dave sprinted after him. The man turned and jumped over a low fence, and Dave followed, bracing his hands on the horizontal rail as he swung his legs over in a smooth movement, and then took off running across someone's back lawn. Well, dirt patch.

He ducked under the low-hanging branch of a magnolia, and ignored the cry of an older woman peering through her kitchen window.

The witch pounded along the driveway, then took a gradual curve across the front lawn, jumping over the fence like an athlete in a hurdle race. Dave sprinted, then inhaled as he leaped over the fence. He didn't break stride as he hit the ground running.

The witch raced along the street. *Look at me.* Dave's jaw clenched. The guy wasn't looking in any direction except straight ahead. Wasn't even checking if Dave was still in pursuit. All Dave could see was the back of the man's head. The witch hit an intersection and turned right, his hand raised to shield his face.

Dave pumped his legs harder, faster. Damn him. He was hiding his face. The witch ducked behind a tall fence, and it took Dave a couple of seconds to reach the spot. Dave skidded to a stop, glancing about wildly.

What? Where the hell had he gone? An old woman, stooped over so much that she could barely make eye contact with him, gave him a friendly smile and wave as she started to cross the street.

Dave went up to the fence, grabbed the top and pulled himself up to peer over it. He scanned the back-yard. A dog lifted its head, then rose when he saw Dave. He barked.

There was no sign of the witch he'd been pursuing, and the dog would have sounded the alarm had some-one tried to scale the fence and run through the yard.

Dave dropped to the ground, then glanced up and down the street. What the hell? He jogged from one driveway to the other, glancing down and around. Noth-ing. Nobody. He tried to summon his powers again, and frustration licked at him like a hot flame at the silence, the cool…the void.

He hurried in the direction of the old woman.

"Excuse me, ma'am?"

The woman slowed, and it took seconds for her to scan the street.

"Ma'am," Dave said again as he jogged up to her. It seemed to take a moment for her to realize he was behind her, and she shifted. Slowly. Little shuffling steps.

"Excuse me, ma'am, but did you see where that man went?"

She was hunched over, her gaze on his shoes, and it took her a moment to try to lift her head enough to meet his gaze. Dave leaned forward to save her the effort.

"What?" she asked, her white brows dipping. She raised her hand to cup her ear.

"The man," Dave repeated loudly. "Did you see where he went?"

"Man? What man?" Her rheumy eyes showed her confusion. She blinked at him, as though trying to understand him. Or remember him. Or...maybe just focus on him.

"Uh, the man—I was following a man round here," he said, gesturing toward the corner.

She shifted. Slowly. Little shuffling steps so that she could see where he was pointing. She blinked, squinting. "Where is he?" she asked him.

He took a breath. "I don't know. Did you see where he went?"

"Where who went?" she asked curiously, angling her head this way and that to peer up and down the street. She reminded him of a bird, with her hooked nose, small eyes and the tilt of her head, first one way, then another.

He sighed. She was nearly deaf and blind, and obviously hadn't seen anything. "Never mind. Thank you," he added. He looked around. The witch had disappeared. Somehow. "Here, let me help you," he said, offering her his arm. She smiled up at him.

"Why, thank you."

They shuffled across the street together, and he cupped her elbow as she stepped up onto the curb.

She nodded at him, then shuffled on her way. Dave turned back to the street, his hands on his hips as he tried to figure out how he'd managed to lose the guy. Lips pressed tight, he started to walk back the way he'd come, then started to jog. He wanted to get back to Sully—and to Jenny.

Sully's friend was going to have to talk with him, now—whether she liked to or not. He wasn't going to take no for an answer.

Sully looked up from Jenny as Dave thumped up the back steps and through the back door. Jenny startled, her tea sloshing in her mug, and Sully covered her friend's hands as they cupped the ceramic mug on the table.

Dave's large frame seemed to darken the kitchen, until he stepped farther into the room. His navy T-shirt sported a damp V-patch on the front, and perspiration dripped down the sides of his face and neck. He'd run hard.

He walked over to her friend and put his hand on her shoulder, bending low to meet her gaze.

"Are you okay?" he asked Jenny quietly. If it had been appropriate, Sully would have stood and hugged him. His tone was low, so gentle, with just the right amount of concern that was heartwarming, but still strong enough that Jenny wouldn't break down into tears—which seemed likely. Sully could feel her friend trembling, and she so wanted to take some of that fear, that residual terror from her. For the first time, she wished she could still use her powers with the nulls.

Jenny nodded, her eyes wide. "Yeah," she said, her voice hoarse.

Dave reached for a high-backed chair at the end of the table, swung it around on a leg and straddled it, his muscled forearms folded across the top as he looked directly at Jenny.

"Mind telling me what happened?" he asked in a mild voice.

Jenny nodded. She opened her mouth, then blinked. She frowned. "I don't—I don't know," she said, then looked uncertainly at Dave, then at Sully.

Sully reached for her shoulder. "It's okay, Jen. Take your time."

Jenny shook her head, her expression becoming distraught. "I—I don't know," she said, her voice rising in pitch. "I remember…" Her gaze drifted to Dave. "You," she breathed. "You, breaking through my door…"

Sully glanced over at the kitchen door. The section of the door where the doorknob was located was rough and splintered, and there was a long crack down the middle panel. From the moment they'd heard Jenny's scream from the front door, Dave had become a force of energy, barreling through the house, and not slowing down for something as trivial as a door. She had entered the kitchen only to see him race through the back door.

For a big guy, he could move like lightning.

And Jenny had been on the floor, shaken and trembling. Sully had made a quick call to Tyler Clinton, and then to Jacob, and then had tended to her friend.

Now, with a cup of tea in her hands, Jenny was beginning to calm, although her cheeks were tear-streaked, and her knuckles were white as she clasped the ceramic mug.

Dave nodded. "Yes, we heard you screaming," he told her. "What can you tell us about the man, Jenny?"

Jenny's hand went to her neck. "My throat is sore."

Sully nodded, smoothing her hand across her friend's back. "You were screaming, Jen."

"The man?" Dave prompted.

Jenny frowned, her gaze caught by a bruise on her wrist, and she turned her hand over to see how far it extended. "The man..." she repeated. She blinked, then looked at Sully. "I don't remember him," she whispered, tears forming in her eyes. "Why don't I remember him?" Her voice held a hint of panic.

"Shh, it's okay," Sully said, knowing it was anything but. "Take your time." Her gaze flicked to Dave, but his face was composed. Neutral. She smiled gently at Jenny. "What were you doing earlier?"

Jenny frowned, looking around the kitchen. "I—I'm not quite sure."

"Why aren't you at school?" Sully tried a different tact.

"Uh, the principal has to do a day each month or so in a class, and today she's teaching my class. She says it keeps her fresh, gives her a chance to see the syllabus in action. She's done it for the past six years." Jenny nodded. "It's a good thing—she can foresee some of the issues when the curriculum changes. So I'm home preparing lessons for next semester."

"Where were you preparing the lessons?" Dave asked.

Jenny blinked. "In—in my living room," she murmured. He rose from his seat and indicated the doorway.

"Would you mind showing us?"

Jenny nodded, and rose, leaving her tea on the table. She led them to her small living room. The coffee table in the center of the room was strewn with papers, and her large diary was opened up to a couple of months away.

Dave nodded, then glanced around the room. "Okay. Can you remember what happened after that?"

Jenny touched her hand to her mouth, then turned to the hallway. "There was a knock at the door…" Her hands trembled, and she pressed her fingers to her temple. "It's so murky. Why can't I remember?"

Dave reached for her hand, and cupped it in both of his. "It's okay, Jenny. We'll figure this out," he reassured her.

Sully watched as her friend seem to draw comfort from Dave's words. He pulled her gently into the hallway. "So, there was a knock at the door…you went to answer it?"

Jenny nodded, and Dave guided her closer to the door. "Can you remember what happened? You would have reached for the doorknob…"

He raised her hand, and Jenny whipped it out of his reach. She stepped closer to Sully, her face pale. "No."

Sully glanced at her. "No? Do you remember something, Jen?"

Jenny shook her head, folding her arms as she looked at her front door with trepidation. "No."

"It's okay, Jenny. He's not here anymore. He can't hurt you."

"Can you remember anything about him, Jen? His hair, his eyes…?"

Jenny caught her lip between her teeth. Sully watched the movement, dismayed. Her friend was so…timid, so afraid. On one level, she could understand—the guy had tried to kill her. But—this was *Jenny*. Her friend was normally so feisty and vivacious, and here she was, too scared to open her own front door.

Memories surfaced, of a similar time when her own heart would stutter at the slightest sound inside her city apartment... She reached for her friend's arm, trying to imbue support and comfort, and feeling nothing rise inside.

Jenny shook her head and took a step back, her gaze fixed on the door.

"Okay, Jenny," Dave said, and Sully was momentarily distracted by the smooth, soothing tone he used. He stepped between Jenny and the door.

"You can remember the knock at the door, you can remember going to answer it. Once you opened the door, what—"

The pounding at the door made them all jump. "Jenny! Jenny, are you okay?"

Sully's shoulders sagged when she recognized Jacob's voice. The doorknob turned, and the door swung inward.

Jenny screamed, collapsing to the floor sobbing, holding her arms up in front of her. "No, please, no," she cried.

Jacob stared down at his sister in stunned shock, and stepped toward her. Jenny screamed again, scrambling back on her hands and feet.

"No! Stop, get out!"

Jacob halted, his mouth agape. Sully glanced between Jenny and the brother her friend adored. Why was she reacting like this?

"Jenny—" Jacob breathed in dismay as flashing red-and-blue lights flickered into the hallway, and Tyler Clinton bounded up the stairs in his sheriff's uniform.

"No!" Jenny screamed, almost hysterical as she backed away.

Dave held out his arms between the siblings, inserting himself between them. "Jenny, it's okay," he said, soothing.

"It was him," she cried, stopping when she backed up against a wall. Her head tilted, and she drew her knees up as though trying to back her way through the wall.

Sully frowned, looking over at Jacob. He looked so shocked, so hurt, so worried. She looked back at Jenny. Her friend was trembling, pale and teary as she tried to curl up and disappear.

Tyler frowned as he stepped inside the house, and looked between Jenny and Jacob. Sully knelt next to her friend, holding her arms out, and Jenny collapsed against her, sobbing. She lifted her gaze to meet Dave's. His expression was grim as he looked between the Forsyth siblings.

"What happened" Tyler asked curtly, surveying those gathered in the hallway.

Dave shifted his gaze from Sully to Jenny. "Good question."

Chapter 13

Dave followed Sully into her home and watched as she rubbed her neck. He closed the door behind them, locked it, then put a magical ward over it, just for the sake of it. Relief swelled through him as he saw the brief bloom of color, the intricate markings of his spell take hold of the door and its frame before disappearing from view. It had felt damn weird not being able to call on his powers when he was chasing the witch.

She turned to look at him. "Nightcap?"

"Hell, yeah."

She turned on the light to the living room, and he narrowed his eyes. She must have seen his reaction, because she turned off the lights, then waved her hand casually. The candles that were placed around the room sputtered to life, and he smiled his appreciation. She crossed to the white timber cabinet, and his eyebrows rose when she pulled out a bottle of Irish whiskey and two glasses. She poured a measure of the amber liquid into each and handed him a glass. She took a seat in the armchair, and he subsided on the folded out sofa.

"What an awful day," Sully muttered as she took a sip of her drink.

Dave nodded. It had been interesting, explaining to Sheriff Clinton about an intruder the victim believed had been her brother. But he'd chased that bastard, and it wasn't Jacob. Wrong height, wrong weight, wrong hair color—just wrong, wrong and wrong. Jacob had been removed from his sister's home to give her a chance to calm down, but with Jenny being a null, Dave had been unable to do any body or brain scans to figure out what the hell had happened.

"He blurred her memory," Sully murmured, incredulous. "She's a null, and he tricked her." Her lips tightened. "And to make her think it was Jacob—that's just plain low."

"While I think Jacob Forsyth is more than capable of being a dick, you're right, he wasn't the man I chased out of Jenny's kitchen."

He took a sip of his whiskey, enjoying the mild burn as it slid down his throat. "I just wish I'd gotten the bastard."

Sully tilted her head. "So, he just...disappeared?"

Dave nodded, and finished his drink. He didn't like failing—hated it, but he just couldn't figure out how the witch had done his vanishing act.

In null territory.

When he couldn't so much as muster a powerpuff punch.

Sully rose and crossed to her library, waving a hand across the front of the bookcase. Dave watched as the camouflage spell glimmered at the movement to reveal the tomes of magical spells and history.

Sully dragged her finger gently across the spines, and for a moment he was distracted by the graceful movement.

"What are you looking for?" he asked, and rose from the sofa. He placed his empty glass on the end table and crossed to her. She pulled out a book and passed to him, then scanned again, pulling two more volumes from the shelf.

"Something isn't adding up here," she said, as she crossed to the liquor cabinet and snagged up the whiskey bottle. "This guy has used my name—I don't understand that part, or why the Ancestors sent you after me. That's number one," she said, holding up the bottle. She poured another measure in his glass, and one in her own, then placed the bottle on the table.

"Number two, he's able to use magic. Around nulls. That doesn't compute. Nulls void any natural magic. Wolves can't shift, vampires can't fang out, witches can't cast spells."

Dave nodded as he sat down on the sofa again. "I know, that's something that's confusing the crap out of me, too," he admitted.

She nodded, then started to flick through one of the books she held as she sank into her armchair. "So, how is he doing it? There has to be something in these books that can help us figure this out."

He eyed her for a moment. He didn't need to ask her why she was doing this. He'd seen her with her friend. She'd been worried. Jenny had been distraught, clutching on to Sully as she'd given her statement to the sheriff. He and Sully had spent hours with the nulls, and he had even walked the neighborhood again, with some of the deputies, in case they could find some trace of the man who'd managed to enter Jenny's home through her front door, mess with her memory and almost kill her.

When Sully had been sitting with Jenny, he'd been trying to soothe Jacob. The one thing he and Sully had agreed on was not to mention the witch aspect. It didn't make sense—yet. They couldn't explain it, and Dave didn't want the sheriff looking at them as potential suspects and distract the man from pursuing the relevant clues—or interfere with his own objective of finding the witch and sending the bastard to the Other Realm.

Jacob, though, had had a difficult time accepting that his sister believed he'd tried to kill her, and was looking for answers—and Sully had wanted to give them to him, and Dave knew how hard it was for her to bite her tongue.

"They're PBs, obviously," Sully muttered absently as she scanned the pages in front of her.

Dave's eyebrows rose. "Really?"

She nodded, her honey-blond braid sliding across her shoulder. "Yeah. Jacob confirmed it. He told me the Adlers, Forsyths, Sinclairs, Drummonds, Maxwells and Tarringtons are the PB families in their community. A member from each family sits on the council."

Dave blinked. "When did he tell you that?"

"When you helped Jenny up, and I had to tell her brother she wasn't really losing her marbles," Sully said calmly. She winced. "Those were Jacob's words, not mine."

Dave's lips tightened. "So when Jacob told us about the PBs, he just happened to forget to mention he was one of them?" That was damn annoying.

Sully shrugged. "They'll tell us stuff when they trust us. We just need to work harder to earn their trust."

Dave frowned as he glanced down at the old and weathered book he held. "And in the meantime, more of them are in danger." It didn't escape his notice that Jacob Forsyth trusted Sully enough to divulge this information, after pretty much telling him to get lost the night before.

Sully played with her braid, and Dave found himself watching her more than reading from the book in his lap. She turned a page, and he forced himself to look down at the book he held. Yet in a moment, he found his gaze lifting to surreptitiously peek at her again. Her slightly crooked mouth was quirked, and a faint line had appeared between her eyebrows as she read through the spells and histories. For some, it took only a momentary scan. For others, she seemed to catch her lip, as though hopeful she'd found the answer, and then she'd press those sexy lips into a disappointed pout and turn the page.

She glanced up at him, distracted, and he glanced back down at his book.

"What about the Ancestors?"

He blinked at the question that seemed to come out of left field. "What?"

"The Ancestors," she repeated, then rose from her seat. She disappeared into her kitchen, and he heard the tap run in the sink, and then she came back into the living room carrying a bowl of water.

"Can you ask them?"

He put the book off to the side, frowning as she set the bowl down on the floor between them. She slipped her flip-flops off to the side, then sat cross-legged on the floor.

"Ask them what?" He leaned forward, bracing his

elbows on his knees as he tried to figure out where she was going with this.

She met his gaze. "The Ancestors directed you to me. They were wrong. Can you ask them for help?"

Dave shook his head briefly, confused as he tried to work through her suggestion until it made sense. He eyed the bowl.

"It's the Ancestors, Sully. They've only ever given me the name, and I take it from there. There's no conversation. It's not like a phone call, where I can chat with them over it."

"Have you ever tried?"

He frowned as he lowered himself to the floor, eyeing the bowl. "You want to scry the Ancestors?" He crossed his legs. He'd never heard of that being done, so he had no idea whether it would work or not—or whether it would just piss off the Ancestors.

Sully shrugged. "It can't hurt to ask, right? This guy is doing stuff that we've never seen before. Surely they can give us a clue."

He gave her a doubtful look, and she responded with an expression full of exasperation. "This guy managed to give you the slip—and I've seen you in action. I even went invisible, and you still caught me. Aren't you interested to see how he managed to evade you?"

He shifted uncomfortably. Admitting to failure yet again was like running a cheese grater over his skin. Damn it, she had a point. He nodded, then settled himself comfortably. Sully did the same, and he closed his eyes, centering his awareness. Once he felt the peace, the warmth of relaxation, he slid his eyes open. He tried to extend his awareness, his senses, to encompass the witch in front of him, but her shields were in place yet again, blocking him off. His brow dipped briefly. It wasn't unusual for witches to combine powers in some-thing like this, but Sully was completely closed off to him. He'd have to do this on his own.

Sully met his gaze, then dipped her finger in the bowl and swirled her finger to create a gentle whirlpool. She murmured a chant in the Old Language, and he shoved aside his surprise at her knowledge and skill, focusing on the water in the bowl that was beginning to cloud over as steam rose from the surface.

Sully kept chanting, and once he could decipher the words, he joined her. The water thickened, and Sully nodded at him. Dave closed his eyes, and using the Old Language, summoned the Ancestors, and asked his question—who was this witch, and where could they find him?

He removed his sunglasses, then opened his eyes. He could feel a coolness sweep over him, the gentle but dizzying sensation as his perception of Sully's living room, of Sully herself, slipped from view, and instead the steam enveloped him. At first it was gentle, its touch against his face whisper-soft, but the pressure increased, and the color faded from white to red. Murky shad-ows, dark and indistinct, danced around him, weaving and ducking, fading and reappearing. Flashes of light snapped and crackled around him, so bright it hurt his eyes, but he remained steadfast, eyes open, until the light dimmed into that *X* symbol he'd seen carved into flesh. Over and over, the symbol flashed around him, and then he saw a face emerge from the red mist. The features were fuzzy, and he squinted, but no matter how much he tried to focus, the features wouldn't sharpen, but would twist and morph as it got closer, bigger, grow-ing larger the nearer it drew.

"Dave," Sully gasped, and Dave blinked.

The red mist dispersed with a soft hiss, and he had to blink again to snap Sully into focus. She was staring down at the bowl, her expression perturbed.

He glanced down. The clear water they'd started with was now thick and red, and the metallic scent was nearly overpowering.

Blood.

It was expanding in the bowl, creeping up to the lip. "There's so much of it," Sully whispered.

He reached for the bowl, sweeping it up as he rose to his feet and strode into the kitchen. He tipped the blood down the sink and ran the tap to get rid of the liquid that had splattered the sides of the basin.

Sully followed him, and he turned to face her. "Well?" she asked him, curious. "Did it work? What did you see?"

He frowned. "I'm not sure. Red cloud. That symbol, flashing over and over," he told her, his fingers spreading out like mini fireworks. "Then there was this face, but I couldn't see it, the features kept twisting and moving." He gestured to the now clean bowl sitting in the sink. "Then the blood."

She shuddered, and rubbed her hands over her arms. "There was so much of it," she whispered. "What do you think they meant?"

He shrugged. "No idea. I've never tried to contact them before, so…" He winced. "I don't understand their code."

Sully gestured to his chest. "So the Ancestors can freakin' spell stuff out, but use cryptic picture codes for the important stuff. Nice going," she muttered, glaring up at the ceiling, as though talking with them directly.

"That symbol is obviously important," he murmured,

and headed back to the books in the living room, then
halted. He turned to her.

"You use your safeguards, even when you're at
home?" Why was she so guarded? She certainly had the
right—every witch could decline a sharing of powers,
it was their prerogative, but it had still been a surprise.
He'd felt a companionship with her, a camaraderie, a
shared intimacy as they worked together to figure out
what the hell was going on. Admittedly, the magical
block had made him realize he'd taken that for granted,
and now was uncertain just how much they could or
would share.

Her expression was surprised for a moment, then un-
derstanding crossed her features. "Yes. I guess it's just
reflex." She scratched her head. "I'm sorry, I didn't even
think to try to link for the scry." She indicated the bowl.
"It's been so long, I just instinctively do it by myself."

He turned to face her fully. "How long has it been,
Sully?" Witches were funny creatures. Mostly, they
gathered in covens, but there were plenty of outliers,
and one could certainly reserve their right not to link.
Sully, though, seemed too sociable, too connected with
the well-being of others to be so isolated. He'd seen her
with Jenny, the amount of times she'd reached out to
touch her friend, and the frustration on her face when
whatever she'd wanted to do to help her was blocked.
He'd seen her comfort her friend, hold her, reassure
her… She genuinely cared for others, and that kind
of witch seemed conducive to sharing, to linking and
bonding. It was almost as though she was fighting her
own instinctive nature.

Sully shrugged as she stepped toward the living
room. "Four, maybe five years."

He reached out and clasped her arm, halting her.

His ears popped, and the hairs rose on his arms and the back of his neck as their magical fields collided once again, awakening and enhancing his senses. He blinked, then swallowed, trying to ignore the physical sensations bombarding his body. He wanted to understand—no, needed to understand why a witch, why Sully, would bury herself in a place where she couldn't use her powers.

"Why?" he asked hoarsely.

She hesitated, and he wasn't sure if she realized her slow shift toward him. "I needed to," she said to him. "I needed…space."

It was that line. *I need space. It's not you, it's me…* he'd heard it a dozen times, and used it himself at least a dozen more. Realization, swift and unavoidable, hit him. "Who was he?" he asked. He slid his hand down her arm and loosely grasped her hand. It was meant to be comforting. Friendly. But her smooth skin beneath his touch was distracting.

She lifted her shoulders in a casual, dismissive gesture. "He was nobody important."

"He must have been, for you to hide yourself here for four, five years," he pointed out. He slid his thumb back and forth over the back of her hand, enjoying the feel of her silken skin.

She frowned up at him, her blue eyes darkening. "I'm not hiding, Dave." She gave a slight shake of her head in denial. Her gaze drifted to his chest, then down to where their hands joined.

His eyebrows rose, and he shifted toward her. "Oh, really? From what I can tell, you're the only witch in this area—"

"You can't know that for sure. This is null territory," she interrupted. "You could have a whole coven here, and they wouldn't be able to practice or reveal their talents. We wouldn't even know."

"Is that why you're here? To conceal your talents?"

"I—" her gaze dropped to his lips, and then she met his gaze again. "I'm not concealing my talents," she said in a near whisper. Her breath hitched, then released in the sexiest sigh, the sound curling down deep inside him, flooding him with a molten desire that had him hardening in his jeans.

How could she make that sound so damn suggestive? So hot? He tried to focus on the conversation, but felt he was losing that battle fast. "Are you sure?" He stepped closer, and brought her hand up to rest against his chest.

She swallowed, and he smiled when he heard the audible gulp. He slid his other hand beneath her braid, cupping the back of her neck. He could see her nipples tighten against the cotton of her camisole, knew he wasn't the only one affected by this attraction, this fascination between them.

"Show me," he whispered, leaning down to kiss the side of her jaw. He inhaled, and her scent, roses, vanilla and sunshine, hit him like a drug.

She rested her hand on his waist for a moment, her eyes dark with confusion. "Show you what?"

"Show me you, Sully," he whispered, his lips trailing down her neck. She angled her head to the side, exposing more of her neck.

"What—what you see is what you get," she murmured, then moaned when his lips found that delicious indent between her neck and collarbone.

His hand slid from where it cupped her head down her back, and he halted when he found her belt with the concealed sheaths, and the blades they contained. His lips curved against her skin. "Oh, I think there is more to you than meets the eye," he murmured, then raked his teeth gently against her shoulder.

She trembled, a slight quivering that set off an answering throb deep inside him, hardening his cock. She slid her arms up over his chest to twine around his neck, her nails raking through his short hair. Her fingers clenched in his hair, pulling his head back up.

"I'll show you me if you show me you," she whispered, then stood on tiptoe to kiss him.

Chapter 14

Sully parted her lips against his, and was rewarded when his tongue slid inside to tangle with hers. His arms enveloped hers, pressing her against his body. She could feel the strength of those arms, those muscles, against the sides of her breasts, could feel the hardness of his chest and hips against her, and could feel the throbbing hard length of him against her stomach.

She could sense his curiosity, his tenderness, as well as the tidal wave of desire and arousal. He'd asked her about her shields. Suggested she was hiding. With Dave, though, there was no hiding. There was no defense against his overwhelming presence, with *feeling*, and there was no way she could fight the burning attraction she felt for this man. It was hot, it was immediate and it was undeniable. And she didn't want to hide anymore.

Her hands trailed down the column of his neck, tracing the breadth of those massive shoulders, and trailing over the soft fabric of his T-shirt. She angled her head, and he deepened the kiss, sucking and nipping with a skill that had her desire pooling in her panties as she arched against him.

"Oh, sweetness," he moaned, kissing his way to her jaw and down her neck. Her head leaned back, and he pulled her tighter against him, leaning forward so that her world tilted. His hands slid down and cupped her butt, and he picked her up, turning to seat her on the kitchen counter.

Her legs wound around his hips, pulling him into the cradle of her groin, and she moaned when she felt him, hot and hard, against her. She tugged at the hem of his T-shirt, and he leaned back, hips still pressed to hers, and helped her pull the garment over his head. Her eyes widened at having his chest so close, and for a moment she was content to place her palms against his warm skin. The mark over his heart looked almost healed, and she traced it very gently.

"So much pain," she murmured.

He winked, grinning as he ducked his head. "Nah, just a tickle." He took her lips in a hard kiss. His hands played briefly over her shoulders before hooking the thin straps of her cami and tugging them slowly down her arms.

She shrugged out of the straps, sighing when he dragged her against him, her breasts mashed against him, and they both moaned. He kissed her shoulder, nipping at her gently, and she shuddered, her breasts swelling at the sharp but seductive sensation. She dragged her nails down his back as he kissed and licked his way across her chest while he slid his hand under her long skirt, dragging the fabric up her legs. She trembled as his hand skimmed over her knee, gliding up her thigh.

Liquid heat pooled between her legs, and her pulse thudded in her ears.

He got to midthigh, then halted. He lifted his head, eyebrows raised. "You're full of surprises, aren't you?" he gasped, before taking her lips again. He fumbled with the leather strap of the sheath she'd strapped to her leg, and she laughed breathlessly.

"Sorry, I forgot that one."

He undid the tie, and she shuddered at the caress of leather against her sensitive skin when he tugged it away from her. He placed the sheath, with her custom-made push-dagger on the bench beside them. He chuckled.

"You are so dangerous," he murmured, gazing into her eyes, his hands rising to cradle her jaw. There was a humor, but there was also warmth, admiration and a little concern, all bombarding her with his touch.

She looked up at him, feeling the answering smile on her lips. "You have no idea," she whispered, then took his lips.

He sighed against her mouth, their tongues tangling. He lowered a hand to her chest, and she gasped, arching her back when he covered her breast with his warm palm. He pressed back, their hips rubbing against each other, and she could feel his hardness, separated by the folds of her skirt and the denim of his jeans.

Heat. Desire. Tight arousal. It hit her, and she wasn't sure if it was him, or her, or that they were just so perfectly in sync.

Panting, she reached for his belt, and within seconds she'd undone it, as well as his button fly. His hands gripped her body as she reached inside his jeans, and her lips curved against his when her fingers slid beneath his boxer briefs and found him.

He growled softly, and she gasped when he pinched

her nipple, just enough to make her tremble with delight. It was as though the floodgates opened. She pushed at his jeans. He tugged at her skirt, and she felt his fingers slide under her panties, felt the brief tug of the cotton as the fabric gave, and then she moaned when she felt those fingers against her, then inside her.

He groaned, then took her lips in a kiss so carnal it stole her breath. He played with her, strummed her, and she shook as she used her feet to shove his jeans down his legs. She gasped when she felt the tension coil inside her. Her nipples tightened, as his tongue slid against hers, his fingers moving with ease inside her, and then his thumb found that secret little pleasure nub, and everything tightened, tightened, tightened, until she exploded. Sensations, so sharp, so crystalized, cascaded over her. He positioned himself between her legs and entered her smoothly.

She tore her lips away from his, crying out with the pleasure as he thrust. Over and over, the waves of intense bliss crashed. Swirls of colors, sparks, everything was exploding—around her, inside her, until he finally groaned his release, his head back, the cords of his neck standing out as he found his own pleasure inside her.

He slid his arm around her waist, pulling her up tight against him, chest to chest, heart to heart, as their panting subsided. He hugged her, and she could feel him. Inside her, around her, it was all warmth and tenderness, an intimate gentleness with the steel edge of determined protectiveness.

She'd never felt safer.

Dave blinked. Hair. Honey-gold hair. All over his face. He brushed it away, blinking some more, then shifted, drawing his thigh up against the warm curves enfolded in his arms.

Sully.

His eyes opened.

Sully. They'd made fireworks last night. He'd seen them. Lots of pops of colors, sparks… While he wasn't shy with women, and thought he could hold his own in the sack, he'd never quite experienced fireworks before with a woman.

He lifted his head slightly, shaking away the last of the tendrils that seemed to want to cling to him. She was asleep in his arms, her back to his chest, her butt resting—he sucked in a breath. Damn, she felt good in his arms.

They were on the foldout sofa, and sunlight streamed in through the bay windows. They'd tried to make it to her bed, but somehow got distracted.

Very distracted. Twice.

His lips curved, and he dipped his head to press a kiss to her neck. She sighed and smiled as she scooted closer. Her stomach growled, and Dave chuckled as he caressed the curve of her hip.

She turned in his arms, her eyes opening, and he pressed a kiss to her lips. "Good morning," he murmured.

She smiled. "Good mor—" she yawned, then blinked "—morning."

"Feel like pancakes?" He was ravenous, and her stomach was making all sorts of hungry noises.

She grinned. "Are you cooking?"

"Yep," he said, and gave her another long kiss. When he drew back she sighed and stretched, then nodded.

"Sure, pancakes sound wonderful."

Dave reached for his sunglasses and slid them on,

then rolled off the foldout sofa and snagged up his boxer briefs, hopping into them as he walked through to the kitchen. Within minutes he had a pancake mix going— they were his specialty—and started to set up the counter for breakfast.

Sully walked in. She was wearing his T-shirt, the navy blue bringing out the blue of her eyes. Her hair was a tussled tangle, her features soft and relaxed. The shirt hit her midthigh, and he paused for a moment, taking his fill of her. She had the longest, sexiest legs he could ever remember seeing in a woman.

He watched as she crossed to the fridge and leaned in to grab the juice, the T-shirt riding up a little to expose a hint of butt cheek. He swallowed. She was a beautiful woman. He glanced back down at his pancakes. They were bubbling. He flipped them, his gaze briefly diverting back to the domestic, disheveled goddess behind him, and was pleasantly surprised when the pancakes landed back in the pan.

He smiled as he got the plates ready for serving. They didn't converse as she got glasses and poured the juice. They worked alongside each other in companionable silence, and he smiled when she caressed his back as she passed. He pulled her back for a kiss, enjoying the feel of her against him, so scantily clad in his T-shirt. The pancake batter in the pan popped and fizzed, and he drew back, winking at Sully's grin as she backed away toward the pantry. This felt…nice. Normal. But a normal he'd never had before. A cozy kitchen, a sexy woman with a heart of gold and a body built for sin. He could get used to this.

He halted midscoop of the pancake. What?

He could not get used to this. He had a job that translated to here today, gone tomorrow. He had a home and business in Irondell, and a task that meant the Ancestors would always take priority in his life. There was no room for a woman, for a relationship, no matter how tempting playing house could be.

He flipped the pancake onto a plate and poured a ladleful of batter into the pan. Sully started to hum as she moved around the kitchen, and he saw her place a bottle of maple syrup on the kitchen counter, along with a basket of strawberries. She even did a cute little dance move when she thought he wasn't watching.

He focused on the pan, watching as the air bubbles popped on the mix. He liked this. He *really* liked this. It was so tempting, just to reach out and kiss her again, feed her strawberries in an indulgent, dreamy little episode of domestic codependency.

And that scared the ever-lovin' crap out of him.

He quickly served up the last of the pancakes. His job—his calling—wasn't something he could just walk away from. He figured once a Witch Hunter, always a Witch Hunter. Everyone assumed his tattoo parlor in Irondell was his main focus, but they were wrong. It was the sideline, the business that bubbled along when he wasn't hunting witches. Eventually, though, his luck would run out. Somewhere along the line, he'd face a witch who was faster, stronger, more powerful...and it would be he crossing to the Other Realm. And another Witch Hunter would be assigned the hit and carry on the duties.

This moment, this side trip down fantasy lane, was exactly that—a fantasy. And he didn't do fantasy. He didn't drift away on daydreams, wishing for what couldn't possibly be. What he did—well, it was a special low, dealing with the excrement of the witch world, but damn it, it was necessary, and he believed in it, believed in the necessity, and that the bad was done for the greater good. He shouldn't be here, cooking breakfast and stealing kisses. This fantasy, this illusion of a different life, was a recipe for a whole world of hurt—at his hands.

"Wow, they look great," Sully said, eyes widening when she saw the stack of pancakes. She smiled as she sat on the stool. "I'm famished."

He gave her a small smile as he sat down next to her. He picked up his cutlery, but sat for a moment, eyeing the food on his plate. He'd lost his appetite.

Sully frowned. "What's wrong?" She eyed the pancakes suspiciously. "What did you to them?"

His lips quirked. "They're fine. Tuck in." He cut out a bit of pancake and popped it into his mouth, his gaze resting briefly on the woman next to him. Sully deserved to be someone's priority. Not someone's booty call, not someone's "between jobs", but someone's first, last and always. He'd eventually hurt her. He'd let her down when he'd have to pursue another witch over spending time with her. Or worse, what he did for the Ancestors could wind up hurting *her*.

He stabbed more pancake onto his fork and shoved it in his mouth. Damn. This sucked. Domestic bliss was obviously some sort of weird mind-meld crap designed to make you assess your life decisions and cry.

Sully eyed him closely as she chewed, then swallowed. "Is everything all right, Dave?"

"It's fine," he said, then put his cutlery down on the plate. "No. No, it's not fine." He turned to look at her. "You and I—we shouldn't have…done. What we did. That." He gestured to the kitchen counter, and then the living room.

Sully's cheeks heated, and she glanced down at her

plate. "Oh." She frowned. "You didn't…enjoy it?" She blinked, then waved her hand. "Don't answer that."

His eyes widened. "We did it three times. Yeah. I enjoyed it. A *lot*." Too much. "We just…shouldn't have."

Sully kept her gaze steadfastly on the glass of juice as she reached for it. "I see," she said. Her voice was low. Calm. Like, dead calm. He glanced at her. Her lips were pursed. Just a little, but that cute crooked little pout of hers was just a little more pronounced.

"No, I don't think you do, Sully. I have—"

"A job to do," she interrupted. She nodded. "I get it." She rose from her stool and placed her plate on the bench with just a little too much force.

"This—" he gestured to the kitchen, to her. "I can't do this. And I shouldn't have done that."

"Because of your job," she said, and folded her arms as she leaned against the doorjamb. "How does sex with me interfere with your job, exactly?" She tilted her head, and although her expression was curious, he could see the darkening anger in her eyes.

Sex. She'd called it sex. They'd made fireworks. It had been more than just sex. Hadn't it? Dave forced himself to focus on the question, and not the quiver of uncertainty that perhaps he was the only one who'd felt the impact of what they'd done, the magical coalescence of their power…

"I need to track down a killer," he told her solemnly. "I'm here having breakfast with you, when I should be out hunting that witch." He rose from his stool and leaned his palms on the counter—the counter where they'd first made incredible, firework-inducing love.

"That other night, when Amanda Sinclair was killed—I should have been out there, hunting, not in here, kissing you."

She gaped at him for a moment. "Are you saying it's my fault Amanda Sinclair was murdered?" Her voice emerged as a hoarse rasp. She folded her arms.

He gaped. "No! God, no! No, not your fault—*my* fault. I should have been out there. I should have been looking. My fault, Sully, not yours." He pressed his thumb to his chest. "None of this has anything to do with you. It's all on me."

Her eyes narrowed. "Ri-ight," she said slowly, although her tone didn't quite suggest agreement. "So this," she said, unfolding one arm to encompass her kitchen, "this was all what? An *oops*?" her voice rose on that last word, and he winced.

O-kay. He'd screwed this up. Monumentally. And he'd managed to minimize the first real emotional connection he'd had with a woman in years. Ever. "No. Yes. Hell, sort of."

She gaped at him. Then she held up a finger. "Okay, first, the correct answer to that was supposed to be a hell, no."

"What we shared meant something to me," he said through gritted teeth. "And that is the problem. I'm not supposed to feel this—" he held up his palms, shrugging. "I don't even know what *this* is, that's how foreign it is," he exclaimed. "I'm supposed to up and go when the Ancestors call, and if we keep going down this—" and again he gestured, palms up "—then I won't want to answer the Ancestors' call."

She stared at him for a moment, and that cute little crooked pout of hers got more crooked, the tighter she pursed her lips. "I see."

His eyes narrowed. "See, I get worried when you say that," he said. "I think you see something that I don't mean."

"Okay, well, let me break it down for you," Sully said, her hands dropping to her waist. The position hiked up his shirt, exposing more of her tanned, toned thighs. "You are hiding from this," she said, and gestured between them. "You feel something, so you are running. You're using your vocation as an excuse to avoid a personal relationship. With…me. You don't trust. You don't trust me, you don't trust us."

His eyes rounded. "Trust?" He placed his hands on hips. "Really? Me? Trust issues?" He found he could only repeat the hot words, so surprised was he by her comments. He was sure he'd get around to forming some rational response.

"Yes. You. Trust issues. You didn't want to tell Sheriff Clinton about the killer witch. Reform law recognizes your authority as a Witch Hunter, Dave—just like they would a guardian enforcer hunting down a werewolf, or a vampire guardian hunting a rogue vampire. Tyler's not going to arrest you for enforcing tribal law on one of your own kind. But you don't want his help—because you don't trust him?"

Dave frowned and opened his mouth to argue, but she was already talking.

"You don't tell the nulls there's a null-killing witch coming after them, you don't want to trust them with the information and still allow you to hunt that witch down. And if I hadn't enhanced that white lie you told about us dating with the breakup factor, you wouldn't have allowed me to tag along in your investigation—because you don't trust me. I'm a witch who wants to help, and you don't trust me to do that. Now, you're starting to feel something, and you don't trust *us*. You want me to believe that all I am to you is some quick screw that you can't get involved with."

"Hey, there was nothing quick about us," he told her, and she shot him an exasperated glare. "And you're not completely wrong," he allowed, holding his hands up. "You're right. I don't trust the sheriff. Nice guy," he said quickly, "but once I approach him, I have to follow Reform rules, and they don't work, not for us. He'd want us to arrest the witch, and have him stand trial with Reform peers—who may or may not be witches, when we already have a higher authority who have made a decision. I trust Tyler—to do exactly what his job tells him he has to do, which doesn't align with what I have to do."

He sighed. "The nulls—I'm not sure about them. Someone is walking among them. Both Amanda Sinclair and Jenny opened their front door to this guy and let him walk right in. He's somehow been accepted by that community, and is able to walk freely among them, so yeah, you're right, I don't trust them. But you…"

He stepped around the counter. "I have never met anyone who is so damn trusting, and that scares me."

Her frown deepened, and he paused, searching for the right words. "You…you're amazing. You're so… big-hearted," he said, shrugging. It was the only word he could think for her. "You can't help yourself, you need to help others. You try to ease people's pain—I saw you with Jenny. You were so frustrated that you couldn't use your empath powers on her and ease her suffering—yeah, I saw that." He nodded at her shift in position, her disconcerted expression. "You tended to my wound, when I'd done everything that should have made you run in the opposite direction. You're wanting to hunt down this killer—to prevent him from hurting others. You're helping me, because I need it. I saw you at the funeral, Sully. When you take on the pain of others, you put yourself at risk. When I visited your shop, you made me tea."

"After I tried to skewer you with a fork," she argued.

He nodded. "Okay, granted. But that's my point. It's so easy to get past your defenses. You sense, therefore you trust, regardless of whether I'm worthy of that trust. You don't really know me," he told her, and he had to force the words out of his throat. "You don't know what I've done. You're right—I don't trust easily, but in my line of work, that's a survival skill, not a flaw." He ran his hand through his short hair. "Which is why I have to leave. The longer I stick around, the more danger I put us both in."

Her blue gaze was dark and solemn, and she sighed. "I would never, ever, beg or force someone to stay with me against their will," she said quietly. "You want to leave, leave." She levered herself away from the wall, and dragged his shirt over her head, and tossed it to him.

He caught it to his chest, still warm from her body. He looked at her, standing naked and proud, her shoulders back, her chin up. And no, he damn well didn't *want* to leave.

"I hope you find your witch," she told him sincerely. "Be safe."

She turned, walked across the short hall to her bedroom and closed the door behind her.

He turned in her kitchen, holding the warm garment to his chest, and stared at the abandoned plates on the counter, the sullied remnants of a glimpse of heaven.

He'd blown it. He blinked, then turned and walked down the hallway to the living room. He scooped up his gear and was dressed in minutes. He looked around for his jacket, and realized he'd left it in the back of Sully's car the night before.

He glanced down the hallway, toward the bend that led to Sully's bedroom. This was lousy. He didn't want to leave her like this, thinking…thinking what? That he thought she was just a brief dalliance? Or that he didn't trust her?

His lips tightened. Maybe that was for the best. If she knew how he felt, that he wanted nothing more than to walk down that hall and crawl into bed with her and never, ever leave—would that change the situation? Would it make her feel better, or worse?

He closed his eyes, letting his senses drift down to that bedroom at the end of the hall. He could sense the peace and tranquility of her room, and he tried to sense her, to comfort her. He gently searched for her essence—a spark exploded in front of him, and he flew across the room, flipping back over the sofa.

Ouch. He looked up from his position on the floor. Okay. She was pissed. He could respect that. He'd knocked, and she'd sent him flying. He got the message. Go away.

He rolled to his feet, pulling up his backpack as he did, and strode out of the house. He shoved his backpack into one of the panniers on his bike, then crossed to the trunk of Sully's car for his jacket. He shook his head. Sully had left the rear window down. The woman had no regard for securing herself or her possessions. He reached in for his jacket and tugged at the sleeve. It caught on the lid of a long metal box in her trunk. He tugged harder, and the jacket pulled free. The lid clanged open, and Dave froze when he saw the contents.

What the—? He reached in and pulled the box closer, frowning at the weight of the darn thing. He peered inside, his jaw dropping.

A supply of swords, axes, knives and arrows—along

with a heap of deadly looking blades, gleamed in the light of day. A cloth bag sat in one corner of the box, and when he pulled at the fabric, he heard a clink, then saw the treasure of Reform dollars winking up at him. A lot of them.

He heard the soft slap of flip-flops on the veranda, and looked up at the woman, that sweet, naive, gullible woman, standing on the top step, hands on hips, as she glared down at him. He glanced back down at the mobile armory and cash stash in the trunk of her car, then back up at her.

"Who *are* you?" he exclaimed.

Chapter 15

Sully padded down the steps and across the yard. "I'm a cutler," she responded shortly, and reached for the lid of the box. First he'd dumped her—although they'd only had a one-night stand, so she didn't think that was the technical term for the one-night-wonder-lover walking out on her. Skunk, maybe. Now he was snooping through her stuff. Dave's large hand flashed out to catch the lid, preventing it from closing.

"This is not cutlery," he exclaimed, pulling out a stiletto blade.

"It's a knife," she pointed out.

"That's one hell of a knife," he remarked. He replaced the stiletto and removed one of her short swords. "Why do you have these in your car, Sully?"

She shrugged. "I made them."

"All of them?" he asked in disbelief, scanning the weapons. She tried to close the lid again, and he braced his hand against the lid, then delved his hand into the cloth bag and pulled out a fistful of coins.

"Where did you get this money?" he rasped.

"Weren't you leaving?"

"Where, Sully?" His voice was low, grim. Determined.

She considered lying, but decided against it. "I made that, too."

He dropped the coins, and closed his eyes as he pinched the bridge of his nose. "Oh. My. God."

She rolled her eyes. "It's not a big deal, Dave."

He removed his sunglasses, and his eyes opened to slits as he peered closely at her. "It's not?"

His voice was quiet, almost conversational. Reasonable. Receptive. And he'd removed the dark lenses that hid his eyes. He seemed open. Approachable. "No, it's not."

He lifted his chin in the direction of the box. "So, that's not really what it looks like?"

She paused, looking at him, then the box. "What does it look like?"

"Well, it looks like you're selling counterfeit cash and weapons," he said.

"No," she said. "I give the money away, not sell it, and I'm not an arms dealer." She thought about it for a moment. She did make weapons on commission, though. "Uh, technically, I might be an arms dealer, but only a little bit." She pinched her thumb and forefinger together to show just how little an arms dealer she was. The thought almost brought a smile to her face, but Dave's expression was so serious she didn't think he'd see the humor in it.

His mouth gaped open for a moment. "Only a *little* bit?" his voice emerged as a high-pitched whisper.

"Well, if I'm being completely honest—"

"Please—"

"I do make weapons for a price, but it's only on a commission basis."

"—don't tell me."

Sully blinked as his words sank in. "Oh."

Dave's shoulders sagged. "You told me."

"You did ask."

"I wanted deniability."

Dave slung his jacket over the rim of the trunk and braced both hands against the car.

"You're not a cutler," he said, shaking his head.

"I am a cutler," she told him, then shrugged. "I also make...other stuff." She leaned back against the car and folded her arms. She'd quickly changed into a cotton camisole and a skirt, and had come outside to make sure he left—or so she told herself. It wasn't because she'd wanted one last glimpse of the man who'd given her fireworks and made her feel safe.

Four years.

"Ah," he said slowly as comprehension spread across his face. "These are the coins you were talking about, when we first met."

She frowned. "What?"

"You mentioned coins on the beach, as though you were surprised the Ancestors had sent me after you for that."

"Oh." She vaguely remembered asking him about it, and feeling confused and hurt that the Ancestors would sic a Witch Hunter on her for such a trivial matter. "Yeah." She eyed the way his biceps flexed as he gripped the edge of her trunk window. She wasn't going to stare. She wasn't going to think about them wrapped around her, or the way she felt when she was in those arms...the passion, the sense of protection. She had to remind herself he was on his way out. Leaving. Adios, amigo.

And she was going to be just fine. This was not a— she pressed her palm to her chest. God, she hurt. No, damn it. This was no big deal.

"Why?"

She blinked, his question bringing her back to the matter at hand. The serious matter at hand. She hadn't expected him to find her...stuff. Only a few people knew about her sideline business, and it was weird, having to explain it to the man she'd shared a bed with. Well, sofa. Kitchen counter. Whatever. This wasn't a conversation she'd expected to have. Especially not when she really wanted to go curl up in bed and cry.

"Why?" She eyed the drive. "I really thought you were leaving," she grumbled.

He turned to face her. "Sully."

She narrowed her eyes against the glint of morning light. "You want me to tell you?"

He nodded.

"Really?"

He nodded again.

"But Dave, I'd have to trust you with some sensitive information," she said, "and I'd hate for you to think I'm too naive and gullible." She glared at him meaningfully, and his lips tightened as he recognized his words thrown back him.

"Sully."

She levered herself away from the car. "No, Dave. You can't have it both ways. You accuse me of being too trusting, while you won't trust anyone, and then you demand me tell you what you want to know." She leaned forward. "Well, guess what? Trust works both ways, buddy."

She turned to walk away, but stopped when his hand

gripped her arm. Not enough to hurt, but enough to turn her to face him. Worry. Genuine concern, flooded her. Damn it, he was doing it again, without even realizing it.

"Are you in trouble, Sully?" he asked earnestly.

"Not if you don't tell the sheriff," she answered honestly.

His exasperation, tinged with frustration, pricked at her, but she could still feel his very real worry. For her. No. He didn't get to do that. He didn't get to worry about her, or feel that warm concern for her, because that made this whole walking out thing really, really suck. But obviously, he wasn't walking out, not until he had some answers.

She sighed. "Look, you've probably noticed the nulls here are really struggling. The fishing season hasn't really hit the high mark, and we have families who are struggling to put food on the table. This," she said, jerking her chin in direction of the coin bag, "is just to get them by until the fish stock picks up. That's all. That's all it's ever been." She wasn't some criminal mastermind, for crying out loud.

His mild relief warmed her, and she pulled her arm from his grip. She didn't want to feel his emotions, didn't want to understand. She wanted to hold on to her anger from earlier. Because if she held on to that anger, the hurt couldn't touch her.

"The weapons?" he asked.

She paused as she considered her answer. "I like weapons," she answered in a low voice. They made her feel…safe. "And I think Jenny and others can use them, right about now."

Dave sighed, his lips firm. "I don't like this."

"You don't have to," she said, stepping away from the car. "You're leaving, remember?"

"Sully, I don't want to leave, I *have* to leave. Every minute I spend with you, everyone else is in danger from this witch, including you."

Damn it. She glanced down at her flip-flops. Buried beneath his need to flee she could see his annoying, frustrating, bloody-minded logic. It didn't mean she had to like it.

Four years.

The words kept repeating themselves over and over in her head. Four years since she'd been with a man, and when she finally surrendered, when she shared something of herself, he ran.

Rode a motorcycle. Whatever.

"Well, don't let me stop you," she whispered. She cleared her throat, then looked out past her front yard toward the headland. "I have things to do, too."

She could see him out of the corner of her eye. His expression was somber, his gaze an almost brilliant silver against his tanned skin and close-cropped beard. She wasn't going to meet his gaze, though. She didn't want him to see how shredded up she was inside.

Silly, silly girl. She'd gone and gotten hooked on a Witch Hunter.

"I'll, uh, get going, then." He stood there for a moment, waiting for her response.

She nodded. Her pose was casual, arms folded, but she could feel the tiny little arcs pressing into her skin as her fingernails dug into her biceps. She wasn't going to cry.

At least, not until after he'd left.

He turned and walked toward his bike, slipping his leather jacket on as he went. He got to his bike, then paused, his hand resting on the handlebar. Then he abruptly turned and stalked over to her. She straightened, frowning, and her eyes widened when his arms slid around her waist, pulling her in for a hot kiss.

Frustration. Anger. Lust. Sorrow. All bombarded her at his touch, his tongue tangling with hers. It was quick, but it was a whirlwind of emotion and passion that left her breathless when he lifted his head. He tilted his forehead against hers.

"I'm sorry," he whispered. He stepped away, and this time he didn't look back when he reached his bike. He slid his helmet on over his head, straddled his bike, and within too few seconds he was riding out of her driveway.

Sully stood where she was, shoulders sagging, by the trunk of her station wagon. She listened as the sound of his bike slowly diminished, to be taken over by seagulls, crashing waves and the sound of cicadas looking for their mates.

Tears blurred her vision. She had done so well. She'd avoided guys—especially the strong, dominant kind of guy. She'd managed to secure her heart, her safety, her *sanity*… She straightened her shoulders. No. She wasn't going to fall apart again. She wasn't going to surrender her peace of mind, her independence, her identity, to a man. Never again.

She turned back to the house. She hadn't been lying to Dave. She did have things to do, and a delivery to make. He was going to pursue this witch on his own. He'd made that clear.

Well, she hadn't said anything about stopping her own search for this bastard. This guy was hurting her friends, and she had every intention of stopping him— with or without Dave's help.

Dave smiled at the librarian who brought forth another old book from the archives and placed it with the others on the table at which he sat. "This is the last one, and contains the first census records since Reformation," she told him in a hushed tone. He glanced about. It must be a reflex for the woman, as he was the only person in the records section of the library.

"Thanks." He summoned forth a slight wisp of power. She was human, and there were no nulls in the library that he could sense. "If there is anything else you can think of that will show me the family trees of the nulls, let me know."

She smiled at him sweetly as she nodded. "If I think of anything else on null families in the area, I'll let you know." He watched as she walked away, her low heels making a slight clack-clack as she lowered her reading glasses. She tucked a strand of gray hair behind her ear as she crossed to the catalogs.

Dave opened the large-paged book. The pages were divided in columns, with neat, meticulous script detailing the names, ages and connections of the residents of Serenity Cove since the town was recognized as part of Reformation society.

He placed one hand on the pieces of paper the librarian had given him to make notes on, and another on the book. There were lots of pages, and more volumes to sift through. It would take him hours, if not days, to sift through all of this on his own.

A little voice whispered that he didn't have to do it on his own, that Sully wanted to help, and that she could get the nulls to reveal the names he was looking for.

He lifted his chin. Well, that would dangerous. For everyone. He'd never had to rely on anyone else to do his job. Witch Hunters worked alone. He'd never had a partner work a hit with him before. Nor had that partner wanted to bring in a whole damn community to help, either.

No. He was on his own. It was better this way. Less... danger. To Sully, anyway.

He closed his eyes, summoning his powers. He murmured a reveal and transfer spell, and could feel the pages warm beneath his hand. He raised his hands from the surface, slowly opening his eyes.

Names on the page started to glow, and he watched as the glow drifted out of the book and onto the piece of paper. Names, dates and connections—they all imprinted on the paper, giving him a list of the purebloods in the area since the town's formation. The pages started to flip, faster and faster, as the names were pulled forth. More books opened, more glowing references. He sat back and waited until the last name landed on the paper, and then he murmured a genealogy spell. He watched as the names reconfigured on the page. Some names faded—individuals who had already passed away.

It took a while, and it was probably early afternoon by the time he had a list of purebloods currently residing in the Serenity Cove area.

He rose from the desk, then waved a hand at the books at the table, sending them back to their homes among the shelves, to save the little old lady at the desk some work. He walked up to thank her, but kept his mouth shut when he heard her snore. He walked out to his bike, opened up his pannier and removed his map of the area. He spread it out on the seat of his bike, then bent down and scooped up some dirt from the ground. Holding his clenched fist over the map, he glanced at the first name on the list, murmured a quick location spell, and let the dirt fall out of his hand in a measured funnel. Within seconds he had the address, and within a minute he was riding out of the Serenity Cove library parking lot.

Chapter 16

"Again," Sully instructed, then brought the wooden blade down toward Jenny's chest in a low-handed grip. Jenny blocked with her arm, pushed Sully's arm outward and stepped in close. Jenny hesitated, then frowned.

"I can't remember the next step," she admitted.

Sully reached for Jenny's other arm. "Your hand. Bring it up and into my armpit—" she stopped talking when her friend followed through with the movements, and was able to bring the practice knife in under her outstretched arm, just beneath the armpit. "Good."

She glanced down at the row of ten or so adults who'd accompanied Jenny over, and were now lined up in her front yard. Kids, including Noah and his sister, were sitting up on the steps of the front veranda watching, or else had taken their cue from the adults and were play wrestling. "Okay, let's do it again."

"So this is supposed to help us, huh?" Jenny said,

as she faced off and started to go through the steps. From what Sully had seen, when she'd piggybacked on Dave's vision of Amanda Sinclair's murder, and from what she'd seen when she and Dave had interrupted Jenny's attack, the killer got his victim on their back on the ground, then delivered the death blow. She was giving the group of purebloods that Jenny had managed to convince to come over for defensive training some choreographed moves to fend off a similar attack that would get them into that kill position.

"Yep." She'd shown them a couple of moves, and was getting them to practice, over and over again. She could hear the clang of metal against metal out in the backyard. Jacob was showing some of the men how to use some of their fishing gear in defensive movements. Jenny was still wary around her brother, and so Sully and Jacob had decided it was best if he was out of sight, out of mind for this.

Jenny looked up at the sound of the mock fighting coming from around the back. "I wish I could remember," she said quietly as Sully slowly made her go through the defensive motions again.

Sully nodded. "We'll figure it out. But you do know that Jacob would never hurt you, right?"

Jenny hesitated, then nodded. "I know. On a rational level, I know. But there's something up here," she said, tapping her temple, "some glitch, and I keep—I keep having these flashes."

Sully narrowed her eyes. "What kind of flashes?"

Jenny performed the block, and a smooth shift to bring the knife up to mock stab her under the arm. Sully smiled and stepped back, assuming the attack position again.

"His face, but—not his eyes. It's...it's so weird." Jenny's lips tightened as she met Sully's gaze. "I'm a null.

This crap has never happened to me before. It's not supposed to happen." She shook her head. "If I didn't know better, I'd say it's…magic." Jenny shuddered. "But then, never having experienced it, I wouldn't know. It's just wrong as all crap."

Sully blinked, then averted her gaze. "We'll figure it out, Jen." After how close her friend had come be being viciously murdered, Sully was even more determined to track down this damn killer witch.

"How the hell do you know this stuff?" Jenny panted as Sully repeated the attack, gradually getting faster and faster.

"I learned it a few years ago," Sully said, then held up a hand. "Okay, let's try something else."

She lay on the ground as the adults gathered to watch. "If you find yourself in this position, and your attacker is kneeling over you, this is what you do."

She gestured to one of the men, Sam Drummond, who tentatively straddled her. She handed him the wooden practice knife. "If he's bringing the knife down at you, he's got the advantage," she told the group. "Grab the wrist with the knife—you want to control that. Use your other hand to strike, preferably punch the throat," she said, showing them slowly a strike to the throat. "Wrap your hand around his neck, and bring him in close—"

"Close?" Jenny exclaimed. "Don't we want to get away?"

"Yeah, but he's got a knife, and close quarters are good. If you try to push him away, that's giving him more room to attack," Sully said, and showed them by gently pushing Sam back to arm's length. "See, here he can stab, strike, etc." She grabbed the back of his neck and pulled him down to her. "Here, he can't, he's too close." She pushed him back so that he straddled her once more.

"So, he's got a knife, and is bringing it down to you.

Grab the wrist with the knife," she told them, wrapping her fingers around the thick wrist. "At the same time, strike at his throat." She demonstrated slowly and gently. "Then pull him forward, wrap your opposite arm over the back of his shoulder, like this, then under his wrist so that you can grab your wrist in a lock." She did the move slowly. "Then, turn his wrist up."

Sam grunted, and tapped the ground as he released his grip on the practice knife. The kids on the veranda cheered, and the adults made noises of surprise and appreciation.

"Then you can control the wrist like this," Sully said, levering Sam's wrist up, and she heard him hiss softly, and his tapping on the ground became fiercer. "You can wrench the shoulder, snap the wrist, move him off you," she said, demonstrating by using the vise-hold to direct Sam's gentle momentum off her body. "You can do various strikes, and run—or pick up that knife and finish him."

The gathered adults gasped, and Sully looked up at their shocked faces. Two of the women shared a look, horrified at the suggestion. Sully rose to her feet. "Guys, this person has killed three of your neighbors. Friends. In some cases, family," she said, eyeing Ronald Sinclair. "If he's coming for you, he wants you dead. Take him out before he takes you out."

Jenny gaped at her, then exhaled. "Well, uh, thanks, Sully." She brightened as she looked around at the others. "Hey, who's hungry?"

The adults nodded, and the kids on the veranda cheered. Sully glanced back at them. Oops. She'd forgotten the kids were there. Not really a conversation you wanted to have in front of the littlies...

She forced a smile on her face. "I have some salad fixings. We could have a cookout. We just need some meat."

The children squealed, then jumped up and down. Which led to a little bit of pushing, and then quickly deteriorated into a game of tag around the house.

"I've got some meat back home," Ronald said.

Sam rolled to his feet. "So do I."

"I've got some bread rolls," one of the women offered.

"I've got more salad—you'll need some more," Mrs. Forsyth suggested. "We could pop home and be back within the hour."

Sully smiled. "Uh, great. That would be great." She blinked, looking at the group as they discussed what to get for the spontaneous potluck meal. It seemed so… big and hearty and wonderful, to have all these people get ready for a large, communal meal. At her place. Like…family.

"Okay, I'll stay here with Sully," Jenny stated as Jacob led more of the adults around to the front. They were all sweaty from their exertions, and most of the men were shirtless, Jacob included.

"I'll help with the kids," sixteen-year-old Rhonda Maxwell offered, winking at her younger cousin, Noah.

"Me, too," Susanne Maxwell, Noah's mother, stated, and Noah pouted, then ran off with his sister, with Rhonda jogging close behind.

"Hey, did we hear something about a barbecue?" Jacob grinned as he rested his foot on the bottom step of the veranda and braced his hand against the railing. Sully watched as Jenny forced a smile to her face, but her knuckles were white as she hugged herself. Jacob's smile faltered when he saw his sister's awkwardness.

"You can come help me pack the car," his mother told him, patting him on the shoulder as she walked toward the street. Some of the purebloods had carpooled, but there were still too many vehicles to fit in Sully's drive. The overflow were parked on the grassy verges on the road beyond.

"I'll start cleaning the grill," Jack Forsyth stated, turning toward the barbecue pit Sully had built shortly after arriving in Serenity Cove. It included a basic grill and metal plate set on a low ring of cinder blocks, and was set in a sheltered corner of her yard that still allowed for a one-hundred-and-eighty-degree view of the ocean.

"I'll take the kids down to the beach," Rhonda sang out as the children ran out of the yard in the direction of the path and stairs that led to the beach below.

The group split up, and Sully led Jenny and Susanne through to her kitchen.

"Do you mind, Sully?" Jenny asked. "I mean, we've all just invited—"

"I love it," Sully interrupted, beaming. "This is great. I miss having family gatherings…"

"Where's your family now?" Susanne asked as she started opening Sully's cabinets. She made a triumphant sound when she located the wooden chopping boards.

Sully smiled, but it took a little effort. "We're all kind of spread out." She crossed to the fridge and started to pull out lettuce and tomatoes and anything else she could use to feed the hoard that was about to descend.

"So, what happened to your family?" Jenny inquired, her brow dipping in curiosity as she reached for a knife in the knife block. "I don't think you've ever told me."

Sully shrugged. "Nothing happened to them. I just… left."

"Why?" Susanne asked as she started to pull off leaves from the head of lettuce. "Wow, that sounded nosy, didn't it?" the woman said, chuckling.

"It's fine," Sully said. "I needed to move away, find my own feet. They're still around, but I don't generally see them unless there's a special event." She'd missed so many birthdays, so many weddings and baby blessings, coven gatherings... She forced a smile on her face. She hadn't let herself think about that, but now, with these people who were being so lovely and warm, so inclusive, she found herself thinking about her family, her coven. Thinking about them...missing them.

But she couldn't go back—she couldn't risk it, for their sake. Something clanged outside, and Jenny smiled. "Sounds like Dad's decided to give your grill a good going-over." She leaned forward. "So tell me, what happened with Dave?"

"Is this the boyfriend Noah was telling me about?" Susanne inquired, and Sully could feel her cheeks heat.

"Uh, he left me this morning." Sully focused on washing the tomatoes.

Jenny slapped the knife down on the board. "What did that son of a bitch do? Where is he? How badly do we need to hurt him? Bruise him up, or make it impossible for him to father children ever again?"

"No, no, it's—it's not his fault." Sully said hurriedly, although she was touched by Jenny's fierce loyalty. "He—he really wants to find the person behind all this," she said, waving her hand around carelessly. "So, he's off—"

"He's dicking around, isn't he?" Jenny muttered, then glanced at Susanne. "He's a private dick."

"Investigator," Sully corrected, then sighed. She could see his point about working without interference, but she still felt like she was not being completely honest with her friends, and hated it.

"Oh, no," Jenny said as she reached for one of the washed tomatoes.

"What?" Sully glanced at the tomato. Was there something wrong with it?

"You have that look," Susanne said, running the lettuce leaves under the tap.

"What look?" Sully frowned, looking between the two women.

"That look that says you've totally fallen all over again for the guy you dated in high school," Jenny said. She brought the knife down sharply on the cucumber, chopping off the end.

"No, I haven't."

"Well, you've done something," Jenny said. Sully's cheeks heated, and she turned away to open a cupboard door, ostensibly to find a bowl. Yeah, and that something had been wicked fun.

"Oh, my God, you did," Jenny exclaimed, and Susanne gasped.

"Whatever it was, from the look of that blush it had to have been good," Susanne said, grinning. "Or very, very bad."

"Guys," Sully pleaded.

"Oh, my God, you did, too!" Jenny squealed.

"Shush," Sully said, looking out the window. She couldn't see Jack Forsyth, but she certainly didn't want Jenny's father to hear the details of her sex life. "It's... over." She pulled the bowl out of the cupboard and placed it on the kitchen counter.

Susanne frowned. "Why, was it bad?"

"No! No, it wasn't bad."

"So it was good, then?" Jenny said, resting the base of her palms on the wooden chopping board.

Sully covered her face. "This is so embarrassing."

"That means it was very good," Susanne explained in a knowing voice to Jenny.

"And he left you?" Jenny asked, a slight frown of confusion on her forehead. She firmed her lips, then nodded. "Fine. Castration it is, then."

"Jen, it's not that simple."

"Yes it is. You can hold him down, and I'll show you how simple it can be."

Sully laughed. "Jen, calm down." She sobered. "We're just—he doesn't trust me as much as I want him to," she admitted quietly.

Jenny hesitated, then placed the knife down on the board. "So *he's* the one with the trust issues…?"

Susanne winced, then leaned her hip against the counter. "Ouch."

"What do you mean?" Sully glanced between her two friends.

"I mean," Jenny said, leaning forward, "you have enough weapons here to arm every man, woman and child in the greater Serenity Cove area, and you showed us some pretty lethal moves out there. That doesn't just come out of a vacuum, Sully. You've been holding out on us."

"What the hell happened to you?" Susanne asked quietly, and for once, her face was dead-set serious.

Sully opened her mouth, then closed it. How did she respond? There was so much she hadn't told her closest friends…

"Hmm, I'm thinking your Dave may not be the only one with trust issues," Jenny stated, then started to resume chopping the cucumber.

There was a knock at the door, and Sully held up a hand. "I'll get it," she said, hurrying toward the hall.

"This conversation isn't over," Jenny called after her.

"I'm already pouring the wine," Susanne sang out.

Sully sighed as she walked down the hallway. Her friends had a point. She'd hidden so much from them—but was she ready to let them in? Was she ready to tell them anything? Everything? And did Jenny have a point? Did her own lack of trust affect her relationship—such as it was—with Dave?

She opened the front door, and raised her eyebrows when she saw the deputy standing on her veranda. He clasped his hat in his gloved hands, and smiled at her.

"Hi, ma'am. I'm looking for Jennifer Forsyth, and I was told she was here...? The sheriff has asked me to stop by with some follow-up questions about her attack yesterday."

Sully's eyebrows rose. "Oh, uh, okay." She stepped aside, gesturing down the hallway. "Come in, she's in the kitchen."

She turned toward the hallway. "I'm surprised Tyler didn't just call," she said.

She heard an agonized cry and turned back. The deputy had stopped just inside her home, and had ducked his head as he clutched his face in pain. She hurried toward him. "What—" she reached for him, but jerked her hand back when he lifted his head.

His features twisted, his skin bubbled and then his eyes flashed rage at her. Her body processed the danger before her mind could quite grasp it. She turned to run, but he grabbed her hair and spun her around. His fist flashed out, catching her in the jaw, and her head smacked against the hall wall. Anger, fury and an evil that was suffocating, slammed into her. Dizzy, she brought her arms up, but his fist struck her again, and darkness crashed over her.

Chapter 17

Dave peered in through the front window. The house really was empty. He stepped back from the front door, and glanced down at his list. Susanne and George Maxwell, not home.

Just like the other purebloods he'd called on. Nobody was home. Anywhere. He glanced down the street. None of the Forsyths—and he'd tried Jenny first—were home. Neither were the Drummonds, or the Sinclairs. Maxwells, and a bunch of others... It was as if they'd all suddenly gone to ground.

He strode down the garden path and had almost reached his bike when his tattoo started to heat. He halted, and pressed his hand to his chest. *No. Please, no.*

"Sullivan Timmerman," he whispered, removing his glasses and staring blindly down the street.

His vision blurred, and then cleared. He was walking up behind a man. The man was stooped over, and using a wire brush on something he held, the grating noise masking the sound of his steps. He reached for the man at the same time he swept his leg out.

The man cried out in surprise as he was grasped, then tripped backward onto the ground, the grill he was cleaning clattering against cinder blocks.

Like lightning, he straddled the man, and Dave grimaced in horror when he recognized the shocked face staring up at him. Jack Forsyth. Bracing one hand against the older man's shoulder, the killer brought down his blade in a smooth arc.

"No," Dave rasped, bracing his hands on his bike. *Damn it.*

Jack's eyes rounded as the blade pierced him, and Dave's hands clenched into fists as he saw the life drain out of the older man's gaze. The killer reached for his wrist, and moved quickly, carving that X symbol into his wrist, draining the blood into that damn horn. The killer rose, turning away from the thicket surrounding them, and faced a house.

Dave's breath caught. He knew that house. The killer raised his horn in a silent toast, then drank its contents. He started to walk toward the house—Sully's house— and murmured those words that blackened Dave's vision.

Dave blinked and shook his head. Oh, God. *Sully.*

Heart pounding, he started his bike and roared down the street, his helmet still dangling from its strap over his handlebars.

Sully was in danger.

The tattoo over his heart began to heat again, and Dave gasped, leaning forward, accelerating out of the null neighborhood and onto the coast road. He blinked furiously, trying to dislodge the vision that was slowly creeping in over the road ahead. "Sull—Sullivan Tim—Timmerman," he gasped.

Sully lay still on the floor of the hallway, her face bruised. "No!" Dave roared, taking the curve of the road at a dangerous speed. The killer walked down the hall, and Jenny turned from the kitchen bench. Another woman was closer, one Dave didn't recognize, and she turned from peering into the fridge.

"Who was at the door?" Jenny asked, and turned back to sliding salad ingredients with a knife along a wooden chopping board and into a bowl.

The other woman smiled. "Sauvignon blanc or—"

The blade flashed, catching the woman in the chest, the smile slowly slipping from her face.

Jenny screamed, and the board she held fell to the floor. The killer worked quickly, laying the woman on the ground and carving the mark into her flesh, then draining her blood. Jenny darted past him, running for the front door. The witch sipped from the horn as he raced after Jenny.

"No," bellowed Dave, his muscles tensing, and he leaned forward, ignoring the high-pitched wail of his bike as it hit maximum speed.

The witch caught up with Jenny in the hall, tackling her to the floor next to Sully's still body.

Jenny screamed and lashed out with the kitchen knife she still held. The witch clasped her wrist, forcing it above her head as he brought his own blade down, and Jenny's scream ended in a gasp.

Within moments, the witch had performed his gruesome ritual with the mark, and was drinking from the horn. His gaze turned to Sully as he murmured those damn words, and Dave's vision again darkened, and he found himself staring at the asphalt of the road unfolding ahead of him.

Sully.

Hands gripping the handlebars tightly, his gut clenching, Dave focused his gaze on the road. He overtook a series of cars all heading in the same direction. One of the cars started honking its horn at him, but he ignored the sound.

He prayed. Prayed for Sully, making all kinds of promises to the Ancestors. He'd never look at a woman again, never get distracted. Keep her safe. He'd walk away, he'd never see her again, just make her safe. Alive.

He heard the squeal of rubber behind him, but didn't turn around to look. The turn for Sully's street was ahead, and he leaned into the turn early, taking it like a motorbike racer on a circuit, before screaming down the road to Sully's house. He turned into her drive and jumped off the bike, not even slowing down to stop it properly. He could hear the bike clatter as it fell, the screech of tires on gravel behind him, and ignored it when someone called his name.

He ran across the yard and up the stairs to the veranda. He shouldered the door open, then raced inside. He skidded on the floor to reach Sully.

"Please, Jenny." Sully was sobbing, clutching her friend's hand. She placed her other hand over the wound in Jenny's chest. Sully's shoulders where shaking, her face tear-streaked as she cried. She started murmuring, and Dave felt his own eyes burn with tears at the grief, the heartbreak in Sully's voice as she tried a healing spell.

A spell that would have no effect on a null.

Dave placed his hand on Sully's arm. "Sully," he

murmured, trying to get the sound past the razor blades in his throat.

She shook her head, the tears streaming down her face. "No, let me help her," she cried, and crawled a little closer. Footsteps pounded on the veranda outside, and Dave looked up as Jacob halted at the front door. The big man had to clutch the doorjamb as he swayed, his face torn with grief and shock as he looked down at his dead sister inside.

"Jenny, please," Sully sobbed, and Dave grasped her shoulder.

"Sully, she's gone," he said softly.

"No, no, she can't be," Sully cried.

A scream, heartrending, full of grief and rage, echoed through the front yard, and Dave looked up at Jacob. The man had turned, and his eyes widened in disbelief. He took a step forward, and more screams, more wails were heard. Jacob took another step, then collapsed to his knees, his face twisted in anguish. He leaned forward, rocking on the veranda, a howl of pain erupting from deep inside him.

"Jenny, come on," Sully gasped, and squeezed her friend's hand in hers. "Let me take it, let me take it," she wailed. She stopped, squeezing her eyes shut, but no matter how much she concentrated, Dave knew she wouldn't be able to take on any of this pain. Not now. Not for Jenny.

"Sully," he whispered, pulling her toward him. "She's gone, love. You can't help her."

"No, no, no," Sully sobbed, and dropped Jenny's hand. Sully's hands clawed over, and she lifted her head and screamed. Her pain, her anguish, her frustration pierced his heart. Dave felt the hot lick of tears trailing down his own cheeks in the face of her despair, and rocked her in his arms.

* * *

Sully poured the steaming water into the mug, and blankly watched the chopped-up leaves and twigs swirl as though caught in a mini hurricane.

A storm in a teacup.

Sully placed the kettle back on the warmer, and took a seat at the table. The tea had to steep. Not for long, but she needed this tea to be potent. A trickle of perspiration ran down the side of her face. She glanced around the tiny little motel room. She'd turned off the air conditioner. It had made an annoying crank-crank-crank noise, and she'd shut it off before she'd screamed.

Her eyes skimmed over the ugliest coverlet she'd seen, its geometric pattern looking like a witch's vision quest on acid. The carpet may have been orange and cream at one point, but now looked brown. Gray. No, baby-crap brown and dead-fish gray.

Her home was a crime scene. She blinked at the tears that welled in her eyes. Correction. Three crime scenes. The tears fell slowly as she stared at the mug, steam curling up from its surface. She watched the steam as it rose, and sucked in her breath as the tendrils roiled, and she saw his face again, the bones moving underneath the skin, his flesh blistering as he stepped inside her home. She blinked. No. She wasn't going to think about that anymore.

She plucked at a loose thread of the long skirt she'd changed into. She'd had to change at her house. Tyler had folded her clothes, covered in Jenny's blood, and placed them separately into evidence bags. She'd given all the information she could to the sheriff. She'd sat through hours of grueling interviews, had flicked through photos...but she'd known it would be a pointless exercise.

Still, Tyler needed to feel like he was doing something, that he was taking action at tracking down this killer. She could understand that. She could give him that, at least.

An image of Jen lying bloodied and still on her hall floor filled her mind. Sully blinked slowly. She didn't want to see that anymore. Didn't want to feel that pathetic uselessness ever again. She'd reached for her friend, but couldn't feel her, couldn't sense her, no matter how much she opened her walls. She couldn't take away any of that pain, that fear and horror that must have preyed upon her best friend in the last moments of her life.

Her gut clenched, and her shoulders shook off a dry retch. Oh, God. *Jenny.*

Hot tears welled in her eyes, before trailing down her cheeks. Jenny. Jack. Susanne. They were all gone.

And it was her fault.

She reached for the mug, her fingers trembling. A knock sounded at the door.

"Sully."

She closed her eyes briefly at the familiar sound of that voice. Dave. She didn't want to see him. Didn't want to speak with him. Didn't want to look him in the eye and see the disappointment, the blame.

"Sully." The voice was louder, as was the pounding on her door.

She pulled the mug closer, but opened her eyes when she heard the lock disengage, the handle turn and the door open.

"Sully." He filled the doorway. So big, so strong. He wore his leather jacket, despite the heat outside. His sunglasses shielded his eyes, but she could guess at the accusation, the recrimination. She deserved it. Hell, she deserved so much more than looks of censure. From everyone. Dave. Jacob... She winced. Mrs. Forsyth.

"Go away," she said, her voice hoarse from screaming.

He stepped inside and closed the door behind him. "I'm not going away."

She cupped her cold hands around the warm mug but couldn't seem to absorb any of the heat. His words sank in, but slowly, like sharp little barbs hitting rubber walls. Some stuck, some didn't, but not quite penetrating the numbness surrounding her. For once, she could feel...nothing.

"You were going away," she said, her gaze fixed on the mug. "Jenny wanted to castrate you." She almost smiled, remembering the conversation, only she couldn't quite get her facial muscles to work. Nothing worked anymore.

Dave paused, then bowed his head. "Yeah, well, I would have deserved it," he said in a low voice.

He crossed over and lowered himself into the seat opposite her at the table.

"I don't want you here," she said in a low voice.

"Well, from what Jacob and Tyler have told me, you don't want anyone here."

She drew the mug closer to her. "I want to be alone."

"You shouldn't be alone, Sully. Not now."

She slowly lifted her gaze to meet his, and decided to ignore the pain and grief she saw etched into his face. "Yeah, I should."

"Sully—it wasn't your fault," he said roughly, leaning forward to rest his arms on the table between them.

This time her mouth did move into a smile, a bitter, self-hating smile that bore no joy or warmth. "But it was, Dave," she whispered. "I let him in."

Dave frowned, and looked down at the table. "Everyone let him in, Sully. Gary let him in close. Mary Anne let him into her home, so did Amanda… Jenny." He clasped his hands together. "I don't know how he does it—"

"He's a skinshifter," she said, and tried to hug the mug closer to her chest. Dave's gaze met hers.

"What?"

"He's a skinshifter," she said, and she moistened her lips.

Dave's eyebrows rose, and he leaned forward some more. "A skinshifter? How do you know?"

"When he—when he came inside, I don't know why, but his facade started to drop." She shuddered. "Literally." She could see it happening again, the way his bones seemed to dissolve, the skin bubbling… She flinched. "He couldn't keep up the disguise." She glanced down at the tea.

Dave sat back for a moment, stunned. "A skinshifter."

She nodded. Skinshifters were a special breed of witch. They could rearrange their features, their physique, to look like anyone they'd physically come in contact with. They couldn't shift into a different species, though, like a bird or a cat, only people. They were the chameleons of witchcraft, and not very well liked. The only time you disguised yourself was when you had something to hide, and these witches had a questionable moral compass. They passed themselves off as others. Sometimes it was a harmless form of mischief, but most of the time it was a form of betrayal and deceit. As such, those witches born with skinshifting abilities were generally outcast—the witch equivalent to a werewolf stray or a vampire vagabond. Tricksters. Imposters. Charlatans.

And in this case, a murderer.

"So that's how he got close to them," Dave murmured.

"Yes." She stirred the tea. "He looked like a deputy. I guess he couldn't pretend to be me with me."

Dave's eyes narrowed. "You say his disguise faltered when he stepped inside your home?"

She shuddered. "If by faltered it looked like his face was melting off his skull, then yes."

Dave rubbed his hand over his mouth. "I, uh—I put a ward on your door," he said quietly.

Sully lifted her gaze to meet his. "What?"

"Uh, the night before, when we got home. I put a ward on your door. A protection spell. You only have a very basic lock on your door, and I wanted to make sure you were safe."

Her lips twisted. "Those spells don't work when the source of dark intent is invited in," she told him.

"No, but they reveal dark intent," Dave told her. He winced. "I, uh, I'm so sorry. About Jenny. And…the others."

She shrugged. "You were right. I should never have gotten involved. I'm just an amateur hack when it comes to catching bad guys."

Dave shook his head. "No, you're not, Sully. This guy is strong, and he's smart." He rose from the table, crossed to the tiny kitchenette counter and picked up a mug. "Mind if I have some tea?"

"Yes," she said sharply, then realized how snappy she'd sounded. "I mean, there's none left."

"Oh." He turned back to the board she'd used to chop her ingredients, and she raised the mug to her lips.

He whirled back to face her, his arm flashing out, and an arc of power zapped from his fingers, blasting the mug from her fingers.

"What are you doing?" she asked shrilly, jumping to her feet.

He stepped up to her, his expression fierce. "Water hemlock? Oleander? What are *you* doing, Sully?"

"Go away, Dave," she cried, stepping away from him.

He grabbed her arm, and for the first time, she sensed nothing from him. He glared at her.

"Why? So you can try to kill yourself again?"

Chapter 18

Sully tried to pull her arm out of his grip, but Dave wouldn't let her go.

"What do you think you're doing, Sully?"

"Let me go," she said, her curled-up fist thumping him on the chest.

He shook his head. "I'm not letting you go, Sully." No. He wasn't going anywhere, he wasn't about to leave her alone, not like this. Maybe not ever.

"Jenny's dead," she hissed, and for the first time he saw a spark in her otherwise dead eyes. She thumped him again on the chest, and he met her gaze squarely. His lack of response seemed to anger her. She thumped him again. "Jack's dead." He remained silent. She thumped him. "Susa—Susanne's dead," she cried, then hit him again. And again. He stood there and let her hit him, again and again, relieved at her anger compared

to the blank numbness he'd seen from her since she'd
accepted that her best friend was dead.

"They're all dead," she cried eventually, sagging
against him. He enfolded her in his arms, felt her
shuddering against him as she sobbed. "It's my fault. I
shouldn't have let him in," she said.

"Shh, it's not your fault," he murmured against her
tangled hair.

"I let him in," she said, and kept repeating it as she
leaned her forehead against his chest. "You shouldn't have
destroyed my tea." Her knees bent, and he caught her.

"Come on, sweetness," he said, scooping her up and
carrying her over to the double bed. He flicked his fingers and the coverlet folded back. He lay her down, then
climbed over her to lie down next to her.

"You should have left me alone," she cried softly.

"I'm not going anywhere," he told her gruffly as he
pulled her back against his chest. "Hate me all you like,
but I'm not leaving you. Never again."

"They died because I invited that evil in," she whispered, and he levered himself up on his elbow so that
he could see her face. He smoothed her mussed hair
away from her face.

"They died because a witch killed them," he told her.
"He's killed before, Sully. Odds are, he would have gone
after them, sooner or later. They just happened to be at
your home when he did."

"I brought them there," she wailed. "I brought them
all there. I may as well have sent up a damn Bat Signal
to the universe that the purebloods were at my home,
come and get them."

He closed his eyes briefly at the devastation, the regret he heard in her voice, emotions that he was all too
familiar with. "You aren't responsible for the bad deeds

of another," he murmured, gently caressing the hair at her temple. "You were trying to help."

"You don't believe that," she said into the darkening room.

He frowned. "Why do you think that?" He didn't believe for one minute that she was responsible for her friends' deaths, and he needed to make her see it, before the guilt ate its way through her.

"You feel guilt," she said in a low voice. "I've felt it. You feel responsible for those witches you kill, and you feel responsible for those they killed. You carry that guilt with you."

His lips parted, stunned at her insight. "Uh…"

"You think you can take this from me?" Sully glanced at him over her shoulder, her eyes dark and solemn. "You think you can carry this weight for me? Make me feel better?" She shook her head. "You can't take this away from me. This is mine to bear. I did this. This is my darkness to carry, not yours."

He leaned forward so that his head touched hers. "This darkness, Sully…it will weigh you down. With me, it's different—"

"Why? Because the Ancestors gave it to you?" She shook her head. "That's a cop-out."

He sighed, stroking her arms. "You can't carry someone else's sins. It doesn't work like that."

"It works that way for you."

"But it doesn't have to work that way for you," he whispered into her hair.

"They were my friends," she whispered. "My family."

"And you loved them," he said, and hugged her just a little tighter. "I understand. Believe me, Sully, I understand. But you have to let it go. The blame is not yours to hold on to."

There was silence for a moment, and then her body jerked, and he realized she was crying silently.

"Sully."

"I can't," she wailed. "I can't let it go. If I let it go, I let *them* go, and I can't do that to them. I can't dishonor them. I can't forget. *I* should be dead, not them. This is so. Not. Fair." She whispered her words harshly, forcefully.

He closed his eyes, drawing her even closer, feeling each shuddering breath. She was so devastated, he couldn't bear it, couldn't bear the guilt that made her want to cross over to the Other Realm. He tried to reach out to her, to draw in some of that pain, to exchange it for some comfort...

He surrounded them with a light cover of warmth, of well-being, tucking the essence around her like a cloak. He took care, making sure he left no gaps, and was surprised when he found it. The slight crack in her shield. He gently pushed the warmth inside her. He heard her gasp, felt her stiffen in his arms and saw the splintering of those walls.

He scooped her up close as she started to cry anew, drawing on the pain and grief. His eyes itched, and he sucked in his breath as the darkness creeped out. Into him.

"What are you—"

"Shh," he whispered, concentrating on rolling the darkness into ball, feeding the light into it and gradually dispersing it. He had no clue what he was doing, but whatever it was, it felt right.

He sensed her relaxing in his arms, and her breathing deepened. He inhaled, slowly, relaxing against her as the warmth spread over them both. He could feel her walls loosen, become more fluid, more flexible, allowing more light inside. She became still against him, so relaxed. He listened as she breathed, deep and regular.

He smiled as he, too, allowed himself to drift off to sleep, and for what seemed his first time in years, he experienced a true sense of peace.

She ran down the hall, her heart thumping in her chest. It was her hall—but…not. No. Familiar, but wrong. Where…? Wait. This was her apartment in Irondell. *No, not again.* She glanced over her shoulder, eyes wide with fear. He was behind her, the deputy with the melting face. She ran faster, but the hall kept getting longer and longer. She looked behind her once more, and stumbled when she saw his face blend into Jack Forsyth. The older man reached for her, and his features twisted, then slid into Susanne. Susanne stared back at her, saddened and disappointed, before morphing into Jenny.

Sully stumbled onto her knees, hands smacking against the tiled floor. She'd fallen in front of the mirror next to the door. She tried to look away, tried to turn back, to face Jenny, to tell her how sorry she was, but her reflection caught her gaze, held it.

Her mouth opened when she saw her own features start to swim, to slide down her face, and she would have screamed, only her jaw felt boneless, loose. She watched in horror as her face melded into masculine features, features she recognized and had prayed to never see again.

Marty.

Sully jolted awake, gasping.

"Hey, it's okay," Dave said, blinking as he reached for her. "It's just a bad dream," he said, caressing her arm in an attempt to soothe her.

She shook her head and sat up. "No, no, I don't think it was," she panted, pushing her hair back off her face. She turned to look at him. "I think I know who's doing this."

Dave frowned. "What?" He sat up in bed, his biceps

flexing as he braced his hands against the mattress and shifted his hips. His silver eyes still bore the shadows of sleep, and a little confusion. Adorable confusion. It took her a moment to get past the fact she'd been snuggled up against this man. And he'd kept his word. He'd stayed.

She didn't quite know why that was so important, but it was a fact that kept reverberating around her skull. He'd stayed.

And he'd…shared her pain. How—? What—? So many things were swirling around in her head, but she plucked the most pressing, the most urgent, out of the maelstrom.

"I think—I think I know who's doing this," she repeated, and threw off the coverlet. She rose from the bed—whoa, headspin—and then lurched for her tote bag, her skirt slowly untangling from around her legs.

"Sully, hold up," Dave said.

Sully shook her head, certainty filling her with determination. "No. I need my books. Now." A sense of urgency sparked inside her.

Sully made her way to the motel room door, but Dave beat her to it. His silver eyes—it took her a moment to really look at him—showed his concern, his bewilderment. "Sully, talk to me."

She met his gaze, still grappling with the shock. "Marty—Martin Steedbeck," she said.

"Who is Martin Steedbeck?" Dave asked, and opened the door for her. He stood aside to let her pass, then followed her out to the parking lot.

"My ex."

"Whoa. What?"

Dave scooted around in front of her, his hands up. "Come again?"

"Marty Steedbeck, my ex-fiancé," she said, and then

fumbled in her bag for her keys. Dave shook his head and guided her toward his bike. "But I need my books."

"I'll drive," he said, and removed a helmet from a pannier. He placed it on her head and connected her strap when her fingers fumbled with it.

They made it to her place in about fifteen minutes. It possibly would have been sooner, but Dave parked the bike near the turn and they ran down the street toward her home. It was past midnight, the darkest part of the night, and the stars were hidden behind clouds, disbursing a dull illumination, full of murky shadows and patches of gloom.

Dave held up his hand, and she halted behind him as they sheltered behind the hedge. A deputy stood by her gate, smoking a cigarette, and she could see Tyler through her living room window. Her front yard was lit up like a football field on a Friday night, and a technician walked out of the front door carrying a number of brown paper evidence bags.

"Can we go in?" Sully asked, and Dave shook his head, his fingers on his lips.

"No, it's a crime scene. It looks like they're about to finish up for the night," he murmured, eyeing the technician who placed the bags in a container in the trunk of a four-wheel drive vehicle, and then started to tug off his gloves. Dave guided her gently behind a bush, squatting down beside her. "We'll wait until they go."

"I feel bad about this," Sully said, eyeing Tyler as he nodded at another deputy, and then they started to walk toward the door. "Can't I just go and ask Tyler to let me go grab my stuff?"

Dave looked at her. "Do you remember talking with him yesterday afternoon?"

Sully glanced at him. "Sort of." A lot of yesterday afternoon was a blur. Evening, too.

Although she did clearly remember Dave blowing the bejeebus out of her tea.

"Your house is a murder scene, Sully. You're not allowed in for several days. You can't remove anything—and they still want an explanation for all those weapons."

"But it's my stuff," she protested in a low voice.

Dave shook his head. "No, at the moment it's evidence. So we wait." He patted the ground next to him. "You may as well get comfy."

He sat down, bringing his knees up and resting his arms across his knees. She followed suit.

He leaned closer, and she caught a whiff of his scent. That neroli did things to her, strange, wicked things. She eyed him. For once, he'd ventured out without wearing his sunglasses. His lips looked soft and relaxed, and his beard had gotten just a little longer, a little scruffier. His leather jacket was open, and his T-shirt was navy. Her brow dipped. Maybe dark gray. Perhaps black. Either way, his shoulders looked broader, and he looked tougher. His short hair and scruffy short beard made him look dangerous. Dangerously sexy.

She looked down at her flip-flops. She shouldn't be thinking about how sexy he looked in the dim light of the stars. Jenny flashed in her mind, sprawled on her hallway floor. She blinked. She was such a horrible person, noticing how good-looking her witch-hunting companion was the day three people had been murdered on her property.

"Mind telling me about this ex?" Dave inquired, his tone low but casual.

She winced. She'd hoped never to have to utter his name again, let alone discuss him in depth.

"It wasn't a healthy relationship," she murmured.

Dave looked at her. "Is he the reason you're hiding in Serenity Cove?"

"I'm not hiding," she argued, her voice low.

"Sully, these people you live among don't know you're a witch. You purposely stay where your powers are restricted, where no other witch will come near you because they'd be powerless...if that's not hiding, it's a damn interesting lifestyle choice that I just don't understand."

"It—it may have started out that way," she admitted, "but I stayed because I wanted to."

"Why?" Dave said, scooting around to face her. "What did he do to you?" His whisper was fierce.

She shook her head. "It was more what I let him do," she said, her eyes on her toes. She sighed. "Marty had...issues." God, just putting into words what had happened, what a monumental failure that relationship had been and how blind, or ignorant, or self-delusional she'd been, was so damn difficult—and humiliating.

Dave's eyebrows rose. "Why do I get the feeling that's an understatement of epic proportions?"

She nodded. "A little. Marty's father was a coven elder. His mother, though, was human. Marty's powers weren't very strong." She rested her chin on her knees. "And his father never let him forget it. The only thing he could really do was skinshift, and even that he wasn't very good at."

Dave leaned back to look up the street, and she followed his gaze. Tyler was now by the drive entrance, talking with the deputies. Dave turned back, and lifted his chin in a silent "go on" signal.

"So Marty started to drink. And when the buzz was dying there, he'd do drugs." She shook her head. She'd been engaged to a drug addict. She couldn't remember when she first noticed the little white lies...and then chose to ignore them. "At first, I didn't realize how much he was drinking when I wasn't there. He was very good at playing sober." She winced. "But the drugs made him...different." She hugged her knees tighter as the memories surfaced. "He'd wait for me to come home, and he'd get angry over the slightest thing."

She hugged herself a little tighter. Maybe it was sitting behind a bush, whispering in the dark while light blazed just a short distance away, reassuring but still hidden. Maybe it was Dave, and this sense of intimacy, of familiarity and friendship on a level that she couldn't remember experiencing before, or the fact that her best friend had died without knowing any of this about her, but for the first time in the longest time, Sully wanted to talk. It was like getting rid of some emotional dregs she'd held in way too long. She'd carried so much darkness with her, but whatever Dave had done earlier that night, it had shone a light on that darkness...illuminated it. Shared it. For the first time since she'd been hiding the reality of her and Marty's relationship from her family and coven, she felt ready to reveal.

"He was in so much pain," she said, shaking her head. "And I'm an empath. I could help him. Like, *really* help him," she said, her hand moving in a smooth roll to emphasize each word. "I could take away his pain." Her chin dipped. "And I'll admit, in some sick way, I felt good about being able to help him." She paused. "But then he'd have more pain, and he needed me to take that, too. I almost think that among his other addictions, my taking away that pain from him, making him feel good, became an addiction in and of itself.

"He'd show me that he was trying, that he was doing some small measures to get better, like taking a different way home to avoid that bar, or showing me where he'd hide his stash so that I could check at any time…" The apologies, the promises…

She shrugged. "But then, he'd stumble again, fall prey to those insecurities, and I'd have to fix him—because the last time didn't work as good as it should have, or my fix didn't last as long as it should have, or I should have known that this would flare up and stopped it from happening… He had me convinced that it was actually my fault. I—I started to feel…useless. He would demand more of me, and would be upset and angry about it." She turned her head so she could look at Dave. "This sounds so pathetic, but he made me feel like I couldn't do anything right, and that—that just wrecks me."

"What do you mean?" Dave asked softly.

"I mean that I know now that he doesn't make me feel anything, I do. So I let him do that to me. That was on me," she said, and squeezed her eyes shut. That haunted her. That she'd fallen so low, and yes, Marty may have pushed her that far, but only because she allowed it. Which only made her feel worse.

"He'd get angry, and we'd argue." Her lips twisted in an ironic smile. "I used to get hurt a lot by accident," she said. "He'd push, and I'd fall into that table, or smack into that door…you know, by accident. He didn't mean for me to end up smashing into the table and knocking myself out…it was an accident."

She swallowed, and Dave moved closer. "How did you get out of there?" he asked quietly.

She blinked back the burn in her eyes. She was not going to cry. Not over Marty. Hell, no. She'd wasted enough tears on that bastard.

"I don't quite know what set it off in my mind, but

I finally figured out the reason he'd call me stupid, or useless, or powerless, or ugly...wasn't because I was actually those things, but because he was afraid of losing me." She held up a finger. "Oh, and when he threw me against a mirror. That may have had something to do with it, too." She still remembered the earsplitting crash, the pain as her head smacked the wall, her back broke the glass, the cuts as she fell to the floor amid the shattered pieces, all showing a warped reflection of her.

Dave sat there for a moment, and she didn't know if he was stunned, or disgusted, or trying to think up an excuse to run down the road, hop on his bike and ride as far away as he could get.

"I left—I ran out the door, with my shoes in my hand, and I ran."

Dave tilted his head. "That's why you make weapons." It wasn't a question, but a statement. A realization.

She nodded. She'd made a promise to herself, all those years ago, that she would never be in a position of weakness with a man—or a witch—ever again. "Yeah. I spent two years learning how to defend myself, how to protect myself... How to shore up my mental shields so that nobody could ever drain me dry again, and then I found Serenity Cove."

"With a null community," Dave finished for her. Sully nodded.

"Yep. You can't scry yourself up a witch if she's surrounded by nulls."

"But—" Dave indicated with his thumb over his shoulder in the direction of her cottage "—you brought your coven's books with you. That means your coven can't access their knowledge base. Why?"

Sully grimaced at the memory. "Marty was so damaged by his father, and was always wanting to prove him wrong—constantly. But he just wasn't that strong a witch. So he used his skinshifting abilities to pass himself off as me, and access our archive."

Dave gaped. "No," he said in horror.

She nodded. "Yes."

"What happened?"

"I found him before he could find the spell he was looking for. There was a fight—and like I said, his talents as a witch weren't as strong as others."

She'd kicked his ass, and protected her coven in the process.

Dave reached for her, his movement slow, as though giving her time to withdraw, or rebuff his touch. She did neither. He cupped her cheek.

"You are amazing, you know that?" he whispered. She closed her eyes, letting herself sense his emotions. The warmth of wonder and admiration. Sorrow and sadness. Anger—but not at her. No. It was tinged with a strong sense of protection. He pulled her closer. "You are the strongest person I know," he whispered against her lips, and kissed her.

She leaned into him, giving herself up to the kiss. His lips were gentle, tender and exactly what she needed from him right now.

The sound of car engines starting interrupted them, and they hunkered low as the sheriff and his deputies drove slowly down the street. Sully looked back at her house. Yellow crime scene tape was draped across her veranda and across her door.

Dave looked at her over her shoulder. "Let's go get you your books. Then you can tell me why you think your ex is killing nulls."

Chapter 19

Dave looked at the array of books strewn across the bed in Sully's motel room. She'd been very methodical in her approach at the house, and had selected volumes quickly. Then she'd performed a transfer spell that had removed the archive from her shelves to a place he didn't know where, and wasn't about to ask.

At which time she'd grabbed some personal items, including a change of clothes and weapons that the deputies hadn't found in their search. Getting the load home on the bike had been a minor miracle. They'd spent the hours since combing through the books. His stomach grumbled. He glanced at his watch. They'd missed lunch. And breakfast. Oh, and dinner the night before.

"I think we need a break." He reached for one of the books. So much…age. He wrinkled his nose at the slightly musty smell. Sort of like old people's stink.

"I think we've been approaching this from the

wrong angle," Sully said as she quickly flicked through some pages. "We know that nulls void any of the natural elements of a shadow breed—werewolves can't shift, vamps can't fang out, witches can't perform their spells..." she said, her hand rolling as she went through the litany. "But this witch has been able to work magic—when no witch working with the natural order can do so."

He nodded. He knew the limitations around nulls, had experienced it personally since arriving in Serenity Cove. That void made him feel almost naked. "I admit, it's one thing that's been driving me crazy, trying to figure out how he's been able to do the spells, bump me out of the visions, etc. I mean, how can a skinshifter even keep his facade around nulls?"

"Especially a skinshifter with limited natural ability," Sully stated. "I think he's drawn on unnatural elements."

Dave frowned. He'd seen the skinshifter carve into flesh and consume blood. "Do you mean blood magic?" Blood magic was a slightly more potent form of magic, and a witch had to be very careful—if their blood supply was killed in the process, it drew the wrath of the Ancestors, and a quick and painful trip to the Other Realm, courtesy of yours truly.

Sully shook her head. "No. From what I saw, he kills his victim, and *then* consumes their blood. I think he's using death magic."

Dave stilled. Oh. Hell. No wonder the Ancestors had called on him.

"The dark arts." It was so obvious, and yet, so damn reckless. Only those on a power thirst used death magic, better known as black magic, and it always—*always*—ended badly. Did this witch not realize that he would eventually pay for his sins? Either in this world or the next… Black magic had a kick to it. As long as you served the dark arts, it served you. One wrong step, though, and it could consume you. Hell into perpetuity. He'd prefer facing down the Ancestors in the Other Realm, thank you very much.

"I don't know why I didn't see it," she murmured, then chewed her lip—*look away from her lips*—before finally lifting her gaze to meet his. He whipped his gaze from her pretty, pouty mouth to her eyes. "Marty used to say that he wanted to find his happy place. When I asked him where that was, he said it was any place where he was the strongest witch—especially stronger than his father."

She shrugged. "I used to think this was a hypothetical what-if kind of conversation, and I'd say to him that even the strongest witch is vulnerable to nulls. He wanted to find a way to be powerful, despite the nulls." She held her hands up in a helpless gesture. "I never thought there was a way to counteract that."

Dave frowned as he flicked through the pages of the book. "You think he found a way to void the null effect." The idea was so extreme, so ludicrous, it was chilling that it might be true. The kind of "sure thing" you bet with a drunk at the bar and then laugh yourself silly as he tried to count out the logic on his fingers. Dave shook his head as he turned the page. He might need a beer or six for this. He glanced down at the page, then froze.

The X symbol was drawn on the side of the page, along with a spell written in the Old Language. Right there, in plain Ancestors-speak.

"Sully."

She looked up at the tone in his voice, then leaned over to look at the page.

"Oh, my God. You found it."

"I need to translate this," he muttered, reaching for the notepad and pen on the table by the bed.

She shuffled around next to him, her head close as he hastily scribbled. Her scent, rose, clove and vanilla, teased at him.

"No, wait," she said, placing her hand on his arm. "That's not liberation," she said, gesturing to the symbol. "That's sacrifice." He frowned, then realized she was right. He hastily crossed out the word and corrected, and then went through the rest of the spell, forcing himself to ignore that teasing, tempting scent.

It took a few minutes, but he finally finished the translation. He showed her the notepad. "Do you agree?"

She scanned the spellbook, and then the translation, line for line, then finally nodded. "Yep."

They both sat there for a moment, staring at the translated spell. "Holy crap," Dave finally murmured in awe. It was—it was—hell, he wasn't quite sure what it was. His brain was having trouble computing it.

"Yep," Sully breathed.

"The Gift," Dave said, his lips tightening. The marking the witch carved on the inner wrist of his victims—the pulse point—was a symbol used by the Ancients, the ones who predated the Ancestors. The symbol, directly translated, meant gift. This spell, though, added some further meaning. A transformative gift, a connection, with the addition of unification.

"He's tying the elements of the null blood—pureblood—to his through the unification spell," Sully said.

Dave nodded. "He's not fighting the null effect, he's accepting it. That enables him to control the effect."

"Like when he bumps you out of the vision," Sully

said, and Dave nodded. This was—this was incredible. Son of a bitch.

"So he uses their sacrifice under the guise of a gift, receiving the qualities and transforming it to become a part of a new...him." Dave met Sully's troubled gaze. "This means that he's warping his magic with a null effect. When others come near him, he nullifies their power and uses it to boost his own." His brow dipped. "An alpha elder." Like elders needed an extra creep-factor. His own mother would love this.

Sully shook her head slowly. "It's...it's ingenious."

"It's dangerous," Dave said. "He can effectively rob supernaturals of their power and convert it to his own, thus becoming the most powerful creature on earth." He frowned as he glanced down at some markings at the bottom of the page. What...what was that?

"But it's only temporary," Sully surmised, reading through the spell. Dave leaned closer to eye the markings, then counted them. Nine. Ni—ine. Three groups of—realization hit him.

"Holy crap."

"What?"

"If I'm correct, the effects can become permanent under certain conditions..." The blood chilled in his veins as he absorbed the meaning of the text.

"What conditions?" Sully frowned as she eyed the page, trying to find the clause.

"Sacrifices," he said, tapping his finger on the markings.

Sully nodded. "Yeah, well, we kind of figured that. He kills for the blood."

Dave shook his head. "No, he has killed six people so far. There are nine markings here."

"The law of three," she whispered, her eyes widening in realization. "Three groups of three—a threefold blood sacrifice."

He then pointed to the circle at the top of the page. "And a celestial event."

He glanced at his watch. When was the next celest—

"The harvest moon," Sully gasped.

Dave closed his eyes briefly. The witch was going after three more purebloods.

This year the harvest moon coincided with the fall equinox. With the day and night being of equal hours, the full moon would rise the closest after sunset, effectively the longest moonshine of the year. A natural phenomenon on steroids. Sheesh.

"So if he completes the blood harvest by harvest moon, he keeps his powers forever." Sully bit her lip.

"Son of a bitch."

"This is massive. We have to do something," she said hastily reaching for the book. "Does this mention anything about a counterspell? There has to be a counterspell—right?" She eyed him hopefully.

Dave shrugged, incredulous. "I didn't even know this spell was possible until two minutes ago. I have no idea about a counterspell."

"We have to do something. This means he's got to kill three more nulls, by moonrise in two days' time."

She started flicking through the book, her movements gaining speed. He tugged over another book and started scanning the pages. "Maybe we should—"

Her murmurs interrupted him, and he glanced over at her. Her eyes were closed, fingers splayed as she tried to encompass all of the books on the bed in her...discovery spell. Damn, she was good.

She growled in frustration, her fingers clenching when her spell turned up nothing.

Okay, so *mostly* good. Nobody was perfect, and you could only discover something if there was something to discover.

Her eyes opened, and he was struck by the panic he saw there.

"What are we going to do? I can't find a reversal."

He smiled. "We do what I do best."

"What's that?"

"Improvise."

"Please, we need to talk," Sully implored. Jacob stared down at her, his brown eyes dark with devastation. His gaze flicked to Dave standing behind her, then back to her.

"Sully, now's not a good—"

"I know." She swallowed. "God, I know. If it wasn't absolutely necessary, I would never come near you and your family ever again." Tears filled her eyes as that treacherous guilt ate at her like a gutful of chilies.

His expression gentled. "Sully, it's not your fault." He lifted his gaze to meet Dave's over her head. "It's not her fault."

Dave nodded, and she felt him place his hand on her bare shoulder. "I know. But you need to hear us out."

Jacob glanced over his shoulder, then stepped out onto the veranda of his parents' home. "I can give you five minutes," he said in a low voice. He shoved his hands in the back pockets of his jeans and leaned against the front wall of the house.

Sully nodded. She'd take whatever she could get, and be super appreciative of it. She turned to Dave, who pulled a scrap of paper from his jacket pocket and handed it to her. She caught her bottom lip between her teeth, and he gave her a reassuring nod. She turned back to Jacob, unfolding the piece of paper. Okay. Deep breath. She could admit that she'd lied, that she'd pretended to be someone she wasn't, that she was, in fact, a dreaded witch implanting herself secretly into the null community to hide her own ass from a psychotic ex. She hated what she was about to do, and was dreading Jacob's reaction. And his mother's. And everyone else she knew. Deep breath.

"We think we know why someone is killing nu—" she halted, "your family and friends." *Nulls* was a generic word, a catchall for the individuals she loved and mourned, and whom Jacob loved even more fiercely. But this was now very, very personal. For everyone.

Jacob watched her. "I'm listening."

She held out the piece of paper to him, and it fluttered in her trembling fingers. She could do this. She wasn't going to hide anymore. These people deserved more. They deserved better. And they'd lost far more than her peace of mind and comfort zone.

"He's carving this into them," she whispered.

Jacob glanced down at the symbol Dave had drawn on the paper. His lips tightened when he recognized the graphic. "I know. I saw it on my sister, on my father," he said roughly.

"He's carving this on them to steal the null restraint for the supernatural."

Jacob's gaze flicked up to meet hers. "Say what?"

"The man doing this—" she took a deep breath "—he's a witch. This symbol allows him to—"

She halted when she realized she'd be going into horrifically gory detail to him about Jenny's and his father's deaths.

"It allows him to use the null effect to cancel out any supernaturals around him," she said the words in a rush.

Jacob frowned. "I don't understand. If he's a witch, it doesn't help him."

"He's figured out a bypass," Dave said from behind her.

"How?"

Sully hesitated.

"He draws on the blood of his victims," Dave stated, and Sully sucked in a breath. His words gave an adequate description without sharing too much more. "He's figured out a spell that can help him absorb the effect without being affected by it."

Jacob frowned, shaking his head faintly. "How do you know this?"

Sully swallowed, then lifted her chin. "Be—because I'm a witch," she said in a whisper.

Jacob stilled. His gaze flicked between her and Dave, and back again. "Say what?"

"I'm a…witch," she finished in a hushed voice.

"A witch."

"Yes, a witch."

Jacob shook his head. "I don't believe it. You've been here for years, and you never—"

"I make remedies," she interrupted. "I know how to do that because I'm a witch, and I'm a student of nature."

"You make teas," Jacob argued. "Ointments. Like a doctor. Or a naturopath. That doesn't mean you're a witch."

Sully's mouth opened. She'd hidden the truth for so long, and it had taken much effort to come clean. She had expected yelling. Rebukes. Anger, betrayal. She hadn't expected not to be believed.

"Uh…" She glanced over at Dave. He shrugged his broad shoulders, a don't-ask-me look on his face.

"I am a witch," she said earnestly.

Jacob shook his head. She wasn't sure if it was in denial, disbelief or disappointment.

"I just didn't tell anyone," she said lamely.

"I don't believe you," he said, and looked at Dave.

"Oh, believe her." Dave smiled, but there was no humor in it. "For the record, so am I."

Jacob closed his eyes briefly, and when he opened them again, Sully saw the betrayal, the desolation in his eyes. And felt yay-high to a slug.

"You lied," he said in a harsh whisper.

She blinked back the tears his tone, his words, brought forth. "Yes," she admitted.

"You pretended you were normal," he accused her.

She opened her mouth. Paused. "When I'm with you guys, I am," she told him truthfully.

Jacob straightened and brought his arms forward to fold them across his broad chest. "You've lived among us for four years, Sully," he said, his voice low and harsh. "And that whole time you never hinted at what you really were." His lips pressed tightly together, and he looked out at the shadows lengthening down the street. "Did Jenny know?" He didn't look at her directly, but kept his gaze fixed on the middle distance.

This time she couldn't blink fast enough to stop the hot tears that spilled down her cheeks. "No," she whispered, ashamed.

Jacob's gaze slid to her, and her lips trembled when she saw the accusation in his eyes. "Liar," he rasped.

She flinched, then looked away. "I know. I'm so sorr—"

"Jenny's dead," he hissed. "My father. Susanne—we all welcomed you. We *trusted* you."

Sully squeezed her eyes shut, her heart clamping at the pain, the grief she heard in her friend's voice.

"There's more," she said, her voice catching. She glanced up at him. She had to tell him. She had to—oh, this was hell.

Dave's hand squeezed her shoulder, and she felt the comfort, the reassurance, the strength.

"The man doing this...is my—" her stomach clenched, and the muscles tightened in her jaw. "He's my ex."

Jacob's eyes rounded, and he stepped forward.

Dave drew her back behind him, shifting forward to stand toe-to-toe to Jacob, meeting his gaze directly. "Calm down."

Jacob's gaze narrowed. "Don't tell me to calm down," he said through gritted teeth. He glared at Sully over Dave's shoulder. "Is this guy here because of you?"

"I—I think so," she whispered.

Jacob swore and closed his eyes in pain.

"I'm so sorry, Jacob," she cried.

"Go." Jacob turned back toward the front door.

"But—"

"Sully, just...go."

Dave glanced over his shoulder at her, and his brows dipped. He turned back to Jacob.

"You need to hear her out."

Jacob turned on the witch, his expression fierce as he grasped the lapels of Dave's jacket. "I said g—"

Dave moved fast. Grasping the other man's wrist, he twisted his body—and Jacob's arms, and shoved Jacob's chest against the wall, the man's arm twisted behind his back. Sully gasped.

"This guy is not a friend of Sully's," he whispered harshly. "She left him for good reason, and she never believed he'd come anywhere near her. She risked her life to work with you guys, to help you guys, and from the moment I've met her, she's only wanted to keep you all safe. I know you're hurting, and I know you're angry. Calm down, and hear her out."

Jacob tried to struggle, but Dave shoved him back against the wall until the man stopped resisting. He looked over at Sully. "Go on." He nodded encouragement.

Sully took a deep breath. "He's coming after more nulls. He needs to kill three more purebloods to complete his spell."

Jacob stilled. She had his attention. "We believe we can stop him," she said, "but we'll need your help."

Chapter 20

Dave dabbed at the pinpricks on the wrist, then smiled at the tear-streaked face of the six-year-old red-haired pureblood. "All done, Noah. And you have a badass tatt to impress the girls when you're older," he said, and winked. He glanced briefly at the boy's father, and he smiled hesitantly back as he rubbed his son's back. Before tonight, he'd never tattooed a kid. Now he'd worked on four. Inflicting pain on kids was now on his "never do again" list.

The boy sniffed, and gave a tremulous smile as he glanced down at the white-inked tattoo. Dave reached for the antiseptic soap and gave the markings a gentle wash. Within minutes he'd taped the adhesive bandages to the boy's wrist. The tattoo was an ancient rune quaternary design, a protective shield. Simple, but effective.

"Does this mean I won't die?" the boy inquired tentatively.

Dave looked up at him, then raised his sunglasses to the top of his head. This was the son of one of the victims—a woman who'd been killed at Sully's house. No wonder the kid was concerned. His mother had been murdered by this sick prick. "This means that you will forever have the witches protecting you," he told the boy in a low voice, his tone sincere. "This guy won't be able to come near you."

"Are you going after him?"

Dave nodded. "Yeah."

The boy frowned, worried. "Aren't you scared?"

Dave tilted his head, assessing the kid. He could appreciate that, living in such a tight-knit community as this null one, the boy had heard about the recent murders, and was scared—as well he should be.

But Dave had discovered he didn't like kids to be scared.

Dave lifted his chin in the direction of the boy's wrist. "That tattoo makes you pretty badass," he said, and lifted up his T-shirt to reveal his own markings. "These make me the king of badass."

The boy's eyes rounded, and he nodded. Dave dropped the garment, then grinned. "Get going." He gestured to the door, and turned back to clean up and put away his portable tattoo kit.

The bathroom door opened, and the kid ran out. His father followed, mouthing "thank you" to him as she went.

Sully peered around the doorjamb. "That was the last one. Can I get you anything?"

"Nah, I'm good." Dave answered as he gently placed the needles onto a little tray, and poured some bleach over them. He snapped the lid on the tray. He'd have to clean and sterilize them properly back at the motel room.

He carefully loaded the kit into his backpack and turned. Sully was waiting patiently, but it was the older woman behind her that drew his gaze. His eyebrows rose. "Mrs. Forsyth."

Jacob's mother smiled tremulously. "I just wanted to say thank you," she told him. He could feel heat fill his cheeks, and he cleared his throat.

"I wanted to say I'm so sorry about your husband, and Jenny," he said in a low voice. If he'd managed to catch him the day he'd first attacked Jenny, or any of the other times before, he would have been able to prevent the deaths of half of her family. Sully had it all wrong. It wasn't her fault her friends were dead. It was his.

He ducked his head as he walked past, but halted when Mrs. Forsyth touched his arm. He looked down at her. Her wrist also bore the adhesive bandages of one of his recent white-ink tattoos. She was so tiny, so frail. How the hell could such a petite woman spawn a giant douche like Jacob?

She smiled sadly as she lifted her hand to cup his cheek. "You're a good man," she told him in a low voice. Her smile broadened, although it was slightly shaky. "Even if you are a witch."

His lips curved briefly. She patted his cheek. "I know you had nothing to do with Jenny's and Jack's deaths. Neither did Sully." She reached her other hand out and grasped Sully's hand. "You both need to believe that."

Sully closed her eyes, her face pained. Mrs. Forsyth pulled them both in for a group hug. "It's not necessary, but if you need it, you have my forgiveness." She took a deep breath, then stepped back from them. "Now, you hunt that bastard down."

She patted Dave once more, hard enough to make him blink, then turned and shuffled down the hall.

He took a deep breath. That tiny little null had just given him more tenderness than his coven elder mother ever had. He frowned. It made him feel…weird. He shuddered. God, he was getting as sooky over these folks as Sully was. Yeesh.

He stretched his neck, then eyed the woman next to him. She wore the same weary expression he suspected he did. "Come on," he said. "Let's go."

They'd been at the Forsyth home for hours. Jacob had rounded up as many purebloods as he could find, but they knew there were still some who hadn't been inked—and that ink would mean the difference between life and death.

He'd been a little wary when suggesting this option for the purebloods. Tattooing involved injecting ink beneath the skin—resulting in a minor contamination of the blood. Most of the shadow breeds would have balked at tainting their bloodlines, but the nulls didn't seem to have an issue with it. And Jacob had been the first to accept the offer, showing his mother it didn't hurt "that much". Dave winced. He'd developed a basic design— something that could be done quickly so that more nulls could be protected in a short time, but also to try to limit the level of discomfort, especially for the kids.

Sully slid her arm around his and gave him a gentle smile. "That looks like it was tiring."

Dave shrugged. "Meh. I think that was a record for me." He'd worked quickly and consistently, and had managed to imprint the warded tattoo onto almost all of the purebloods in this area. He'd be coming back in the morning to work on anyone else who came forward. It was the Harvest Festival, with streets blocked off and stalls already being assembled. The nulls were determined to go ahead with the celebration. Which meant there'd be lots of purebloods walking the street fair, among many others. A skinshifter would be next to damn near impossible to locate in such a large crowd. All the witch would have to do is come into physical contact with a person, and he'd be able to take on their facade. It would be like having a haystack and looking for the needle—no, the ax—no, now the nail…

At least, if Dave was a skinshifter, that's how he'd do it. But with this protection ward tattooed onto the purebloods, they'd both tainted the blood supply with ink, which meant technically the purebloods were no longer pure of blood, but they also had a blocking ward to prevent attacks.

Take that, skinshifter.

They just needed to make sure they found all of the purebloods. If there were three left untattooed, this witch could still complete his spell. And that would make it incredibly hard for Dave to send him to the Other Realm. Sully claimed Mental Marty—his name for the witch, not hers—wasn't a skilled witch. He wasn't so sure he'd agree. He'd managed to come up with a really twisted plan, find an ancient spell and become almost undetectable in the process. It was like hunting and fighting a shadow—a shadow that had proven time and time again just how lethal he could be. Sully was so damn lucky she'd escaped him when she did.

He eyed her. Sully had dark circles under her eyes, and that crooked pout was just a little more pronounced, the lines a little more drawn, her complexion just a little more pale.

"You look tired."

"Gee, thanks."

He winced. Oops. "Sorry. But it's understandable."

She'd had very little sleep since Jenny's murder, and had startled awake with nightmares. "Do you need to recharge?"

Witches used nature to feed their energy. Finding a place to sit with exposure to the elements…sun, wind, rain, earth. Even moonlight helped. It was a chance to be still, to meditate and to become a little more present. After his inking marathon, he could do with a recharge, too.

She nodded. "That sounds great. I usually go the headland at the end of my street, but…" She shrugged, wincing.

He nodded. Her home was still classed as a crime scene, and she wasn't technically permitted access to it. If you followed the rules.

He didn't really follow the rules.

"Sounds great. Let's go."

Sully led him downstairs, but she halted when she saw Jacob coming out of the living room. The tall man paused when he saw them, his eyes on Sully. Dave stiffened. If this guy was going to threaten Sully—

The fisherman shoved his hands in his jeans pockets as he took a step toward Sully. He gazed sheepishly at her for a moment, then sighed. "Sully, I'm so sorry—"

"Shh," Sully said, shaking her head. "You've got nothing to apologize for."

"No, I do. You were Jen's friend, you're my friend. I shouldn't have said the things I did."

"You had every right to—" Sully's words were cut off when the big man swept her up in a bear hug.

"No, I didn't. I was being a royal dick."

Dave's eyebrows rose. Well, he wasn't about to argue with a royal dick.

Sully hugged Jacob back. "You've lost your sister

and your father," she whispered. "And you're my friend.
You can always speak freely with me, especially when
I deserve it."

"But you didn't."

Jacob lifted his gaze, and met Dave's over Sully's
head. Dave arched an eyebrow. He sure as hell wasn't
going to give the guy a hall pass for being a royal dick.
Sully had been so worried, so heartsick about telling
the nulls the truth. And the big jerk had hurt her feelings when she was already feeling so much pain and
guilt over the recent deaths.

But the big jerk had just lost his sister and family.
He guessed if Sully could cut Jacob some slack, he
could, too. He relaxed his features when he met Jacob's
gaze. And then realized the man's hands were smoothing down Sully's back. Dave narrowed his gaze. Well,
there went that warm and fuzzy moment. He narrowed
his eyes as he met Jacob's, and this time it was Jacob's
eyebrows who rose.

He gave Sully one more squeeze, then set her back.
"Thank you," he whispered. "For everything."

Sully ducked her head and nodded as she stepped
past.

Dave made to follow her, but stopped when Jacob
stuck out his hand. "Thank you," the fisherman said
sincerely. Dave eyed the extended hand. Aw, darn. The
royal dick was being halfway decent. He grasped the
man's hand and shook it, giving him a nod, then he followed Sully out into the night.

He handed her a helmet, and within minutes they
were back on the coast road. The motel was on the other
side of town, so passing Sully's home and pulling in at
the headland was virtually on the way.

He slowly drove past the house. It sat, dark and silent,

at the end of the street, the crime scene tape blocking off the drive fluttering in the night's breeze.

He pulled over onto the grassy verge, and waited for Sully to dismount before doing so himself. He removed his sunglasses and gazed out over the water. Light gray clouds drifted slowly across the sky. Stars glittered, and the moon cast a silver swathe across the water. The breeze was soft and still bearing the final warmth of a summer on the wane.

He sucked in a deep breath. Held it. Slowly exhaled. Salt and sweet blossoms. He glanced about. Yep. Sully's garden backed up to the fence.

"What do you think?" Sully asked as she sat cross-legged on the grass. He joined her. He could feel the night dew soaking through his jeans.

He looked out over the water. "It's beautiful," he said quietly. Even if he did have a wet seat.

They sat there for a while, soaking in the serenity. Dave's lips curved. No wonder this area was called Serenity Cove.

He tilted his head back, enjoying the feel of the breeze ruffling his short hair and the stretch of his neck muscles after the long day of bending over to ink up nulls. He watched the stars for a moment, then closed his eyes. He put aside his thoughts on Mental Marty, his very grave concerns that Sully's ex would find an unprotected pureblood—or worse, get desperate when he couldn't, and strike out in a much more dangerous and lethal way. He put aside his thoughts on Jacob, of the teeniest spark of jealousy that had awoken when the man wrapped his arms around Sully... He put aside the torment of fulfilling another task for the Ancestors, and the self-doubt and guilt over the six people already killed by the target he had yet to dispatch.

He let nature have its way, let the calm and peace soak in, let the delight in a breeze against his skin take hold. He opened himself up, dissolving his mental wards, letting the energy gently roll in to fill his reserves.

He sensed a lightness, a warmth that was sweet and pure, with the cooling edges of worry and anxiety.

Sully.

Instinctively, he touched those cooler, darker edges with his own energy, feeding her reassurance as he drew in her worries to make them his own—and then realized what he was doing.

He snapped his eyes open and sat bolt upright. "I'm sorry," he blurted. After what she'd told her relationship with Marty, he could well understand her resistance to link with another witch, to have that witch consume anything from her, especially without her permission. They hadn't fully linked, but he'd forged a connection, one that hadn't been invited.

Sully sucked in a breath, her gaze fixed on the sea that glittered with silver diamonds under the moonlight.

"It's—it's okay," she said in a small voice.

"No, no it's not. You've never invited me in, and after hearing about Marty, I understand that. I—I didn't intend for that to happen."

She nodded, and her bottom lip disappeared between her teeth again. She tilted her head, and it was almost as though she was wanting to look at him, but trying to avoid him at the same time.

"You—last night you—" She sucked in a breath, and he watched as her breasts quivered beneath her cotton camisole top.

He whipped his gaze back to the sea. First he intruded on her mentally, and when she's trying to talk to him he's ogling her. *Bad form, Dave.*

"I don't know what happened last night," Dave admitted in a low voice, and this time it was him averting his gaze. "I just know that you were dealing with so much pain, more pain than I'd ever felt in a person, and…and I wanted to help ease it." He grimaced. He'd intruded on her then, too. Had no idea how he'd done it—he'd never done it before.

She remained silent, and he didn't know if she was mentally screaming "I hate you" and trying to map out her escape route. What she'd endured with her prick of an ex was on his mind, her vulnerability, the abuse of not only her generosity, but her body, her mind and her powers…and for a witch, that was a painful violation.

He raised his knee and rested his forearm on it. "I know—I know there's a protocol with power bonding," he said in a low voice. "I've bonded with other witches, like my sister, when it was necessary—and agreed to, but I haven't lived in a coven." He shook his head. "That's not an excuse, it's—it's that sometimes I'm ignorant of the process, and for some folks, I take shortcuts that can be…confronting."

It was a constant source of frustration for his coven elder mother—something he'd rather enjoyed doing, up until now—when someone he was beginning to really care about was affected.

Sully turned, and reached put her hand on his arm—and there it was. That little pfft of a power meld that he still couldn't get his mind around, but that awoke every single one of his senses and focused them on her.

"It's okay, Dave," she said, and gave him a tremulous but reassuring smile, and gave his arm a gentle squeeze. He felt an answering throb in his groin. Felt the want, the need for her, and battled it. He met her gaze, saw the tenderness, the interest. He raised his hand to cup her cheek. Her skin was so soft, so smooth, her eyes so dark, full of wariness, full of curiosity, and yet showing him a hunger he wasn't sure she intended for him to see.

But he did. He leaned forward a little, then halted.

He wanted her—desperately, but thoughts of Mental Marty, of what he'd done to her, bubbled up. He never wanted her to feel forced around him—for anything.

As though reading his mind, Sully moved. Tilting her chin up, she closed the distance, her lips pressing against his as she slid her hand up his arm and over his shoulder.

Dave closed his eyes, content to let her lead, let her set the pace, the level of intim—

Her tongue slid past his lips, and heat flooded him, tightening inside him, flooding his body with an arousal that was so damn gripping, so tight, it had him panting as he angled his head.

Without breaking contact, Sully rose up on her knees, her arms sliding around him, under his jacket. He shrugged it off to give her access—*oh, please, access*—and dropped it to the ground behind him. He raised his hands to her hips, guiding her as she straddled his hips. He wrapped his arms around her, crossing them over her back as he pulled her against him. Sully sighed, her breath drifting across his lips as she tilted her head first in one direction, then the other, as though trying to find the best position.

He groaned at the teasing contact, and slid one hand up into her hair. He could feel the damp heat of her pressed against his groin and his cock stiffened. She moaned, her hips writhing against his, and he shifted beneath her, trying to get even closer, despite their clothes.

She drew back, tugging at his T-shirt. He brought

her lips back to his, impatient at the loss of contact, and ripped his shirt from neck to hem, shrugging out of the scraps. She laughed huskily, and the sound had to be the sexiest he'd ever heard, that playful rasp against his neck.

She pushed him back, and he lay down across his discarded clothing. She made that sexy, crooked pout with her lips, and he raised a finger to trace her mouth. She captured his fingertip with her mouth, sucking on him in a way that almost made him delirious with need.

She pulled back for a moment, scanning his chest, running her hands over his body. He closed his eyes, enjoying the feel of her caressing her skin, until he felt her lips against his nipple.

Oh, wow. He bucked beneath her, and she chuckled throatily as she kissed her way down his torso. Her fingers fumbled with his belt and fly, and then suddenly she had him, all of him. He gave himself up to the intense pleasure as she took him into her mouth.

She tugged at his control, teased at his restraint, until he could feel himself swelling in her mouth. He reached for her and found the straps of her camisole instead. He pulled gently at the garment; she helped him draw it up over her head. He grasped her head, tugging her up to him. He skimmed his hands over her back, dispensing with the clasp of her bra, and the bra itself. Her skin was so warm, so smooth, and he ran his fingers down her back. His lips curved as he felt her shudder.

He pulled up her skirt, dragging at the lacy band of her briefs until they skimmed over her bottom.

Sully moaned, shifting so that they could pull her panties off, and then she straddled him again.

He looked up at her. Bathed in the silver glow of the moonlight, her skin looked pearlescent, and he reached out to touch his midnight goddess. She gasped when he caught her breasts with his hands, and he fondled them. She quivered, head tilting back, and her hair cascaded down her back. She writhed against him, and this time he could feel the molten core of her pressed against his cock. God, he wanted her.

She caught her lip between her teeth as she quivered above him. Looking up at her, seeing her body, the way she undulated against him, was setting off a fire in him that he needed to control, before he exploded. He grasped her hips, rolling over so that she lay beneath him, and she panted, surprised but smiling at the move. He gazed down at her for a moment, and they both paused, catching their breaths.

He stared at her face, the gentle arch of her eyebrows, those beautiful blue eyes, the straight nose and that crooked, sexy smile. She was magnificent.

"God, you're beautiful," he whispered, and she smiled, almost shyly.

"You're pretty gorgeous yourself," she whispered, her gaze skimming his body, before her eyes once again met his. In that moment, in that infinitesimal connection, something shifted inside him, something he couldn't name, but seemed to rock him to his core.

Slowly, he dipped his head and pressed his lips to hers.

Chapter 21

Sully closed her eyes, her arms twining around his neck. The kiss was tender, hot, slick and carnal, but yet she felt something, a weight, an impact that seemed to set her senses to overload and her emotions into a headspin. It was the perfect kind of kiss, full of emotion, passion and sensuality. Meaningful.

And so not what she was expecting.

She sucked in a breath as he pulled away from her, and kissed his way down her body. He carefully undid her skirt and belt—avoiding the daggers—and pulled the garment down her body, following it with his lips and tongue. She shuddered as the fabric slid down her legs, and then off her body. He shoved at his jeans, discarding them, and then was kissing his way back up her body until—

Her eyes widened as his lips kissed her. There. His hands stroked her, drawing out her reactions, making her tremble as the heat, the tension, coiled inside her. Oh. My. G—her neck arched when his tongue slid inside her, and she groaned, long and loud into the darkness. The stars above them were swimming as he laved her, over and over, until she was a hot, wet mess in his arms. He used his hands and mouth to wring extreme pleasure from her, and her back arched when that tension suddenly snapped, sending her spiraling into a cloud of bliss.

He didn't give her a chance to catch her breath. He crawled up her body, stroking her breasts, then biting and sucking on her breasts, until his hips found hers. He braced his arms on either side of her, his silver eyes meeting hers, and she gasped as he slid inside her. She brought her thighs up to his waist, and they both moaned at the change in angle, the deeper penetration. She reached for him, her breath hitching each time he withdrew, then slid back to the hilt. He covered her body with his, his hips thrusting, and she cried out as the passion once again swept over her, pulling her body taut with need.

He held her in position, hands grasping her shoulders as he slid home, and the heat exploded. She cried out, a sound snatched away by the breeze. Her nipples, her core, her very mind seemed to overload on sensation. She heard him groan as he thrust once more, his body hard and tight against hers, and then he, too, found release. Lightning crackled above them, and the air practically snapped with energy.

Heart thudding in her chest, she embraced him, trembling, as she tried to catch her breath, her reason, some modicum of control. She gazed up at the stars, and realized even her toes were clenched, and it took conscious effort to get her muscles, everywhere, to unclench.

"Oh, my," she panted, and he chuckled, setting off little rockets of sensation as he kissed her softly.

"Oh, my," he said, nodding.

He rolled onto his back and pulled her into his side, and they lay like that for a while, letting the wind play over their naked bodies. Dave stroked his hand down her arm, and she stretched against him, enjoying the contact.

"Well, that's one way to recharge," he commented, and Sully started to laugh. She definitely felt...renewed.

He pulled his T-shirt on over his head, then looked across at Sully. They'd arrived at the motel room in the wee hours of the morning, and had managed to catch a couple of hours' sleep. Which was hard when curled up to a soft, warm, luscious body like Sully's. Now, though, there was nothing warm, or remotely soft about the woman. Still plenty of lush, but as she strapped her weapons to that luscious body, he wasn't about to mention it.

She slid a dagger into her boot, and she was carefully drawing a long-sleeved blouse on over the interesting-looking contraptions strapped to her arms. He also noticed she wore her tricky little belt with the twin blades. The woman was a damn walking armory.

"Do you really think all that's necessary?" he gently asked her.

She eyed him, her expression set in an implacable expression. This woman before him was so far removed from the moaning siren in his arms from just hours before. She'd been like this, so grim, so focused, since she woke.

"Today—tonight—Marty will either finish off his spell and become the most powerful creature walking among us, or we will have killed that nutter."

He frowned, and stepped around the bed. "*We* are

not killing him, Sully. I'm the Witch Hunter, remember. If you see him, you tell me. Don't go after him."

She tilted her head as she returned is gaze. "I don't want to see him. Just the idea that I will see him again makes me...nervous," she admitted. Then her chin dipped, and her stare became intent. "But I will do whatever I can to protect these people from him."

He didn't know whether to kiss her or criticize her. Sometime overnight, his sweet little Sully morphed into a fierce warrior woman. He eyed the leather pants, the boots, the black singlet with the gray overshirt. Her hair was pulled up into a braided bun on top of her head, and the severe style highlighted her cheekbones and drew attention to her bright eyes and that gorgeously crooked mouth.

He couldn't deny this whole badass vibe he was getting from her worked. He was a confident guy, he could admit when a woman turned him on, and right now Sully was ticking all the boxes. And that secretly worried him. He didn't want her anywhere near her psycho ex.

"This is why I'm here," he told her. "If you see him, let me know, and then let me do my job." He gestured to her outfit. "I don't want you to hurt yourself."

Sully's eyes narrowed. "Excuse me?"

He walked up to her. "These weapons—they're not toys. You could be in more danger from yourself with all these sharp blades than from anyone attacking you."

Her jaw slackened, as though she was lost a little for words. He sighed, and gestured to the guards strapped to her forearms. "Do you even know how to use these things?"

Her eyebrows rose. She thought about his words, then gave him a small smile. "If you can take them off me, I'll leave them."

Dave cocked his head to the side, both annoyed and pleased with her challenge. "Really?"

She nodded. "Really."

He moved quickly, reaching for her right forearm. She moved so damn fast, her movements almost a blur as she flexed her wrists, and the pronged swords slid from their sheaths. She caught the handles, the blades moving in a wicked twirl as she easily evaded his grasp. He stepped after her, then hissed when he felt the flat of the blade smack his arm away. The blades twirled, and suddenly the tip of one was against the indent of his collarbone. He halted.

She eyed him coolly. "Yield?"

His eyes narrowed. "Never."

He dodged the tip, bringing his arm up to hit hers away from him. She turned, the blades flashing. He raised his arm to block her strike, and she hit him again with the flat of the blade. And then smacked him in the thigh with the second blade. He grimaced, and caught her wrist.

The world tilted, and he had a vague impression of the room flipping upside down, and then he landed on the floor, with a blade at his neck and one over his heart.

She arched an eyebrow. "Yield?"

He pursed his lips. That was…impressive. "Only if you show me that move," he said, and she grinned as she straightened.

"Let's get through today, first." She slid the pronged swords back into their sheaths, then extended her hand to him.

He grasped it, moving smoothly to his feet. "Fine. You…wear those." He gestured to the weapons she'd now hidden behind her long sleeves. He got the impression that she'd taken it extremely easy on him.

She nodded. "I'm glad we sorted that out."

She turned for the door, but he stopped her. "It's going to be okay," he told her. She smiled and nodded, but he knew neither of them were fully convinced. They were going up against a guy who could easily neutralize their powers, if the surrounding nulls didn't do it already. He grabbed his mobile ink kit and followed her out, his eyes on the leather-clad hips swinging in front of him.

Damn, but this look worked on her.

Sully stared at the street scene. The road had been closed to traffic, and people milled about, strolling from stall to stall. There was a fish market section down the end, and local farmers had brought produce. There was apple-bobbing, pumpkin-carving, clowns, wood-chopping, animals, bake stalls, food stalls…the scents and sights were like a colorful burst to the senses.

"I don't like this," Sully said, lifting her gaze from the crowd to the darkening clouds skidding across the sky. Talk about portent. The clouds had started to skid across the sky after lunch. A storm was coming.

Which was surprising, as the forecast called for a faux summer day.

She turned to Dave. He wore leather pants and a black T-shirt beneath his leather jacket, his dark sunglasses shielding his eyes. Tall, muscular…dangerous.

Badass sexy.

She ran her gaze over his body. Last night had been… wow. She had to admit, sex with Dave was…cosmic. Fireworks, lightning…she'd never experienced anything like that before with a lover. But there was something else, something more…like the buildup of a spell before the effect was visible. Full of magic, full of meaning and fraught with just as much danger. When this was over, though, she didn't know what was to come next, and that scared her. She'd lived her life quietly, safely, since leaving Irondell and Martin. Well, except for the two years she spent on the West Coast learning how to defend herself. But the four years since arriving in Serenity Cove had passed in idyllic peace and, well, serenity.

Dave had turned that all on its head. He'd threatened her—physically. And then had vowed to protect her. He challenged her, with every word, with every touch...he was able to get to the heart of her, the heart she'd successfully shielded from everyone. Until now. She was in very real danger of losing her heart to the Witch Hunter. She gazed around the crowd. And that was the problem. Marty had figured out a way to close down the Witch Hunter's vision. He'd figured out a way to nullify the null effect—which was pretty damned clever. He'd killed six people. He'd avoided the law, Dave and any number of nulls out searching for him. If they didn't find the other nulls before he did, they could be looking at a new world order by sunrise.

"There's Jacob," Dave said, raising his chin. Sully looked. Jacob was standing beside a chair and table set up, with a Free Tattoos sign. Dave grimaced. "Free?"

"They needed something to use as a cover," Sully said. Jacob had called them earlier that morning at the motel. He and his mother had convinced the mayor to let them set up another booth on the street so that Dave could tattoo the last of the purebloods under the guise of a market stall.

"But free?"

She smiled at the mock whine in his voice. "You're being very generous, whether you like it or not."

He turned to face her, his smile dropping a little.

"I'm going to be at that stall pretty much for the rest of the day."

She nodded. "I'll be helping Jacob and his mom round up the rest of the purebloods."

Dave pursed his lips. "Don't stray too far. Stay with the crowd, no wandering off by yourself. This guy is using your guise to get close to these nulls, and I don't think that's by accident."

Her smile faltered. Dave was right. Marty had tracked her down, had tricked her friends to get close enough to kill him. Apparently her departure must have been a sore point for him. She nodded. "I understand."

"Good." Dave leaned forward and pressed a quick kiss against her lips.

"Dave!"

Dave startled at the call and drew back. They both turned. Noah was hurtling down the street, weaving his wave through the crowd.

"Hey, Noa—oh." Dave grunted when the kid ran into him full tilt. Noah clung to his legs, and Dave stooped down to hug him back.

"How's my little badass going?"

Sully winced at the language, but Noah laughed. "Great. How is the king of badass?"

Oh, my God. Now the kids were repeating it. She watched as Noah's father—George, Susanne's husband—shook his head as he approached, overhearing his son.

"The king is good," Dave remarked, then dropped Noah to his feet. He shook hands with George. "Hey, how you doing?"

George nodded. "We're…getting by." Sully could see the haunted look in his eyes, the dark circles and deep grooves. His wife's death had hit him hard. She ruffled Noah's red hair.

Dave looked down at the little boy. "Hey, do you want to come help me at the booth? Folks might be a little braver if they know you've got one of my tattoos…?" He raised his brow at George, who nodded in relief. "Thanks. I've got to go watch his sister in the pumpkin fairy production."

Sully blinked away a tear. Susanne was usually one of the stagehands for these things, working behind the scenes to get all the kids into costumes, soothe fluttery tummies and offer all sorts of encouragement. Noah's sister, Cherie, would be facing her first concert without her mom.

"Take your time, Dave and I can watch Noah," she told him.

George patted her on the arm. "Thanks," he said hoarsely, his eyes red, and hurried away before his son noticed.

Dave stretched his hand out to Noah. "Come on, LB, let's go get our ink on."

Noah scrunched up his nose. "LB?"

"Little Badass." Dave put a hand up over his mouth and mock whispered, "It'll be our secret."

Noah nodded. "Okay, KB."

Dave tilted his head. "KB?"

"King of Badass," Noah explained, his tone suggesting it was obvious.

Dave chuckled. "Yeah, that'll definitely be our secret."

Sully watched as the tall, leather-clad man led the little boy over to the booth. Noah was practically skipping. Jacob greeted both of them, then went and got a stool for Noah to sit on as Dave set up his kit.

It was sweet, in a weird, testosterone-laden way.

She pulled a piece of paper out of her pocket and glanced at the list of twelve names. Mrs. Forsyth was already trying to locate the older purebloods, and as soon as Dave was ready for clients, Jacob would be out combing the crowd.

For now, it was her turn. She was on the hunt for purebloods.

Dave taped the adhesive bandage over the new tattoo and smiled at the twentysomething-year-old woman. She flicked her hair over her shoulder and eyed him.

"I'm thinking about getting a tattoo…here," she said. His gaze dropped to where she indicated. She was drawing her denim skirt higher up her thigh.

His eyebrows rose, and he gently grasped her wrist, stopping her from baring any more leg. "Uh, another time. It's best to let the body recover a little before going for the next tatt."

She pouted. He was sure she was trying to be flirtatious, but all he noticed was that her mouth didn't have that cute little quirk in it like Sully's did.

The woman sighed. "Fine. Maybe later, then?"

He gave her a noncommittal nod. "Maybe."

He turned away to clean and sterilize the needles, and looked up when Jacob joined him.

"How many is that?"

"Seven," Dave said, washing the needles in a solution before placing them in the pot on top of the camping stove Jacob had provided. It was rough, it was rudimentary, but the end result was sterilized needles ready to be used on the next pureblood null to make it to his booth.

Mrs. Forsyth had managed to locate the older purebloods, and Sully had tracked down three. Jacob had found two.

Dave leaned back to look behind Jacob. "Where's Noah?"

"Oh, he's right—" Jacob jerked his thumb over his shoulder as he turned. He frowned. "He was right behind me."

Dave closed his kit with a snap and rose. He lifted the cloth on the booth to look under. No Noah. He straightened to scan the crowd. "Well, he's not there, now."

Jacob paled. "I swear, he was right behind me."

Dave nodded, holding up a hand. "Okay. He's a kid. There could be lots of explanations, from deciding to go watch his sister in her concert to being distracted by a funny-shaped bird poop. Let's look."

Jacob nodded. "I'll go look around the stage," he commented, and strode off in the direction of the area designated for performances.

Dave sighed. "Great. I'll take the bird poop." He walked around the booth, scanning the crowd. He wasn't going to panic. Sure, the kid was cute. Pretty cool, actually. And tatted up with his own special ward. Noah was also full of curiosity, if his gazillion and one questions about tattooing, motorbikes, sunglasses, laser eyes, magic powers, leather underpants—how the hell that had come up, he still didn't know—and needles maybe turning into ninja spears for grasshoppers were anything to go by.

"Noah!" he called out the boy's name as he made his way through the crowd. The colors of the booths started to darken, and he looked up. Storm clouds were skidding across the sky.

Dave glanced about, his pace quickening. He didn't like this. He didn't like this, at all.

"Noah!"

Chapter 22

Sully glanced down at her paper. She, along with Mrs. Forsyth and Jacob, had managed to find eight out of the twelve remaining purebloods. Four were still outstanding. Marty needed only three. The paper in her hand darkened, and she looked up. Dark clouds, thick and voluminous, skittered across the sky, as though the Ancestors were angry and frowning down at everyone. She frowned. That cloud action was too fast to be natural. The night would arrive early.

Marty.

Damn him. She started to walk back toward Dave's booth. She waved to Cheryl, who was manning the Brewhaus Diner coffee stand. She noticed Tyler, in his sheriff uniform, standing beside it. She almost went up to him to ask him when she might be able to get into her home, but he was frowning as he tried to catch Cheryl's attention, and Cheryl was steadfastly ignoring him as she chatted to a young man who'd received his coffee but didn't seem in any hurry to move along.

Sully turned away. She'd have to catch Cheryl later for an update, but it looked like something had definitely changed between those two. She took two steps and halted. Was that Noah?

The red-haired boy was being led away from the crowd, toward the head of the walking trail that led down to Crescent Beach. He was being led by a woman wearing a long flowing skirt and a billowy top. A woman who looked a lot like Sully.

Sully blinked. No...

Noah tripped, and the woman turned to tug on his hand. Sully's heart seized in her chest, then started hammering.

"Noah!" She started to run after the pair, and stumbled a little when the woman looked casually over her shoulder. It was like looking into a mirror, or at a long-lost twin. The face staring back at her was her own.

Except for the eyes. Where Sully's eyes were blue, this woman's eyes were jet black. The woman spotted Sully, and her lips lifted in a smile. Then her features started to waver, and the boneless mass morphed into masculine features she knew all too well, and Marty scooped up a surprised Noah and started running.

"Noah," Sully screamed and bolted after them.

Dave stared around the petting zoo in frustration. Noah wasn't here, either. He moved his arm away from a donkey whose attention was becoming way too personal. Jacob hurried over to him, with George, Noah's father, close on his heels, his face pale with worry.

"I take he's not watching his sister's concert?" Dave commented.

Jacob shook his head, and George ran his hands through his dark hair. "Where is he?" The man's tone was panicked, his eyes wide with consternation. The man had lost his wife in a violent crime—Dave couldn't begin to imagine how he was processing the disappearance of his son.

"Is everything okay?"

Dave turned at the query. Tyler Clinton, in full sheriff's uniform, was eyeing George with concern. His normal reticence to involve the police, to involve others, disappeared. A little boy was missing.

"Sheriff, we need your help." Dave quickly informed him of Noah's disappearance, along with the fact that he may have been taken by a man who can change his appearance, by taking on the facade of anyone he came into physical contact with, and who was responsible for the recent murders in Serenity Cove.

To his credit, the sheriff took it well.

"You son of a bitch," Tyler hissed, eyes flashing with anger, his fists clenched. "You've known all this time—" he bit the words off, his gaze taking in George and Jacob. The sheriff pulled the radio from its holster on his hip and called for all available deputies to attend the festival in search of a missing six-year-old, believed to have been abducted. Then he pointed a finger at Dave. "You're with me. You withheld vital information to an ongoing murder investigation. That's obstruction."

The sheriff turned to George. "Do you have a recent photo of Noah? I'll need to distribute to the guys when they get here. We'll also make announcements from the staging area, and see if we can get everyone to help." He placed his hands on his hips, then looked at Dave. "Can this guy really play swapsies with his face?"

Dave nodded. "Yep."

Tyler sighed, then turned in the direction of the stage. "Let's get to it, then."

It wasn't long before most of the activities at the Festival were shut down—not because Tyler called for it, but because pretty much all of those attending the street fair wanted to help in the search of the boy. Tyler split the crowd into groups and assigned the groups areas to search.

Tyler beckoned him, and Dave followed him down the length of the street.

"You should have told me." Tyler's voice was low, and full of controlled anger.

Dave shot him a look. "Yeah, I can totally see how that conversation would have gone. 'Hey, Sheriff, your killer is a witch—I don't know who he is, or what he looks like, or why he's doing it, but I'll take it from here.'" Dave shook his head.

Tyler peered through the glass windows of a store. "You still should have told me."

"You were already suspicious of me," Dave reminded him.

"No, I wasn't."

"How many tourists do you ask when they're leaving?"

Tyler's lips curved as he looked back at him, eyeing the bike leathers. "You were never a tourist."

"But you see where I'm going with this. I have a job to do, too."

"You could have just told me."

"We witches don't air our dirty laundry." Dave looked inside the window of the next store. Most of them were closed for the festival holiday. "Just like the wolves, the vampires, the bears…"

"So you were really going to kill your witch and leave me with an unsolved murder?"

"I'm a Witch Hunter."

Tyler grimaced. "No wonder people don't trust witches," he muttered.

"Hey, people trust witches," Dave protested. Tyler arched his eyebrow. "Mostly," Dave added, trying to be as truthful as he could.

Dave held up both hands. "Witch Hunter." He didn't like playing that card, would prefer to just drift in and out of a mission without pissing off the local law enforcement, but the reality is that he had a duty that, while focused on witches, had the recognition and enforcement from Reform authorities.

"The path of least resistance," Dave told him as they crossed the street. There was a break in the buildings, with what looked like a trail down toward the beach.

"So keeping this from me was to avoid an uncomfortable conversation," Tyler said, his tone dry.

Dave nodded. "Like this one? Hell, yeah." He squinted as he scanned the beach briefly. The wind was picking up, the temperature had dropped several degrees and the waves were crashing against the shore as though being hurled at the beach. He was about to move on when a figure running in the distance. Black pants, gray shirt.

Sully.

And she was bolting after something.

"Sully!" he cried out, taking the trail. His words were snatched away by the wind.

"What is it?" Tyler asked as he reached the top of the trail.

"Sully. Something's wrong."

Sully wasn't jogging leisurely along the beach. She

was running at full pelt and was almost at the end of the beach where the headland started to rear out of the water. Dave took off after.

Sully clambered over the rocks. She heard Noah cry out, heard the fear in the little boy's voice. She hurried, her feet scrabbling over the wet stones slick with seaweed. The waves rolled in, smashing against the rocks, and she ducked under the spray.

She had to wait for a wave to recede before she climbed around a larger rock formation and stumbled when she landed on wet sand. A hole loomed in front of her, the entrance to a cave. The sand was drier up near the mouth of the cave, and she ran, plowing through the sand until she reached the cave and entered.

"Mar—"

An invisible force pushed at her, sending her flying against the rock wall of the cave. She landed heavily on the sandy floor, coughing as she tried to catch her breath.

Wicked laughter echoed through the cave, and she raised her head. The cave was huge, with various rock formations that created bridges and ramps within the space, so it was almost like a multilevel labyrinth, resident monster included.

She eyed Marty who was presently carrying a struggling Noah up a ramp. Had he—had Marty just magically blindsided her while carrying a null? His powers were getting stronger. Her shaking hands clenched fistfuls of sand. This was Marty. The guy who'd almost drained her dry, who had scared her so much, had hurt her so much, that she'd run from him. Not walked out. Not left. *Run*. All those years of training on the West Coast, all those hours of practicing with the weapons she created, all of that fled her in the face of the man she'd once trusted, and who had abused her so much. Memories, of him screaming in her face, of him pushing her, of her falling over furniture, against walls and doors, of glass breaking, cutting…they all surfaced, along with her sense of powerlessness, of the very real danger she faced with this witch.

"Let him go, Marty," she called out to him, and rose to her feet. She quickly bolstered her shields as she ran over to the base of the rocky ramp. The closer she got to Noah, though, the harder it was to maintain the protection.

Marty turned to face her. "I'm afraid I can't do that, Sully." He looked different. His skin was almost radiant, his eyes flashing. As though power itself was coursing through his veins, bringing with it a confidence and brashness she could never feed him. "I need him. He's the last."

Did that mean he'd killed already? She didn't think so. Each time she'd delivered a null to Dave at the stand, he'd seemed in good health and not reeling from the wound on his chest. Did that mean he'd captured the nulls? Is that why nobody could find the remaining purebloods?

"No, you don't." She started to jog up the ramp, and Marty whirled, his hand out.

"Stop right there," he told her. He reached behind him and pulled something out from the waistband of his jeans. Sully swallowed when she recognized the ceremonial knife she'd seen used in the vision to kill Amanda Sinclair. "Admittedly, I don't like using kids, but I'm working with a short time frame, here."

"You have to see this is crazy," Sully said, panting as she slowly advanced, arms up, palms out in a nonthreatening pose. Even she could see how much her hands were shaking.

Marty's eyebrows rose. "Crazy, huh? Crazy like a fox, maybe."

Noah squirmed, and Marty shook the boy. Sully took a couple of extra steps forward.

"I know what you have planned," she told him. "And it's clever, I have to admit—but it's so wrong, Marty."

Marty smiled grimly. "Only those in a weaker position would say that. To me, this feels very right—and long overdue."

Sully stepped closer again, and she had to lock her knees to stop from collapsing. Everything felt so unstable, so...shaken. "Why, Marty? Why are you doing this?"

Marty's smile turned into an unattractive twist. "Do you remember what you called me, Sully? Remember that day you ran out like a rat scurrying in a sewer...?"

Sully glanced at Noah. The boy was looking between them, his face pale, but his eyes—so like his mother's—showed a spurt of rebellion. She held out her palm in his direction, trying to make her warning to the boy to hold still look casual in the eyes of his captor. She'd learned that if you didn't move, didn't make eye contact, just burrowed down and let him vent, the storm would eventually pass.

"I remember begging you to stop," she told him quietly. "I remember you throwing me against that mirror."

Marty huffed. "Well, that was an accident," he told her. "You got me so mad."

She pursed her lips. So him throwing her up against a wall mirror was her fault? She shook her head. "You hurt me."

"When my father found out the Alder Keeper of the

Books had cast me aside, he banished me from my coven," he rasped, and Noah cried out as the grip on the back of his neck tightened. "You called me pathetic."

Sully took a deep, quivering breath. "I realize that must have sounded harsh," she allowed. She couldn't agree with him, but she didn't want to outright challenge him, not knowing how he'd react.

His comment, though, brought a lot of things into sharp relief. He'd been cast out. For a witch whose powers were limited, he needed the safety of a coven to ward off threats. He would have been vulnerable. Alone. Although she thought that was a fitting outcome for this guy, she wouldn't have actually wished it on anyone. After living so long without her own coven, she knew how lonely, and how scary, it could be on your own.

Marty sneered. "You called me a pathetic vessel of puerile misery."

"I'd have to agree," a deep voice called out from behind her.

Relief flooded her when she recognized Dave's voice. She didn't turn, though, didn't take her eyes off Marty and little Noah.

Marty's eyes widened, and his hand moved. A fireball burst from his palm, and Sully ducked. She heard a grunt, a hiss and then a thud. She glanced over her shoulder. Dave was on the sandy floor of the cave below, and steam was rising from his jacket. Dave shot Marty an exasperated glare.

"Hey, watch it. This is my favorite jacket."

"Stand back," Marty shouted, and Sully turned in time to see him angle the knife toward Noah's throat.

She met Noah's eyes and saw a familiar terror, one she recognized from her own experience with this man. That day he'd pushed her down the hallway, and she'd fallen in front of the mirror… She'd seen her expression, seen the fear, the desperation…the depths she'd allowed herself to sink to. She saw that same fear, that same desperation in her friend's son. Something snapped inside her. Rage—but not fiery and unpredictable. No, this anger filled her like a cold, calm curtain of control.

She stepped closer. "You can't hurt him," she told Marty, her eyes on his.

"Oh, and who's going to stop me? You?"

She shook her head. "No." She lifted her chin in Noah's direction. "He is."

"He's a little badass," Dave called as he grasped the lip of the ramp and pulled himself up and over. He rose to his feet and winked at Noah. "Aren't you, buddy?"

Noah looked at Dave, then nodded faintly.

Marty smirked, then brought the knife down.

The blade halted about half a foot away from his body. Marty frowned and tried again. Again, he faltered, as though the knife encountered an invisible barrier.

Marty looked up at her and Dave, his eyes wide. "What have you done?" he rasped.

"You're not the only one who can draw symbols," Dave responded as he came up to Sully's side. "Only I'm better at it."

"He's protected," Sully told Marty. "It's over. You can't make your quota."

Marty shook his head. "No," he bellowed, his face blooming with the heat of his rage. He shoved Noah, who screamed as he stumbled and fell over the edge of the ramp. Dave launched himself over the edge, diving for the boy. He caught Noah midfall and twisted so that his body bore the full brunt of the landing on the cave floor about twelve feet below.

Sully screamed, racing to the edge of the ramp to look down. Dave wheezed, but he gave her a thumbs-up signal. She turned around to see Marty running farther up the ramp. The witch leaped across a divide to a rock ledge. He scurried along to a tunnel opening and disappeared.

She hesitated, then Dave groaned.

"No," he gasped, his hand to his chest. He lifted his gaze to Sully. "I'm warming up. He's got someone back there."

She turned and ran, heart in her throat as she jumped over the gap between ramp and rock ledge. She hissed as her hands slammed into the rock wall, and she almost bounced back. She clasped a rock bulge to prevent herself from plummeting backward into the cave. Taking a deep breath, she scurried along the ledge, hugging the wall until she reached the tunnel, and then started to run.

It was so dark. Sully braced her hands outward, using her contact with the wall of the tunnel as a guide. A strangled scream echoed down the tunnel, and she sped up, stumbling along until the tunnel opened up into another smaller cavern. She skidded to a halt. A shaft of light came through an opening in the roof of the cavern, almost like a natural skylight. The light was weak, though, and growing dimmer.

A man lay cowering on the floor, Marty straddled his body. His hands and feet were tied, and his yells were muffled by his gag as he shook his head rapidly at Marty. A woman lay on the ground nearby, her wrists and ankles bound, tears streaking her face. Marty raised his hand and the blade gleamed in the weak light.

Sully reacted. She ran toward him, her hand pulling out one of her belt blades as she did. She raised her hand behind her ear and flung the blade.

Chapter 23

The woman screamed. Marty cried out in pain as the blade sliced across the back of his clenched fist, and he dropped his knife.

Sully leaped, her legs out in front, and caught Marty in the back with her foot. He tumbled off the man, and Sully landed heavily on the rocky ground, rolling with her momentum to gain her feet and spin around.

The null on the floor rolled rapidly away from Marty and kept rolling until he hit a boulder.

Marty reached for his knife as he rose to his knees, then his feet. His face was grim and full of anger as he faced Sully.

"You bitch," he said through gritted teeth. Sully put both her hands out, knees bent, waiting for his move. Marty started to laugh. "You think you can fight me?" He tossed the blade, letting it turn in his hand. Sully flinched at the nonchalance of his movement. "These are nulls, Sully. You have no power here."

Sully licked her lips, her gaze darting to the couple on the ground to the left. The man stretched his hand out and grasped the hilt of the blade she'd thrown at Marty. She brought her gaze back to the maddened witch in front of her. As long as she had his attention, he wouldn't realize the purebloods were cutting through their restraints.

She just had to keep him occupied long enough for them to escape…her, against the only witch to ever be able to use the null effect to his advantage. She swallowed.

"See, this is your problem, Marty," she told him, shaking her head as she sidestepped to the right. His gaze followed her—away from the bound couple on the ground. "You never got it."

He smirked, and she had to wonder what on earth she'd ever seen in this man who was becoming even more unattractive to her. "What's that, Sully?"

"You were always thirsty for magic, you always craved it and you never realized that magic isn't the only form of power," she said softly. She flexed her wrists, and her sai swords ejected from their sheaths, sliding along her arms until she grasped their hilts.

He grinned and his left eyebrow rose at the move. "You think you can take me on?" he asked silkily. "Do you forget all those times, Sully, when you were cowering on our living room floor, or beside the bed, quivering?" He spread his arms out. "That—that was power. And you always gave it to me."

Her eyes narrowed. "Well, I guess I'm taking it back."

She launched herself at him, and he brought his blade

up. The clink and clank of blades striking each other filled the cave, little sparks coming off as the metals collided. Sully moved rapidly, spinning and ducking. A movement caught her eye. The couple had freed themselves, and were running toward the tunnel.

Her distraction cost her. She hissed when she felt the hot slice against her forearm. Marty had cut her.

He gave her a triumphant grin—until he saw the couple dart down the tunnel behind her. He shifted his gaze back to hers. "You bitch."

This time she smirked at him. "You have no idea."

She flicked her wrists, drawing her blades along her forearms in a defensive yet elegant move. His eyes narrowed and he came at her again, his blade flashing. Over and over, she blocked his strikes, the clash of metal ringing through the cave. He was forcing her back, his eyes wide with fury, his teeth bared.

She stepped back and halted. Her back was to the wall. Marty smiled.

Sully flicked the sai swords around to an offensive position, then started twirling them. She got faster and faster as she stepped forward, and Marty was forced to step back, unable to penetrate her wall of whirling blades.

"Martin Steedbeck," a familiar voice bellowed from within the tunnel. Dave.

She waggled her eyebrows at Marty. "Ooh, you're in trouble now."

"In accordance with Nature's Law, passed down by the Ancients, you have been found guilty, and for your dark crimes, the Ancestors call upon your return to the Other Realm, to a place of execution—"

Marty roared, lashing out with his feet and kicking Sully's knee out from under her. She fell to the floor, her knee landing hard on the rock surface. Marty smacked one sword out of her grasp, and grabbed hold of her other wrist as he stepped behind her, his knife at her neck. "Drop it."

He squeezed her wrist, and she could feel her fingers tingle. Her grasp relaxed on the blade, and it clanged as it fell to the stone floor.

Dave emerged from the tunnel. He stopped talking when he saw Sully on her knees, Mental Marty's knife to her throat.

"I don't recognize Nature's Law," Marty rasped, panting.

"It recognizes you," Dave said in a low, dangerous voice. He removed his sunglasses, sliding them casually into the inside breast pocket of his jacket. Son. Of. A. Bitch. He had to fight the natural instinct to go berserk all over the witch's ass.

The tip of the blade pressed under Sully's chin, and she had to tilt her head back to avoid it piercing her skin.

"Get up," Marty hissed to her. She rose to her feet, very carefully. One stumble, one awkward lean, and she could end up with a knife in her skull.

Dave's heart was in his throat. His fists clenched. He could still sense the nulls in the cave system, although their effect was weakening. Tyler was guiding Noah and the couple he'd almost cannoned into on the rock ledge outside. He'd told the sheriff to clear the area of nulls. If there were any nearby, they'd mute his capacity to fight this witch, and Marty would have the advantage.

"You're going to be fine, Sully," Dave said, trying to keep his voice calm and warm for her benefit, when he really wanted to bellow with rage at this witch putting the woman he loved at risk. He tried to convey all the hell he was going to visit on this witch with his eyes. "Don't even think about hurting her."

A clap of thunder reverberated throughout the cave. Sully glanced upward. The sky that she could glimpse at the end of the shaft was dark gray, and a flash of lightning jolted across the diameter of the shaft.

"Can you feel the power in the air, Witch Hunter?" Marty asked as he started to back toward the shaft. "That's *my* power. I created that."

Dave advanced, his shoulders moving in a way that made him look like a big cat stalking prey. Sully shuffled along with Marty, the knife at her neck silently urging her movement.

"But you can't complete the spell," Dave told him. Noah was protected. The other two nulls had escaped.

Marty shrugged. "Then I simply complete it between now and the summer solstice. I only need two more." He stepped up on a rock, and Sully hissed at the painful little prick under her chin. "Up."

"Sully," Dave's voice was low.

She gave him a shaky smile. "Trust me," she said in a tremulous voice. "It's going to be all right."

Marty laughed. "I don't think you're going to be able to make this feel better, Sully."

Dave frowned, his silver gaze full of concern. Sully was…calm. Alarmingly so. She slowly slid her hand to her belt. *Trust me,* she mouthed at him.

His mouth opened and his gaze flicked between hers and Marty's. Aw, hell. She could get herself killed.

He'd heard their fight through the tunnel, and he'd seen her display back at the motel. He'd been fairly confident she could protect herself—until she wound up with a knife at her throat. He wanted to blast Mental

Marty. He wanted to annihilate the bastard. That was his job. He did this alone.

His gaze met Sully's. She was pleading with him with her eyes. It wasn't like he didn't *want* to trust her, but…she was in a vulnerable position.

And she's armed to the teeth and knows more about personal safeguarding than he may ever learn. Damn it. He hated this. It was anathema to him, letting a woman—a woman in a vulnerable position—call the shots. But it was Sully. He had no idea what she was thinking, but she knew *something*…this was the woman who'd managed to hold her own against him, who could block an invasive threat to her mind and magic as easily as swatting a fly.

His frown deepened, but then he nodded. Just once. He kept his gaze on Marty. He could distract the witch, at least. "The Ancestors call upon your return to the Other Realm, to a place of execution, until you are dead. May the Ancestors—"

Sully's movement was graceful as she slid her blade from her belt and caught Marty's knife-wielding hand. She jerked it back, and Marty roared—and Dave winced—at the audible snap of bone. The knife fell to the ground, and she held his hand close to her body as she twisted and knelt. Marty flipped over her head, his feet flying through the air, as she used that same move on the man she'd used on Dave in the motel room. Marty yelled, his head tilting back as he cried out in pain. Dave ran forward, but the witch sat up, hands outstretched, and a wave of power rolled through the cavern. Dave was knocked backward, as was Sully. By the time he rolled over onto his back, Marty was hastily climbing the shaft toward the darkened sky above.

Dave bolted across the floor to Sully, who was just sitting up. "Are you all right?" he asked.

She nodded, then pointed at the shaft. "Go. I'm fine."

Dave sprinted across the cavern floor, leaping up over a boulder to grasp a bulge in the wall, and he started hauling himself up after the witch.

Sully stumbled to the bottom of the shaft. She wasn't anywhere near as fast as Dave, or that skunk, Marty. Her heart was pounding. Dave. All she could think about was Dave. Marty was strong. She could sense it in him. She would have tried to draw some of that power out of him, when he held her, but he would have sensed it immediately, and she couldn't get her magic on with a knife in the brain.

Her foot slipped and she gasped, clinging to the rock face. A ladder. A ladder would be really good about now. She kept climbing. The light was almost nonexistent now, and she was feeling her way up the rock wall.

Her arms were shaking by the time she got to the top and could feel the grass around the edge of the hole. She raised her leg, using it to lever herself out awkwardly. Panting, she looked around.

Oh. My. God. Clouds were swirling as though caught in a twister. Lightning flashed among the fiercely spinning clouds, illuminating the dark strands of a lethal magic. The sea at the bottom of the cliff showed white peaks as the waves roiled and rolled, as though caught in Mother Nature's washing machine. The wind was biting, and she had to bend forward to avoid being pushed back by its gale force.

Marty had tried to blast Dave with a ball of power, and Dave was currently holding it off. Streams of dark red fire were swirling toward him, but she could see they were slowly getting closer to him. She forced one leg in front of the other, her arms up to protect her face from the wind whipping at her. Her shirt cracked like a sail caught in a thunderstorm, and she could feel the fabric tear.

She had to help Dave.

As though sensing her, Dave turned his head, his silver eyes bright in the darkness. "Go away," he called to her.

She shook her head. She summoned her power, raising her hands toward Marty. He noticed her, and braced one hand in her direction. She reeled back under the impact of the blast, but managed to stop the dark fire from consuming her.

"Leave, Sully," Dave roared, his focus now on the witch.

Sully slowly crept forward, gritting her teeth as she tried to find her wedge through the wall of power Marty had thrown up. Marty was able to keep them both at bay, and his eyes brightened when he realized this. He was strong…too strong. Tears filled Sully's eyes at the realization.

She couldn't fight him off, not in a power struggle. His death magic was too powerful for her, and for Dave. A dark flame danced across her arm, and she screamed at the burn. Marty was going to kill them.

Dave shifted toward her, protective to the last. An idea hit her. She dropped her shields and mentally reached out for Dave. She felt his surprise, his confusion and then his acceptance. He reached back for her, and she grasped his hand. Marty started to fade in her vision as shards of light transferred between her and Dave. Blues, pinks, purples, the spears of light brightened. She sent Dave a mental image, and he squeezed her hand. Together they started to recite a spell, the Old Language glowing across her vision, like a magical teleprompter.

Marty frowned, wincing as his right hand started to glow. The force coming from him stuttered a little, then flicked on to high wattage, before stuttering again. Marty glanced down at his hand, turning it over. Sully and Dave continued to chant, but then spread their arms out, calling on the tempest around them, drawing in the elements—the wind buffeting them, the water crashing below them, the spark of lightning fire and the solid ground beneath them.

Marty's eyes widened when he saw the mark Sully had carved onto his hand when she'd thrown him in the cavern below. His gaze flicked to hers, and full comprehension dawned on him.

"No," he cried, trying to blast them away. Harnessing the power of the tempest, they rebuffed his attempt to incinerate them.

The mark on his hand glowed, and his skin began to blister. His face roiled, and he screamed in pain as his bones melted into another's features. First Jenny, then Susanne... Jack, Amanda, Mary Anne and Gary. Each time his face twisted, Marty screamed. He clutched at his skull, but the fire from within consumed him, his flesh melting as his bones turned to ash, plucked away in all directions by the wind.

Sully weaved on her feet, her hand gripping Dave's until they both fell to their knees. Sully dropped his hand, catching herself before she face-planted in the wet grass. Thunder roared, and lightning cracked, the blade of light spearing downward from the spinning clouds above.

The lightning hit Dave square in the chest, and he

arched under the shock, his silver eyes glowing as the energy coursed through his body. Sully screamed as his lips pulled back, and for a brief moment his teeth glowed, his veins glowed, even his bones seemed to glow. And then the charge was gone, and Dave sagged to the ground.

"Oh, my God, Dave. Dave!" Sully hurried over to him, reaching for him carefully. She pressed her hand to his neck, her eyes closing when she felt his racing pulse, but even as she held her fingers against his skin, she could feel it start slow down.

"Dave, please be okay," she whispered as she cupped his cheeks. His eyelids fluttered, and it took a few attempts before he was able to force his eyes open. His silver-gray gaze met hers, and he gave her an exhausted smile.

"Well, that was shocking."

She laughed, her hands trembling, and she had to blink away tears of relief. "You are such a dick."

He lifted his shoulders.

"No, no, lie—"

He brushed aside her attempts to make him lie down, and she helped him sit up. She glanced up. The lightning was no more, and the clouds were no longer a whirling mess. They drifted slowly across the sky, revealing the night stars and the harvest moon.

"What was that?" she asked. Where had that lightning come from? Marty was dead. Incinerated. She didn't think it had been his hand that had called forth the spear of lightning.

Dave hissed, pulling at the neckline of his T-shirt and ripping it down the front.

Sully gaped. All of the markings on his body glowed on his skin, and then slowly faded, disappearing into smoke. All save one.

In the Old Language, emblazoned across his heart, was one name.

Sullivan Timmerman.

Dave gaped at his chest, then slowly raised his eyes to hers. "I—I think I just retired."

"What?" Sully gasped. She stared at his bare chest. His glorious, smooth, muscled bare chest, adorned with just her name. She smiled. All of those names, the proof of the Ancestors' hold over him, had disappeared.

Dave touched himself, then shrugged out of his jacket and the remnants of his T-shirt. He twisted about, turning his arms over. "They're gone," he breathed, stunned.

He looked up at her, and she smiled. "They're gone," he shouted, then clasped her head and brought her in for a kiss. She laughed against his lips, and collapsed against his magnificent chest. She smoothed her hands over him, testing for herself. The names were definitely gone.

Dave ended the kiss and rested his forehead against hers. His chest rose and fell with his pants, and she felt him shake his head gently against hers.

"You linked with me," he breathed.

She nodded. "I wanted to help you."

He closed his eyes in relief, in gratitude. "Thank you," he whispered, and kissed her sweetly.

Shouts drifted across the cliff top, and they both turned to the source. Flashlights were cutting swathes in the darkness, and Sully smiled when she saw the familiar faces of Tyler and Jacob, and Noah being carried by his father.

"Oh, look. LB." Dave slung his arm around her shoulders, and leaned in close to her ear. "I might be the king of badass, but you're the queen of whoop ass."

Chapter 24

Dave watched as the tall, dark-haired men emerged from the null council meeting. Both men had dark hair, both men had blue eyes, but both men were as different as night and day.

"Who are they?" Sully asked, curious. Dave slung his arm over her shoulders as the men approached, lazily inhaling her entrancing sent of rose, vanilla and... sunshine. She was wearing a pretty red summer dress, with buttons all the way from the V neckline to the hem. She looked so beautiful, so...feminine. He still marveled at the way she'd fought Mental Marty, and just how damn lethal she could be. She was smoking hot and fought like a ninja. He was in love.

"Friends," he said, finally answering her question.

One of the men shuddered, shaking out his shoulders. "I want out of here. It's weird," he muttered.

Dave's smile broadened. "Sully Timmerman, allow me to introduce Lucien Marchetta."

The lean vampire nodded at her, his smile quick and almost nonexistent. "Sully."

Dave gestured to the other man strolling toward him. He had a slightly more muscular build, particularly across his shoulders and in his arms. "And this is Ryder Galen. Ryder, this is Sully."

Ryder smiled and held out his hand. "Hi, Sully."

Sully shook his hand out of politeness. Cheers erupted inside the town hall, and her eyebrows rose. "Does someone want to tell me what's going on?"

A blond-haired woman skipped out of the hall, a wide smile on her face, and she caught up with the men, sliding her hand into Lucien's.

"And this lovely lady is Natalie Segova," Dave said, gesturing at the woman by Lucien's side.

"Marchetta," Lucien corrected, frowning. He glanced down at the woman by his side, and his frown disappeared, replaced by a genuine smile. "Her name's Natalie Marchetta, now."

"Hi," Natalie said, extending her hand. Dave's smile broadened. Natalie was a sweetheart, and her warm smile was contagious.

Sully shook the woman's hand, smiling back at her. "Hi, I'm Sully." His gaze stayed on Sully. She looked so relaxed, so…happy. He couldn't stop looking at her, and he could see out of the corner of his eye that Ryder was smirking at him. He would have frowned at the guy, but that would mean looking away from Sully, and well…he preferred this view.

There were more cheers inside, and Sully's brow dipped in confusion. "Okay, now I'm really curious. What's going on?"

Lucien shuddered again. "I'm paying my debt." He arched an eyebrow at Dave. "We're even."

Dave nodded. "Yes, we are."

Lucien strolled over to a dark car and opened the passenger door for his wife. Natalie slid inside, and waved at them as Lucien climbed in, started the engine and drove off.

"Wait—did you say Marchetta?" Sully gasped as she finally recognized the name. "The vampires?"

"Well, technically Lucien and Natalie are hybrids. Ryder here is a light warrior."

"But, why are they all here? I would have thought vampires—sorry, hybrids—and light warriors would want to avoid Serenity Cove."

Dave shrugged. "I think Lucien Marchetta was overcome by a sudden desire to contribute to the community. The Marchetta Corporation has just established an investment program with the fishing co-op here."

Sully gaped. "Why?"

He grinned. "Because Lucien Marchetta owes me one, as does his wife."

"What did Natalie do?" Ryder queried calmly.

"She's researched the requirements for a request of recognition of the nulls as a breed on their own, and will oversee the submission process."

He enjoyed Sully's stunned expression. "Seriously?"

He nodded. "Seriously."

Sully turned to Ryder. "So…why are you here, if you don't mind me asking?"

Ryder smiled. "I'm also paying my debt. Dave mentioned that your closest medical clinic is over an hour away. My brother and I will help set up a clinic here for the nulls, and run the training programs for staff."

Sully turned and gaped at him. "You did this?"

Dave frowned. She was looking at him weirdly. "Not by myself—I had help."

"Dave, this will help them so much," Sully exclaimed softly.

He shifted uncomfortably. This is why he'd preferred to stay outside while the hybrids and the light warrior made their announcements. He didn't need the thanks, he preferred just quietly getting on with things and then disappearing.

The town hall doors were flung open, and Mrs. Forsyth scanned the street. She squealed when she saw them standing across the road. Darn. Was it too late to disappear?

"I'm out of here," Ryder said, and quickly jogged to his car.

Dave glanced about. His bike was down the block, and him running away would look fairly obvious to the little lady who was now hurrying across to them. He eyed Ryder's car enviously as his friend drove away. Darn, he could move fast.

"David, thank you."

He tried not to cringe outwardly as Mrs. Forsyth hurried up to him, her arms open wide. Only his mother called him Dav—

"David, you are so lovely," she said softly as she hugged him, and he had to lean down, she was so short. He patted her shoulder awkwardly. This was sooo uncomfortable. But nice, in its weird little way.

"It's nothing, Mrs. Forsyth," he said, embarrassed as Jacob walked out of the town hall, arms folded. The fisherman grinned when he saw Dave's discomfort. Dave shot a pleading look at Sully, who shrugged, grinning.

Traitor, he mouthed.

"You have to come over for dinner," Mrs. Forsyth exclaimed as she stepped back. Dave straightened and tried to make his disappointment look sincere.

"Oh, I wish we could, but Sully and I are on our way out today," he told her.

Mrs. Forsyth blinked. "You're leaving?"

He nodded, then grunted when Noah threw himself against Dave's legs.

"Don't leave, KB!" Noah cried, hugging him fiercely.

Damn it. He hadn't bargained on the kid. Something warm flared in his heart, and he smiled tightly. He wasn't going to get sucked in. He was the rolling stone that gathered no moss. The tattoo artist that could up and leave at the drop of a hat, the retired Witch Hunter who could disintegrate another, how could—

Noah looked up at him. "Please?" the boy begged. Those green eyes, that quivering bottom lip…those freckles. That warm spot turned into goop. Mushy, fluffy goop. Dave was touched, so touched that these people were welcoming him so warmly. He could understand how Sully viewed these people as family. He'd had more physical contact, more interaction with this community than he had any of the covens back in Irondell—including his mother's.

"We'll come back," Dave promised.

"You swear?" Noah demanded.

Dave grinned. "I swear."

A shadow fell over him, and he looked up. Aw, darn. The royal dick.

Jacob held out his hand. "Thanks," the fisherman said. Dave accepted his shake, and winced as Jacob also thumped him on the shoulder. "For everything." Jacob's gaze slid to Sully, who was now talking to Mrs. Forsyth. "Take good care of her."

Dave nodded. "I will."

Then there was George, and Noah's sister, the sheriff and a whole bunch of others who wanted to come shake his—oh, wow, a hug. He nodded at Cheryl, the waitress, then stepped back toward Sully. He didn't miss the sheriff's gaze narrowing as he eyed the farewell.

"We should get going," Dave whispered in Sully's ear.

"Where are you going?" Jacob asked, squinting against the sun.

"Holiday," Dave informed them without giving too much information away, then waved as he and Sully managed to step away from the group. He handed her the helmet from his pannier, but hung on to it until she met his gaze.

"Are you sure you want to do this?" he asked, solemnly. It was a big move, for Sully. They'd decided to take a break—his first. Ever. Wherever they wanted to go, whatever they wanted to do...together.

She glanced down the street toward the small crowd gathered outside the town hall. She sighed. "You were right. I was hiding here. I love it here, but...you're right. This was my bolt-hole. I think I'm ready to travel, see some sights. Maybe even visit my coven." She nodded. "I want to do this."

He leaned forward and kissed her tenderly. "I'm looking forward to meeting your coven," he murmured. Then he grinned. "I'm also looking forward to introducing you to my family." He tilted his head. "Just don't mention your books."

She laughed as she slid the helmet on over her head. "I won't."

Her coven's archives were in a very safe place, and she'd pointed out to him that she could set up her factory…anywhere. They were going to keep things casual, see which way the wind blew.

He grinned. "Come on, sweetness. Let's go."

Sully stretched as Dave drove onto the grassy shoulder. He kicked down the bike stand and she slid off the bike as he cut the engine. She removed her helmet.

"Wow," she breathed, taking in the view. Chains of islands could be seen in the distance. "This is beautiful."

Dave made a sound of agreement as he removed his own helmet and straightened, his legs still straddling the bike. He crossed his arms over the helmet and lifted his face to the sky.

She took the time to appreciate the view—of him. His short hair ruffled in the light breeze. His sunglasses hid his eyes, but his face—it was probably the most relaxed she'd ever seen him.

"How are you?" she asked him as she walked toward him.

He looked at her. "I'm feeling great."

She gestured to his chest. "How do you feel about… the names?" They hadn't really spoken about anything in great detail. Nothing concrete about the future. Nothing concrete about a commitment—although this was the first time she'd up and left with a man. She wasn't quite sure how she felt about his change in circumstance, or what he wanted to do about his future…about them.

He shrugged out of his jacket, and then drew his T-shirt over his head. She looked about. They'd left the main highway about forty minutes ago, and hadn't seen a car since. Nor were there any buildings within view. This place, watching out over the ocean, seeing land in the distance…it felt like they were the only two people left in the world.

Dave glanced down at his chest. "It's...weird," he admitted.

"Weird, how? Like you've lost an arm, or something?" She couldn't begin to imagine what it would be like, having something that was such a part of you, that defined you, to a certain extent, suddenly disappear.

Dave shook his head. "No, not quite. More like an ache that you noticed you had, but only when it's gone."

She stepped close and ran her hand over his shoulder. "What do you think you'll do, now that you're not a Witch Hunter?"

His arm slid around her waist, and he tugged her close so that she was pressed along his side. Emotions fluttered at her. Attraction. Desire. Contentment. And something warmer, something deeper she was too afraid to identify. He removed his sunglasses, and his silver eyes stared at her intently. "I think I want to live a little, remind myself that life's not all about death." He leaned forward and kissed the corner of her mouth.

She sucked in a breath. "Oh?"

He nuzzled her ear. "Yeah. You taught me that." His voice was so deep, it practically vibrated in his chest.

She swallowed. "I did?"

"Yeah. You taught me...not to piss off a chick with a knife," he said, kissing along her jaw. Her nipples tightened in her bra, and she forced herself to focus on his kiss. *No! Words. Focus on his words.*

"Oh?"

"Yeah. You also taught me...that nulls are kind of nice. Even the ones called Jacob." He ran his lips down her neck, and she trembled.

"Uh, okay..."

"But mostly you taught me that I don't have to do this alone. Any of it." He lifted her over the bike, so that she straddled it, facing him. The skirt of her dress hiked up with the movement, baring her thighs. He pulled her close, and she wrapped her legs around his hips. He cupped her cheek.

"Sully, I don't care what I do, or where I go—as long as it's with you." His stare was so solemn, so full of promise. "Whatever my life holds, I want to share it with you."

She blinked, overcome with the weight of his words... A weight that, if uttered by another man, at another time, would have felt crushing, but here, with this man, right now, it felt...right.

"You've taught me a few things, too," she murmured shyly.

His eyebrow arched, and he gave her a wicked look that heated her from the inside out. "Oh, I'm listening."

"You taught me that not all men in sunglasses are douchebags," she said, and his lips curved. Amusement, light and teasing, tapped at her. He leaned forward and kissed her, long and slow. He pressed her back, and she found herself lying back against the bike. "Uh-huh," he said, a soft, husky sound of encouragement.

"You taught me that leather can look good on, but much better off," she said, trailing her hand over his bare chest.

Desire. Hot. Hard. Gripping. It flooded him, and it flooded her. Her fingers trailed over the tattoo above his heart, her nails lightly scraping his nipple. She smiled when he swallowed, and then closed her eyes as he kissed his way across her collarbone.

His fingers slid beneath the neckline of her dress, and she felt the top button pop out of its loop.

She opened her eyes, staring up at the blue, cloud-less sky. "But mostly, you taught me that I had closed myself off, that I didn't have anyone to truly share my-self with, to talk with, to laugh with…"

He raised his head, his gaze meeting hers.

"You taught me that it was okay to trust again, Dave," she told him earnestly. "You taught me that a man could be safe." She smiled. "You taught me some-thing that I hadn't even realized about myself…that I'd become a shadow, closing myself off to everyone. You taught me to open up, again."

He kissed her hungrily. "I love you," he whispered, kissing her over and over again. She arched her back, pressing her breasts against his chest, feeling his cock harden in his jeans. His fingers slid to the next button, and the next, and he peeled her dress open.

"I love you, too. So much," she said. She pulled back her mental walls, letting in his light, letting in the warmth of his love and feeding it back to him, firmly establishing their link. He groaned, caressing her, kiss-ing his way across her chest. His hands slid under her, unclipping her bra and pulling it down her arms and off. She fumbled with the zipper of his jeans, sighing when she could feel the heavy, hard weight of him in her hand.

He drew back, just a little, his expression raw. "I will always be there for you, Sully. You're my everything."

"And you're the light to my darkness," she whispered against his lips, then kissed him, her tongue sliding in to tangle with his. The lace of her panties pulled taut across her hips until the fabric gave, the soft tear caus-ing her to shudder as her desire turned her core into a slick channel.

She guided him inside her, and she moaned with pleasure as his length slid inside. When he was buried to the hilt, paused, then withdrew. His thrusts were long and slow, gradually quickening. She held on to his arms, and he grasped the handlebars. She moaned, the delicious friction of his body against hers, inside hers, sent her tingling. His eyes met hers, and they moved against each other, panting, linked physically, magically, emotionally, until it was too much, the pleasure, the sensations and sparks exploded around them. Sully cried out as she orgasmed, and Dave shouted his pleasure, out there in the middle of nowhere, bare to each other.

Dave swallowed, and Sully laughed with delight, experiencing a freedom, and a lightness of heart she'd never felt before.

Dave grinned and pressed his forehead against hers. "I give you my heart, sweetness."

She grinned back as she stroked her hand over the one tattoo that still marked his body. "You'd better. It's got my name on it."

He put his hand over hers, holding it there. "This is permanent, you know."

She wasn't sure if he meant the tattoo, or if he meant their commitment. Either way, she agreed. She nodded. "I know."

He leaned down, and they kissed, under a clear blue sky—with not a storm cloud in sight.

* * * * *